Just Right

SHON

Cover Design: Alessia and Mya

Formatting: Mya

ISBN: 979-8-9913348-0-8 (paperback)

ISBN: 979-8-9913348-1-5 (ebook)

BLURB

Okay, so maybe I *shouldn't* have broken into their house.

Maybe I *shouldn't* have made myself at home and eaten through enough food for two people in twenty minutes.

But after being lost for half the day, I was hungry. And I needed their electricity to charge my phone so I could use the GPS to make it back to my car.

So, I did what I had to do. Besides, it didn't look like anyone was home. I'd be gone in thirty minutes, tops. And I'd leave a note apologizing about the broken window.

Except, that food knocked me out. And when I woke up it was with a gun to my forehead and three unnecessarily attractive men staring down at me.

Naturally, I expect them to want answers and kick me out. But instead I end up with a proposition I can't refuse.

CONTENTS

AUTHOR'S NOTE

Hey sugarplums, thank you for picking up this book. I've wanted to write this book for a very, very long time. And I finally put all my other projects on the back burner to do it. I love this world and this characters. That being said, this story may not be for everyone. Take a look at the Tropes, Tags, and Content Warnings on the following page

TROPES, TAGS, AND CONTENT WARNINGS

Just Right is a MMFM why-choose novel that takes place in a fictional mountain town a few hours from New Hope. It is my longest books as I will be alternating between four different POVs and weaving their story together. That doesn't mean it's a long book, LOL. Just longer than anything I've written.

Two of the men are already in an established relationship. The other man is their best friend. Our FMC is involved with all three.

Tropes: Modern fairytale retelling, why-choose, forced proximity, instalust, slow burn (with one of the MMCs), friends with benefits to more…so much more

Tags: That time a fine ass woman broke into our lake house and we kept her for the summer, MF, MFM, MM, MMFM, summer fling, bookish FMC, she's only theirs for the summer until…, MMC with golds

Content warning: This is a cozy, fluffy and filthy story, but it contains explicit content that may not be suitable for all readers. This content includes, but is not limited to, mention of recreational marijuana use, difficult family relationships, estranged parents, mention of past biphobia, somnophilia, mention of absentee parents, auralism, endometriosis, painful periods and fibroids. There is a smidge of angst between Goldyn (FMC) and one MMC in particular, but overall, the vibes are lovey-dovey and gentle.

Safety

If sharing is not for you, please put down this book. No other woman drama.

"…But someday you will be old enough to start reading fairytales again."
— C.S. Lewis

JUNE

I was lost.

That much I knew for sure.

Yet, I didn't know how to *undo* that fact. Hiking to the lake to celebrate summer solstice seemed like a good idea. *At first*.

I sat by the water, wrote down my manifestations for the new season, and got lost in a comfort read while the sun kissed my skin.

But then it came time for me to walk back, and I realized all that precious battery power I'd used to reread *Glory* for the third time had completely depleted my phone down to one percent.

Fuck. Was that my payback for obsessing over a fictional triad every chance I got? If I was wrong for envying Glory for having two boyfriends who were also boyfriends, then I didn't want to be right. I knew that kind of thing only happened in books, but it was my comfort read anyway.

And that comfort read had left me with a completely black screen five minutes into my trek back to the main road.

I couldn't say that I'd ever been good with directions. I relied way too heavily on technology to navigate spaces, even the spaces I should have been familiar with by now.

After living in Bliss Peak for the past year, I'd made this journey countless times. And yet, I still needed assistance on getting back to the paved trail that led to the public entrance.

Letting my head fall back, I stared up at the canopy of trees above me and squinted at the sun. That was a good sign. If the sun was still high enough to peek through the trees, I had time. Surely, I could figure a way out of these woods before nightfall.

I held firm to that hope until I passed the same tree three times and realized I was walking in circles. How that was even possible in the woods was beyond me, but I was kinda good at pulling off the impossible. And I knew it was the same tree because I'd left a red Sharpie at the foot of it after the second trip to make sure I wasn't losing my mind.

I mean, I *was* kinda losing my mind, but not to the extent that I didn't realize I was going in circles.

"Damn it, if I brought my Kindle instead of reading on my phone, I wouldn't be having this problem." Except the reason I didn't bring my Kindle was because I forgot to charge it last night.

This little predicament was the result of a domino effect of bad decisions, and there was really no need obsessing over things I couldn't change now.

Fragrant pine trees surrounded me on every side,

and each possible path looked identical to the one adjacent.

Blowing out a frustrated breath, I stood in place for a few beats and decided to go straight. No more turns, because apparently I didn't know this place by memory like I tried to trick myself into believing.

If I went straight, I would either end up deeper in the woods or back where I needed to be. Enough daylight remained for me to feel good about my odds.

So, I left my Sharpie right where it was and walked straight.

What felt like an hour passed before the rustle of pine needles under my sandals gradually faded, replaced by the crunch of gravel. The paved trail was nowhere in sight, but the winding path in front of me intrigued me enough to keep walking in that direction.

It only took me a few seconds to realize I was on the opposite side of the lake than where I usually ventured. The side with the lake house I could only admire across the water. It always looked like a black speck from my vantage point, but now that I was up close and personal, I realized just how wrong my expectations were for the "quaint little cottage" I imagined.

There was nothing quaint or cottage-like about this house. It was sprawling and beautifully modern with black siding, and enough square footage to house at least three large families comfortably.

For a while, I stood there with my jaw unhinged as I took it all in.

The rocky path morphed into their driveway where I found an old Bronco and matte black G-Wagon.

Hope ballooned in my chest.

"Somebody's home," I said to myself as I walked up to the front door.

Large, open windows spanned the house and not a single one of them was covered.

"Why don't rich people like curtains?" I asked no one as I drew closer to the house.

Decidedly, it was *none of my business* as long as the rich people in question were generous enough to let me charge my phone.

My stomach chose that exact moment to rumble and I placed a hand over it, trying to quiet the sound before I raised my other hand to knock on the front door.

Maybe they could spare a snack or two while my phone charged.

I stood there, knocking so long my knuckles ached. But nothing happened. Nobody came to the door and no one yelled from the other side to tell me to get the hell on either.

One glance down and I saw the bane of my existence—a digital keypad instead of a lock. I couldn't put my lock picking skills to use on it.

The rational thing to do would be to *get the hell on.* But there was nothing rational left in my brain after the last few hours I'd endured.

As it turned out, my sore ankles, rumbling stomach, and sweat slicked skin didn't know what *rational* was.

Add in my sudden urge to pee and I was fresh out of decorum. I needed relief. From...everything.

At the very least, I needed a bathroom break and a place to charge my phone.

At most, I needed a meal and a little air conditioning to cool off before I braved the walk back to the other side of the lake. Because now that I knew where I was, I kinda—*sorta*—knew how to get back.

Fighting the urge to squirm, I made it to the back of the house and my jaw dropped yet again. The whole deck was raised, leaving enough space under it for a boat, two kayaks and a bunch of other stuff I didn't have time to identify.

After climbing the stairs, I was greeted with another keypad instead of a lock and resisted the urge to scream. Instead, I pressed my nose against the window closest to the back door and sighed when I didn't see any signs of life.

Until now, I thought someone might have been inside and they were just ignoring me, but now that I could see no-one was home, I did what I had to do.

Do you know how hard it is to break into a house when your bladder is trying to embarrass you? It was the most humbling thing I'd done in a while. And when I got in through the broken window, I couldn't even marvel at the beautiful kitchen. All I could focus on was the small miracle of me not cutting myself on any stray glass in the process.

Then I ran straight for the hall in search of a bathroom. Luckily, the second door I flung open was a half bath.

A stunning forest view greeted me as I relieved myself, and I almost got lost in how magical it was.

As I washed my hands, my eyes traced over the raised stone covering the wall in front of me and the warm lighting provided by the two fixtures on either side of the mirror.

In a word, it was...perfect. If the spare bathroom looked like this, then what about the rest of the house?

As I trekked back to the kitchen, I pulled my phone and charger out of my crossbody bag and plugged it into the first outlet I saw.

Then I spun in a slow circle, admiring the double height ceiling and the panoramic views of the lake and forest.

Breathtaking. Everything was so tastefully extravagant. And somehow, warm and inviting at the same time.

A massive staircase separated the living and kitchen areas. It was lit by sconces that explained the soft, amber light illuminating the tall windows when I walked up. A familiar, woodsy scent permeated the air, adding another layer of cozy, rustic charm.

It always amazed me to see how other people lived.

Whoever owned this home had it made. This house was the epitome of postcard material.

And I couldn't help the guilt gnawing at me now that my bladder was relieved and a sliver of rationality crept back to the surface.

I'd broken into someone's house.

Eyes darting to the center island, I bit my lip at the red battery sign flashing on my phone screen.

It was still too soon to leave.

But the second I *could* leave, I would.

Right after I wrote a note apologizing for the window.

My stomach filled the silence of the home with another obnoxious growl. One that was harder to ignore now that I'd taken care of my other needs.

Okay, I'd write a note for the window and the food I was about to eat.

One turkey sandwich turned into two. And I needed a side with those sandwiches, so I devoured an entire bag of SunChips. Then I washed it down with the best iced tea I'd ever had. I was sure I could taste lavender and lemon on my tongue. It had no business being as refreshing as it was, and after the hours I'd spent walking through the woods, I was thirstier than I thought. It wasn't until I was done with my second full glass that I realized I'd put a nice dent in the pitcher.

The least I could do after my ungraceful binge was clean up after myself.

I washed the plate and utensils I used, content to grab my phone and get on about my evening. But then a glass dish on the far-end of the butcher-block counter caught my eye.

Cookies.

Just like that, my mouth watered at the thought of *something sweet*.

Walking over to the dish, I peered down at the dessert, content to just look and not touch. But then I noticed what kind they were.

Blueberry cookies?

And—oh my god—they tasted really good. So good I ate two of them without thinking and fully tipped myself over the edge from satisfied to full as a tick.

A drowsiness set in when I replaced the lid on the glass dish and it was all I could do to make it to the couch without tripping over my feet.

I grabbed my phone along the way and went through the motions of setting a fifteen-minute timer.

I'd rest my eyes for fifteen minutes and then I'd be out of these people's house. Long before they ever got home.

That was the plan. A cat nap and then get the hell out of dodge.

Except, I slept right through that alarm and the next time I opened my eyes it was because of the cold press of metal against my forehead.

I WISH I COULD SAY THIS WAS THE FIRST TIME I'D WOKEN UP with a gun to my head, but I'd be lying. There was that failed robbery sophomore year of college in that dodgy off-campus apartment. Then there was the time a month after I started traveling in my van full-time when the cops woke me up in the middle of the night to tell me I matched the description of someone who had just robbed a convenience store.

Neither time had been fun.

However, at least then my body had woken up ready to fight. But right now? Right now, a thick fog clouded my brain and it felt like someone had just submerged my body in a tub of molasses.

I felt drugged, subdued, not like myself.

Like my brain and body were on two different pages. In two different books.

My fight or flight instincts were nonexistent, and all I could do was lay there and will my eyelids to open.

"Holy shit, Rome. The gun is unnecessary," a male voice complained, the silky timbre doing more to rouse me awake than my own will.

"We could be harboring a fugitive. A fugitive who broke into our fucking house and you're worried the gun is too much?" came a curt response, his voice dry and devoid of anything remotely pleasant.

A fugitive? That was dramatic.

But he was right, I had broken into their house. And now I was stuck in some zombie-like state on their couch.

Lord help us all.

A weird knot formed in my stomach.

"At least get it away from her head." That sounded like a third voice. How many of them were there? And why couldn't I just open my eyes to see?

"Would you want to wake up with a gun to your head?"

"If I broke into someone's home and fell asleep, I'd say the owner had the right to wake me up anyway they pleased."

Their bickering would have made me giggle if it wasn't *me* they were talking about.

A collective, exasperated sigh came from across the room.

The person closest to me did *not* drop the gun, and it was just as well. Because something about my perilous predicament finally clicked in my head and allowed my body to function enough to exit its freeze state.

Finally...*finally*, my eyes popped open and I stared directly at the underside of the weapon and the hand gripping the butt of it.

"Shit, she's awake!" one of the friendlier voices announced.

Squinting, I flexed my jaw and sat up slowly. My

gaze darted to the person closest to me and I winced when we made eye contact.

The man holding the gun studied me with a tight expression, his eyes cold as I imagined, but at least he dropped the weapon to his side.

He didn't speak, he just stared at me until I looked away. But my reflexes were still kinda shit, so I got a good eyeful of him. He was…mesmerizing. Tall and solid with skin dark as night. Undeniably beautiful, but he was the exact kind of man I never wanted to piss off.

Yet, here I was…

"I can explain," I croaked in a voice that didn't sound like my own. "I'm not a fugitive."

Rubbing a hand over my neck, I cleared my throat and tried again.

"I'm sorr—"

"Get her something to drink, Sin."

It was then that I finally let my gaze travel to the other side of the living room and land on two men. I caught a blur of the one walking toward the kitchen. The other one was standing near the staircase, calm and collected with his arms crossed over his expansive chest.

He was just as tall as the man beside me, but his siena skin was covered in ink, inviting me to drag my eyes over the colorful tattoos. My eyes widened when he readjusted his arms and his biceps bulged.

Oh.

"Are you in danger, Goldyn?" He asked me, his voice calm to match his demeanor.

"H-how do you know my name?"

He reached in his pocket, his movements unhurried, and pulled out my sunflower card carrier.

"We found this in your bag while we were trying to wake you up."

I looked down, mortified that my bag was no longer slung across my torso and that I hadn't even noticed until now. "Oh."

"We turned off your alarm too," the third man announced, reappearing with a large mason jar full of water.

He handed it over to me and I took a grateful gulp. It felt as if someone had crawled inside my throat and rubbed sandpaper everywhere.

"You were *knocked out*. Must have needed the rest."

Why was he being so nice to me?

He dropped to his haunches in front of me and sent me a dimpled smile. "I'm Sincere."

Sincere looked me up and down and heat flamed my skin under his scrutiny. I know he didn't mean it to be unsettling, but his attention—hell, all of their attention—made me feel like a museum exhibit.

The man holding the gun—Rome, if I remembered correctly—finally tucked it in his waist and cocked his head to look at me with...curiosity?

I didn't know if that was better than the iciness from earlier, so I took another gulp of water to help me process it.

Jutting a hand over his shoulder, Sincere said, "This is Rome. Sorry about the gun. He's overprotective." Then he turned and smiled at the man still hovering near the staircase, like he was afraid to overwhelm me by joining the other men huddled around me. But there was unmistakable gentleness in his gaze that instantly put me at ease. "And that's my husband, Lorenzo."

"Oh. Nice to meet you?" I posed it as a question, because while I was charmed by their hospitality, I couldn't say I expected them to hold the same sentiment.

"Likewise," Sincere smiled. "What are you doing in our house?"

"Um, I got lost. I knocked. But when you didn't answer I got desperate and broke a window. My phone died when I was hiking and I don't know how I ended up on this side of the lake and—"

"Breathe, Goldyn," he interrupted, an amused lilt to his words. "We're not in a rush."

Romeo scoffed at that, but said no words otherwise.

I cut him a glance and then refocused my attention on Sincere. "I'll pay for the broken window. And the food I ate. And the tea—"

"What *tea*?" Romeo interjected, his brow hiked and demanding.

"The purple sweet tea that was in the fridge. I had a couple glasses after I ate."

"Ah, hell," Romeo muttered under his breath while Sincere's dimples went missing for the first time since he'd introduced himself.

"Define a *couple*," Lorenzo prompted, walking over to us.

"Two of these," I answered, holding up my mason jar as a reference.

Why was everyone looking at me like I'd suddenly grown five heads?

Lorenzo stopped beside Sincere and mirrored his squatting position to stare up at me with probing eyes.

For someone surrounded by three unknown men twice my size, I didn't feel the least bit afraid. Now that the gun was out of the picture, I even felt calm. But maybe that had more to do with my drowsy state than anything else. I was too sleepy to be scared.

"You had more than four times the serving size."

"Oh." I shrugged. "I probably needed the calories after the day I had," I said off-handedly.

"It's a sleep elixir," Romeo added gruffly.

"What?"

"I'm an herbalist and I was trying out a new recipe. It wasn't *sweet tea*, it was an herbal blend to help people with insomnia."

"Oh," I said again. "That explains a lot."

I thought it'd been the Itis, but this made more sense. A lot more sense.

It definitely explained why I got sleepy so fast, slept through my alarm and could barely wake up even when I knew there was a gun to my head.

The three men stared at me, perplexed awe shone on all their faces.

"I'm gonna go." My voice broke the awkward silence and prompted Sincere and Lorenzo into action.

"I think you should stay."

"*What?*"

"Just for the night," he clarified. "So Rome can check

you out in the morning to make sure you're good. Then one of us will drive you anywhere you want."

I opened my mouth to object and then closed it when my jaw felt heavy.

"We have a guest room. You can take a shower, relax and sleep off the tea a little more."

"I feel fine," I protested.

"You're slurring your words, mamas," Lorenzo said, laughter apparent in his tone.

I couldn't even react to the endearment because my head felt heavy again, and I knew they were right. I needed to sleep this off. And then I would wake up, go back to my van and pretend this never happened.

"Get her in the guest room, I'm going to find something for her to wear after her shower," Enzo said, his fingertips brushing over my lower back in a barely-there touch before he disappeared up the stairs.

Goldyn gave me a lopsided smile and then fell back against the sofa, the mason jar slipping from her grasp in slow motion.

Before I could react, Romeo caught it and placed it on the end table next to the couch. He swore under his breath.

"A shower might be ambitious," I mumbled as I looked at the half-asleep woman. How she woke up long enough to talk to us was a mystery. But I was just happy she wasn't on the run from something or someone.

I leaned down and hooked my arms under her knees and around her back, grunting from the dead weight her half-conscious body created. It was like lifting a heavy log full of wet sand.

"*Careful,*" Romeo warned when I had her nestled safely against me.

I narrowed my eyes at him and offered in a dry tone, "*You* wanna carry her?"

He muttered something slick under his breath, narrowed his eyes, and sidestepped me as if I'd just offered him poison.

Exactly.

Instead of hitting him with a smart ass retort, I focused on the woman in my arms and walked across the house to the guest suite.

"Can you come turn on the light and get some fresh towels?" I called over my shoulder, knowing he would already be in action doing what I asked. He passed me walking swiftly and disappeared down the hall leading to her suite.

Her suite? I shook my head, telling myself I was way too gone in the head to be thinking clearly and that was why I slipped up.

Goldyn nuzzled against my chest in her sleep, making me readjust my hold on her. It'd been too long since I'd been around a beautiful woman and it was showing, even if she wasn't awake to notice.

My heart had been thumping since I laid eyes on her. And when she woke up and spoke to me with that sweet, lyrical voice? I thought I'd entered another realm and still didn't know how to process it.

I snuck another glance down at her and my gut tightened.

Calling Goldyn 'beautiful' felt reductive, but I was too tired to try to find a new word. I'd gone from tipsy and ready to lay up with my husband all night to surprised, and then intrigued when our guest finally woke up.

There was nothing more sobering than finding a

strange woman on your couch when you lived in the middle of the woods.

I still couldn't believe Rome pulled a fucking gun on her. Then he wanted to act protective when he saw me carrying her.

Walking into the guest room, I sat her on the bench at the foot of the bed and hovered to make sure she didn't topple over. Whatever Rome had put in that elixir was giving her hell.

With a soft smile on my lips, I waited for her to steady her bobbing head and brushed my knuckles over her cheek.

"Hey, love," I called softly. "You think you can manage a shower?"

Slowly, her eyes eased open and confusion was quickly chased away by more fatigue. "S-shower?" she stammered.

"Yea, seems like you were outside all day." The scent of outside clung to her coupled with her natural scent. She didn't smell bad, per se, but I knew I would appreciate a shower after being lost in the woods all day.

"I don't have a change of clothes," she said, her voice clearer now, but I could tell it was taking everything in her to remain lucid.

"Enzo is getting you clothes. You just focus on the shower and I'll have some clothes waiting at the foot of your bed when you get out."

Rome chose that moment to enter with fresh towels and walked right past us without a word. I heard a faint *beep* and then a lid closing. The towel warmer.

"And you'll have warm towels when you get out," I added with a reassuring smile, hoping the gesture was more comforting than creepy.

Still ignoring us, Rome exited as quietly as he arrived and I smirked when Goldyn's eyes lazily tracked his journey out of the room.

When Goldyn finally stood up to go to the bathroom, I slipped out of the room and smiled with my back against the door when I saw Enzo rounding the corner.

"All I could find was your old student gov t-shirts and a pair of boxers and briefs. Any of our shorts woulda fell off of her."

Eyeing the assortment of clothes draped across his forearms, I smirked.

"What? Why are you looking at me like that?"

"You couldn't just bring one?"

"I wanted her to have options," he answered, cutting me a look and then moving me out of his way so he could knock.

But we both heard the water running at full force and assumed it was okay for him to go in. He eased inside and came back shortly after with full hands instead of empty ones.

"Her clothes," he supplied before I could ask. "I'll wash them so they're clean for her in the morning."

"I love the way you take care of people. This is why I married you," I teased, grabbing the back of his neck to pull his mouth against mine. Before I knew it, our tongues tangled in a familiar dance and I leaned into him, our torsos colliding.

"I'm sure there were other reasons," he said, biting my lip when I tried to kiss him again.

Then he was gone, leaving me to watch his retreat with the same smile from earlier stretching my lips.

I WOKE UP TO WARM SUCTION ENVELOPING MY MORNING wood. Wet sounds filled the silence of the early morning quiet, and I didn't need to open my eyes to know Sincere was under the covers with his jaw unhinged to fit me inside. I heard a gurgling sound when I hit the back of his throat and my hips involuntarily lifted off the bed.

"Shit, Sin," I groaned, my eyes popping open when he deliberately sucked the tip, spitting and using it as lube to jerk off the rest of my length.

Then he pulled his mouth off me entirely and pushed the sheets out of the way to slide me a knowing smile. "Oh, you're up."

"You knew that would wake me up."

His smile slipped and I bit my bottom lip while he continued to run his hand up and down my erection. I was hard and glistening with a sloppy mix of his spit and my precum.

There was enough lubrication for the movement to create a nasty soundtrack as his hand worked up and down and then up again.

When he sat up and used his knee to widen the space between my legs, I hissed at the first press of his forefinger against the sensitive stretch of skin just beneath my balls.

I was wound tight as hell, my body tingling and taut with the need for release, but I didn't want to do it like this.

"I don't want to come in your hand," I grit out, reaching for him.

Sincere ignored me at first, squeezing and stroking and applying just the right amount of pressure to make me see stars every time my eyes fell shut.

"Get the fuck up here." My voice was harder, more demanding and it was enough to get my husband exactly where I wanted him—on top of me.

Together, we kicked the blanket and top sheet away until they tangled at the foot of the bed.

As soon as his torso was aligned with mine, I locked my arms around his waist, holding him tightly in place.

"You know how I feel about you waking me up like that," I groaned against his lips, my eyes rolling back when his dick slid against mine.

"Mmm," Sincere moaned when my hips rose, meeting his languid movements. "Remind me of how it makes you feel, Enzo."

"Like—fuck," I broke off on a hiss and held him against me tighter, not caring if it inhibited his breathing. I didn't want him anywhere but right here, doing exactly what he was doing.

Sincere sucked my neck, his full lips fixated on my pulse point, and I'm sure it only skyrocketed under his attention. He grinded against me, dragging his hardness along mine. The friction we created was a sensation I'd do anything to prolong.

There was nothing like being wrapped up in Sincere Davenport. Ten years and I'd never gotten tired of being with him…like this. He was my partner for life, and I only ever wanted to give him everything. Whether that was a nut or the entirety of my trust fund, I didn't care. He took care of me like no other and I would *always* return the favor.

I felt the instant his precum joined mine in the mess of everything happening between us. It leaked against my stomach in a trickle of warmth and ran along the underside of his thick, veined dick. And I whimpered— fucking whimpered—like a bitch when he bucked his hips so I could feel him spreading the mess between us even more.

He braced his hands on either side of my face and looked down at me with lust and love and everything I adored shining in his eyes.

We stayed like that for a while, hips rocking as we maintained eye contact. Bliss edged into my senses and the same chemical reaction I had whenever he looked at me for too long took over.

"I fucking love you," I panted, my breath shallow and my heart in my throat.

"I know you do. That's why you're gonna come for me." He licked my lips, moving his head when I tried to turn it into a kiss.

"Don't tease me," I pleaded hoarsely. "Please… kiss…me, Sin."

His face softened and I knew he relented the second he groaned, "Fuck, baby."

Those were the last words either of us spoke before our tongues sought each other out and we lost ourselves in a nasty French kiss as our bodies rocked.

And rocked.

And stilled.

My orgasm built, my muscles contracted and my balls tightened with the need for release. But I wouldn't —couldn't—come without him.

Panting, we pulled away from the kiss and locked eyes again.

"You gone come for me?"

Throat dry, eyes burning, and heart pounding, I nodded and shifted so I could rut against him from below.

Sincere's eyes dipped low, until they were almost slits and then that little telltale frown furrowed his brows.

"Ahh, shit," he moaned, dropping his forehead against mine. Then he wined his hips in a slow circle, pushing his dick up and against mine. "Yes, Enzo—shit. Just like that."

The pressure building was almost painful at this point. And I wanted—no, *needed*—to come with him. Needed to feel him freeze up and let his cum paint my stomach so I knew I made him feel as good as he made me feel.

Finally, I gave in and threw caution to the wind, seeking the pleasure we both craved.

I jerked my hips against his, fast and hard, driving

us to a simultaneous orgasm that left my head spinning and eyes watering.

Oh, fuck. That was perfect.

It was always perfect with him.

Ropes of cum shot out of us, wetting up my stomach and his. Satisfaction trickled through me, a slow smile spreading my lips.

Sincere stayed on top of me for a while, his forehead still resting against mine until his breaths became more than desperate pants as he rode out the aftershocks of our shared release.

Loosening my hold on his waist, I kept my left arm around him in a lazy grip and reached up with my right hand to cup the side of his face.

His *perfect* fucking face. I would do anything for this face.

"Morning, baby," he murmured softly.

"Morning, Sin."

We kissed again, quickly, before we rolled out of bed and went to clean up in the bathroom. After a quick shower together, we stood at our sinks, brushing our teeth.

Sin paused with his toothbrush lifted in front of his mouth.

"Was I drunk or was there a stranger in our house when we got back from the restaurant last night?"

"You were drunk," I confirmed, sending him a lazy smile through the mirror. "We *both* were. But there *was* a stranger in our house last night and she's sleeping in our guest room right now."

It was funny because we'd gone out to celebrate

Rome's apothecary anniversary and he ended up DD'ing for us like he always did. Even when I offered to get us a car for the drive home, he claimed the one glass of red wine was enough for him for the night.

"Shit, I thought I was hallucinating."

I snickered and bent down to rinse my mouth. He went back to brushing his teeth as I reached for my face towel.

"Would be one hell of a hallucination if we all remembered it, Sin."

"Goldyn," he recalled her name thoughtfully. "She's pretty as fuck."

"Oh, that part you remember, huh?"

"Hell yea," he grinned before rinsing his mouth out.

Unfortunately, I couldn't disagree with my husband. Goldyn was pretty as fuck. And she had the sweetest voice. I didn't know if she'd be as subdued as she was last night whenever she woke up, but I was curious to be around her again. More than anything, she impressed me, but I hadn't missed Sincere's reaction to her last night.

He'd jumped at the chance to take care of her.

I could always tell when he was into a woman because he went from zero to a thousand in half a second. Pretty women were his kryptonite. And that was apparently true even if the pretty woman had broken into our home.

Sin and I were both bisexual. And while we were committed to each other for life, we still liked to date women from time to time. As long as she was open to being shared. We hadn't done that in a while though.

The past two years had been hectic, getting used to living in the mountains and adjusting to a slower lifestyle after living in King's Town for most of our lives.

No women had really caught our eye, but I couldn't say we were looking either.

But last night...

I knew what the fuck he looked like when he was smitten. And it happened on the spot with Goldyn. Maybe it had been the alcohol. Or maybe it had just been instant infatuation…

We'd see how the next few minutes went.

As if reading my mind, Sincere rushed past me, tugging off his towel to go in the closet. "Come on, let's get dressed and go see if she's okay. We can't leave her alone with Rome. He'll scare her off and I want to make her breakfast."

Shaking my head, a chortle passed my lips. Still, I joined him in the closet to find something to wear. "Something tells me she can hold her own. She wouldn't have been on our couch yesterday if that weren't the case. Goldy has self-preservation skills."

GOLDYN

When I woke up, instant confusion riddled me. This bed was too comfortable and the room was too cool.

I loved my converted van and everything it had allowed me to do in the past three years, but it wasn't a luxury sleeping experience. I couldn't say the same for wherever I was right now.

The sheets were soft as butter against my skin, the room was freezing, making me burrow deeper under the plush duvet. It was perfect.

Too perfect.

My eyes popped open.

"Where am I?" I croaked, looking up at the wood beams spanning the ceiling. A ceiling fan spun slowly, circulating the cool air.

Slowly, bits and pieces of the night before played in my head.

Getting lost.

Breaking a window.

Eating.

Drinking.

And falling asleep like a fucking creep in somebody's house.

I groaned, sinking deeper into the heavenly mattress and further under the safety of the blanket.

A few seconds later, a loud thud made me jump. It was the unmistakable sound of iron hitting the floor. Like someone had dropped a weight after a set in the gym.

Palm pressed flat against my forehead, another tortured groan greeted the air.

The last thing I wanted to do was confront any of the three men I met briefly last night.

Especially Romeo. He looked pissed, for good reason, when his housemates were helping me.

I knew I didn't deserve to be taken care of after what I'd done, and now I needed to find a way to sneak out before anyone noticed.

On a mission, I tossed the covers off me and walked to the bathroom in the far-right corner of the suite.

This time I was greeted with a lake view that took my breath away and I realized the guest suite faced a different direction than the bathroom I'd used in haste when I first broke in.

I winced at my own word choice, but shook my head as I emptied my bladder, washed my hands and face and tiptoed back in the room, trying to make as little noise as possible.

The clothes I found folded on the bench at the foot of the bed made me want to jump for joy. They were *my* clothes and they'd obviously been washed and dried while I was knocked out.

Pulling the soft gray t-shirt up over my head, I pulled on my t-shirt bra, cropped top, and leggings.

Everything still felt warm and fresh from the dryer, and that made me wonder how long ago someone had come in my room to leave them for me.

Tossing that thought aside, I neatly folded the t-shirt and boxers I'd worn last night and set them on the bench in place of the clothes I'd just put on.

Then I grabbed my bag from the chair by the bed and walked into the hall.

Relief washed over me when I found the place mostly silent. The only noise came from a gym I was assuming was on this side of the house. It took a few tries, but I made it to the main hall leading back to the kitchen, made a turn and speed-walked through the empty kitchen and living room.

My sandals were neatly lined up by a rack full of expensive men's shoes. The worn Teva's looked sorely out of place, and it was just as well, because I was leaving and never interrupting their world again.

I pushed my feet into my hiking sandals, leaned down to adjust the straps, and turned for the door.

My fingers made it as far as the handle when a deep voice boomed behind me, freezing all the blood in my veins.

"Going somewhere?"

THE PEOPLE IN MY LIFE WERE TOO TRUSTING. THERE WAS no other way to justify what happened last night. And no other explanation for my uncharacteristically early workout, either. I usually worked out in the dead of night. But after the events of the last ten hours, my schedule was thrown off and I woke up in need of the satisfying burn my muscles were currently enduring.

I knew I was being loud enough to potentially wake Goldyn up, but that didn't stop me from letting the fifty-pound dumbbell in my grip fall against the floor with a loud *bang*, either.

She was a guest in my house, not the other way around.

And really, *guest* was a stretch. She broke in to our house and Sincere and Lorenzo were too soft to turn her away.

And I saw that look in Sin's eyes when he first picked her up. He was already halfway in love with the woman and she'd barely said two words to us.

Pacing in a tight circle with my hands at my waist, I calmed down from my last set and was about to grab the weight for my next one, when I heard a soft, barely audible *click*, a few doors down.

It was only because I forgot my headphones upstairs that I was able to hear it.

Workout forgotten, I walked to the slightly ajar door and pulled it open to look into the hall.

On tiptoe, our houseguest made her way down the long hall and turned toward the kitchen.

An involuntary smile touched my lips before I knew what was happening. I reached up and physically *wiped* it away before I followed in her wake, purposely hanging back to give her a perceived advantage.

A head full of loose golden-blonde ringlets brushed her nape as she walked, moving in a mesmerizing sway as she tried to make her escape. I stood by the stairwell and studied her unsuspecting form while she went through the motions of putting her sandals on.

I'd been the one to put them near the shoe rack last night.

According to the ID we'd found in her bag, Goldyn was five-foot-four. She was slim and toned, if the glimpse of her abs in that shirt was any indication.

I couldn't see her face right now, but last night I'd had plenty of time to study her while she slept on our couch.

She had a damn near angelic face. Perfect features all around.

Light golden-brown skin, a smattering of dark freckles across her nose and cheeks, full lips and doe eyes I was sure she used to her advantage every chance she got.

They'd certainly worked on my best friends last night.

All they needed to see was the way those eyes rounded with fear when we woke her up and they were fucking goners.

Sad.

Tired of watching her like a creep in my own house, I stepped forward and asked, "Going somewhere?"

Goldyn stilled, her whole body tense. The closer I got, the more a familiar scent overwhelmed me, almost stopping me in my tracks.

She smelled like *me*.

That's when I remembered I'd hastily stocked the guest bathroom closest to the gym with duplicates of all my favorite stuff, thinking no one but me would ever use it.

Now, I had regrets.

I tried to shake the thought away and take smaller inhales. "You break into our house, spend the night, and you weren't even going to say bye first?"

She spun around then, and I might have imagined it but she did a double take when she saw I wasn't wearing a shirt. I hadn't even thought twice about following her without one. Sweat still dampened my chest as her eyes found my face. She cleared her throat, looking contrite. "I didn't want to impose anymore than I already have. The sun is up now, I can find my way back to the other side of the lake."

My eyes scan her from head to toe again, and I didn't bother trying to hide my suspicion.

"I never got to ask you last night," I started, fixated on her shoes. "You went hiking in sandals?"

For the second time in as many minutes, she cleared her throat.

"These sandals are made for hiking. But for your information, the trail to the lake is on a decline. I didn't expect to get lost," she replied defensively.

"Right."

"Is that all?" she questioned, gaze darting to the door.

I ignored her question and asked one of my own. "How do I know you didn't plan this break-in? It's very convenient that you picked our house of all houses."

It was no secret our lake house had been the talk of the town for the past few months. And even though Sin, Enzo and I kept to ourselves, it was also no secret that people were curious and wanted to see it. Some had flat out invited themselves when we were out shopping or running errands. And every time Sincere had politely told them to fuck off. This place wasn't an exhibit, it was our *home*. Even though I suspected an even bigger reason people wanted to see it was to understand our relationship. No-one could quite wrap their head around three men in their early thirties living together in the woods.

"Hello?" A small flicker in front of my face caught my attention and I realized it was Goldyn waving her hand.

Shit, I zoned out.

"Look, I don't know what elaborate scheme you're trying to unearth, but you won't find it. It's simple, I was lost. This is the only house I saw. I told you, I've never been on this side of the lake. I just needed a bathroom and a place to charge my phone. I apologize for how it turned out."

I didn't speak as I processed her explanation. There was a southern lilt to her melodic voice that made me want to hang on to her every word. She had a storyteller's voice. One I could get lost in and listen to all day.

"You're not gonna say anything?"

"What would you like me to say, *thief*?"

She laughed dryly and ran her tongue over her front teeth. "It would be nice to acknowledge when someone is speaking directly to you, but I can see now that may be asking for too much decency."

"Decency is overrated," I told her, shoving my hands in the pockets of my sweats. "And your parents did you a disservice if you walk around expecting everyone to be just as nice as you are."

Her tenuous smile fell before she gripped the strap of her bag tighter. Her knuckles turned red before she spoke again and all the forced cheeriness in her voice had vanished. "My parents couldn't be bothered to raise me. So I guess, in a way, you're right. They did me a *lot* of disservices."

Guilt formed an annoying knot of pressure in my chest.

Goldyn assessed me coolly, her whisky eyes intent before she blinked and looked away.

"Listen, I understand that just because I offer an apology it doesn't mean you have to take it. The good news is that you never have to see me again. So, if you'll excuse—"

Her departure was interrupted by the sound of bounding footsteps. Seconds later, Sincere and Enzo appeared at the foot of the stairs, fingers loosely intwined before they turned around and noticed us in the foyer.

Sincere spoke first, his smile so bright I had to look away as guilt continued to gnaw away at me. I was a fucking dick and now Goldyn wouldn't meet my eyes, after so brazenly holding contact up until now.

"Is everything okay?" Sincere asked, his gaze ping-ponging between us.

I spoke before Goldyn could, scared she would try to leave again. She couldn't do that before I got a chance to apologize. In *private*.

"Everything's fine." I infused my voice with levity I didn't feel. "Our houseguest was just trying to sneak out before breakfast."

Did I fall asleep and wake up in the Twilight Zone?

That question was the only one in my head as I looked around the dining room table at the family-style feast the guys had whipped up in less than an hour.

It made me believe they'd done it often and I was just witnessing their daily coexistence.

After talking me into staying for breakfast, Romeo disappeared upstairs to shower while Lorenzo and Sincere guided me back to the living room, gave me a remote and told me to watch whatever I wanted while they made a "quick" breakfast.

When Rome reappeared, he surprised me by walking right over to where I sat and kneeling in front of me. "How did you sleep?"

His quiet voice was so deep, it sent chills scattering over my skin.

"Good," I answered as his eyes swept over my face, clueing me in to the fact that he was physically examining me to make sure the tea didn't have any dramatic lasting effects.

"Did you wake up after your shower during the night?"

"No, I slept straight through to morning."

Romeo nodded.

"I'm just checking your pupils," he said by way of explanation as he moved in closer.

I didn't exhale until he backed up.

"Dreams?"

"Yes. Very vivid dreams actually," I said.

"And how do you feel now? Sluggish? Confused?"

"I feel great." It was the truth. I'd gotten the best sleep of my life and my mind was as clear as it'd been in a while.

"Good," he responded curtly before standing to vacate my personal space.

Just as abrupt as it started, the exchange was over, and Romeo walked into the kitchen without another word.

Now, I stared wide-eyed at my full plate after Sincere passed me yet another dish. This one was laden with muffins.

"Here you go, love. Have a muffin," he offered gently, moving to put one on my plate when I didn't reach for it quick enough.

My plate was already full and now I had a comically large muffin hanging off the side of it. I was going to be bursting at the seams whenever I pushed away from this table. But Sincere's soft-spoken nature wouldn't allow me to tell him no. Especially when I knew he'd made them.

"Take as many as you want," he offered, his kind eyes shining.

Something dawned on me then.

Oh, God.

Were they feeding me because they thought I didn't have food? That I'd broken in and eaten because I didn't have food at home?

"It's lemon blueberry," Sincere added, oblivious to my spiraling thoughts.

Those words triggered another thought and my mind detoured from its embarrassing track to the dessert I inhaled last night.

"Did you make the blueberry cookies on the counter too?"

He paused and looked at me with a subtle lift of his lips. "Yes. Why?"

"No reason." I cleared my throat. "I tried them yesterday. That's all."

He set the plate of muffins down and his smile bloomed. "Did you like them?"

"Yes. They were amazing. I've never had a blueberry cookie before." My mouth watered just thinking about them, but then the heat of embarrassment flushed my cheeks when I remembered what I did after eating them.

"I'm happy you liked them, love," Sincere said quietly, his expression unreadable as he picked up his fork to eat again.

"Sin is the best baker I know," Lorenzo chimed in, casting a loving glance at his husband. "But Rome and I are the only ones who ever get to try his stuff because he won't put himself out there."

It was clear there was more to it, but I wouldn't be the one to pry.

A companionable silence fell on the dining room as

we went back to stuffing our faces. The only sounds were of forks clattering against porcelain and the occasional thump of a plate being returned to the center of the table after someone took more of what they wanted.

Sincere and Lorenzo sat opposite me and Romeo, giving me a front row view of all their sweet touches and soft murmurs. Even if Sincere hadn't told me they were married last night, there'd be no doubt in my mind after sharing this meal with them.

Which led my musings to wander in a different direction. Where did Romeo fit into all of this?

Was he just their best friend or had I broken in to the home of a tr—

"What's on your mind, mamas?" Lorenzo's cool voice snapped me out of my thoughts. "Looks like you have questions."

When I glimpsed his face, I found nothing but an inviting smile.

I bit my lip, thought of how to phrase my curiosity and then just went with the straightforward approach. "So, what is your dynamic? Are all three of you in a relationship?"

Romeo cleared his throat.

Lorenzo raised an amused brow.

And Sincere, who was quickly becoming my favorite, actually answered, "Something like that. It's… unconventional. Technically, only Enzo and I are married. But we're nothing without Rome. We've been inseparable since college and just because we're not together in that way doesn't mean I love him any less. I still consider him my partner, one of my soulmates, and so does Enzo. We go where he goes. Which is why we're currently living up here in the mountains. He wanted to live here while he got his herbal apothecary off the ground. We were out celebrating the two-year anniversary last night." A fond smile touched his lips when he looked over at Rome and then back at me.

"I see." I didn't. Not really. But like he said, it was unconventional and therefore, really none of my business. They didn't even owe me an answer to that question, but my curiosity thanked them anyway.

"Most people don't get it. Think we're some sick codependent freaks, but..." he trailed and I dropped my fork to cut in.

"Fuck what other people think. It doesn't matter if they understand it as long as the three of you do. What you have sounds...special." My voice dipped and I ignored the longing trying to form a catch in my throat. I couldn't imagine going through life having one—let alone, *two*—partners I knew would be beside me through thick and thin. By design, my life had been a solo one for the past three years. I was tired of it. Hence, why I'd been in Bliss Peak for so long. It was time for me to put down roots, but I doubted they'd ever be as strong and interwoven as the ones these three had grown. I toyed with the end of my fork, the gold blurring as my eyes grew misty.

A sad smile lifted my lips and I reached for my orange juice. I didn't make eye contact with any of them again until I knew the annoying moisture in my eyes had subsided. "I hope you cherish that."

"We do," Enzo and Sincere said in unison. Romeo just gave me a sidelong look before lifting another piece of bacon to his lips.

"So what do you do if you're not a baker?" I asked conversationally.

"I take care of them," Sincere answered without missing a beat. There wasn't a hint of resentment or regret in his tone and the genuine smile that followed made me smile.

"Oh."

"Rome stays busy creating and testing products. And Lorenzo is always in the middle of ten meetings at once. They work hard as fuck and I like knowing they're good, even when they forget to be good to themselves."

"You're their center."

His brilliant smile brightened even more and I couldn't help but notice how straight his white teeth were. The man was criminally easy on the eyes with the most soothing energy to match. "I've never thought of it that way, but yea, I guess I am."

The rest of breakfast was pretty quiet. I didn't eat anything else, but I couldn't pull myself away from the table. I was too enraptured by their familiar dynamic. The way they finished each other's sentences. The way they refilled each other's drinks. The way Romeo got up and cleared everyone's plates without a word, and the way Enzo thanked Sincere for making breakfast with the most tender kiss I'd ever seen before he got up to answer a call.

My mind was so caught up in everything they were that I forgot everything I wasn't. Well, almost.

Until Sincere cleared his throat and I came to the realization that it was just the two of us in the dining room now. I'd been zoned out and he was watching me with a playful smile. "You aight, love?"

Honestly? No, I wasn't okay when he called me love and looked at me like that.

And that was how I knew I needed to get the hell out of dodge. This man was very happily married and I was sitting here all giddy and flustered from a friendly smile. He was not flirting, yet my synapses weren't firing the way I needed them to, so that message got lost in translation. "Yep, perfect. I should be going."

Sincere nodded, his gaze still locked on mine. "Enzo has a meeting and I need to call our supplier to get the window fixed, so Rome is going to drive you back into town before he heads to his shop. Is that okay?"

Call our supplier to get the window fixed. I gulped as guilt speared through me. Those words were the exact reminder I needed about my place in all…this. I was an intruder. I didn't belong here. And the sooner I got that through my head, the better.

It didn't matter how nice they'd been to me or how good it had felt to feel like I was a part of something. This wasn't real and I needed to *go*.

Patiently, Sincere waited for my approval, genuine interest shining in his brown eyes as he waited for my response.

"Sounds good," I managed tightly, hating the lump

in my throat. "Thanks again…for everything. You really didn't have to."

"It was my pleasure, Goldyn." He hesitated like he wanted to say something else, but thought better of it at the last minute. Then he stood, rapped his knuckles against the solid wood table and disappeared.

A sense of loss washed over me the second he was gone. I looked around the dining room like someone who'd just been left at a party where they knew no-one. I needed to leave…if for no other reason than to get away from this feeling invading my senses.

The feeling of being alone in a space where everyone else felt welcomed. Of being the spare. Of being here because I was tolerated and not actually wanted.

Everything in me told me to run. So that's what I did.

I pushed my chair away from the table, grabbed my purse from the arm of the couch and tried to walk out of the front door for the second time that morning.

This time I didn't even make it to the door before Romeo's presence at my back stopped me in my tracks. He hadn't said a word and his energy alone had made me freeze in place.

"Trying to escape again, thief?"

"Not escaping, just getting out of the way."

Something in my tone must have been cold enough for him to drop it because all he did was grab a set of keys from the brass hook on the wall.

"Let's go," he said gruffly, and left me with no choice but to follow him out the front door, down the stairs and to a violet BMW M4 I hadn't seen last night.

Romeo opened the passenger door for me, waited for me to get inside and then closed it before walking over to the driver's side. I observed his confident gait as he walked and gulped when he sat in the car beside me.

His earthy, masculine scent clung to everything inside the vehicle and made me feel surrounded by him on all sides.

How did that simultaneously rile me up and calm me down? It didn't make sense.

God, his jawline was sharp enough to chip ice. I was sure of it as I watched the muscle at the base tick. Unlike Sincere and Enzo's low-cut Caesars, Romeo's hair was long on top and tapered short on the sides. And he was so fine, it broke my brain a little bit.

Forcing my eyes away from his profile, I took in the pristine interior of his car. Nothing was out of place and there was even an oil diffuser in the center console, emitting mist as he expertly found his way through the woods and back to a main road.

When we did reach the road, I squinted, realizing we were on a completely different side of the mountain than where I started yesterday.

"Where am I taking you?" he finally asked.

"The library across from the farmer's market is fine."

He didn't bother responding and we rode in silence for fifteen minutes until…

"I'm sorry for what I said about your parents. I didn't know—"

"It's all good," I said, waving him off.

"No, it's not. I shouldn't have been rude to you. I'm just a creature of habit and I don't—"

"Like disruptions to your routine."

He cut me a glance, his jaw flexing as he nodded. "Yea. That."

"I get it."

More silence loomed and I occupied myself with staring out the window at the jagged rocks jutting out from the mountain, closest to the street. Rome handled the curves on the road with ease I was still trying to learn. It was nerve-racking getting adjusted to the narrow lanes and ever-winding roads. Especially when you drove a van as old as mine with questionable power steering.

"Congrats on your two year anniversary." I didn't know why, but I wanted to talk to him, hear his voice a few more times, before we said goodbye.

"Thanks," was all he said. But his jaw wasn't clenched anymore and I took that as a sign to continue the conversation.

"What's the name of your shop?"

"Soulstice Apothecary."

A gasp left my throat. "*Oh*, I've been there! You make my favorite hibiscus tea blend."

I tried to contain some of the excitement in my voice, but it was impossible. I loved that place. I bought all my incense, teas and body balms there. It was my little monthly treat to myself.

"How come I've never seen you at the shop or farmer's market?"

"I like being behind the scenes."

"Hmm. I get that."

The shop was always quiet with a single attendant near the front whenever I stopped by. But I knew they had an impressive online shop that brought in most of their revenue. They made everything in-house and shipped their tinctures, teas and herbal supplement capsules all over the state.

It was strange that he didn't even man his weekly booth at the farmer's market though. At least he wasn't there whenever I popped by.

Still, I couldn't believe I'd unknowingly come in such close contact with him so much over the past year.

It was a good thing though. If I knew the owner looked like Romeo, I probably would have found my way in that cute little shop way too often to spend unnecessary money just to get a glimpse of him. I *still* couldn't get over how beautiful he was. I hadn't met many people with a complexion as dark and mesmerizing as his in my life. I was so enamored I kept catching myself staring without knowing it. The muscles pulling his skin taut didn't help, either.

Before I knew it, we were in the library parking lot. I smiled when my Volkswagen bus came into view.

Just as I suspected, it hadn't been towed or booted overnight. The public library was one of the few places I could count on in any city not to be a stickler for extended parking.

"This is me," I said, pointing to the blue and white van.

Romeo frowned and pulled into the parking spot beside it.

"This is your car?"

"This is my *home*. But yes, I drive it too," I told him, digging around in my purse to find my keyring. "Thanks for everything. Tell Sincere and Lorenzo the same."

He didn't say anything as I climbed out of his luxury car and headed straight for the side door of my van.

Pulling them open to air out the stuffiness of the past twenty-four hours, I didn't notice when Romeo drove away. But he was gone when I finished opening all the doors and something about that was a relief.

It was back to the real world now.

As reckless as my little stunt was, the most comforting part was that I'd never seen them around town in the year that I'd lived here. And that gave me solace because it meant that I would never—ever—see those three fine ass men again.

TWO DAYS LATER, LORENZO SMILED AT ME AS I ENTERED his home office with lunch in my hands.

"Thank you, baby," he said, distracted by the line chart dominating his computer screen. A few minutes passed before he pushed away from the desktop and swiveled his chair to the part of his L-shaped desk where I'd sat the food.

My husband must have felt my eyes on him as he went through the motions of sanitizing his hands and grabbing his fork because he paused and looked at me with a quizzical stare. "What's up, handsome?"

"Do you think Goldyn would date us?" I asked, getting right to the point.

It'd been forty-eight hours since she left our house. The window was fixed. Romeo had dropped her off at home. And yet, I couldn't shake her or her infectious presence from my head. I'd spent too much time in the past two days wondering what she was doing and who she was doing it with. Whether she thought about that night or that breakfast we shared at all. Maybe it had been a normal day for her, but for me...

Enzo speared a piece of cubed steak with his fork

and brought it to his smiling lips. "Why did I know you were gonna ask me that?"

"I don't know." I sat forward in the chair facing his desk and rested my forearms against the edge. "Maybe because you wanted to know too."

His expression turned thoughtful, but he said nothing as he added potatoes to his bite.

"I know it's crazy after meeting somebody once, but I can't stop thinking about her."

"I met you once and knew I wanted to spend the rest of my life with you, Sin. So, I don't think it's crazy. When you know, you know. But I'm not gone lie to you and say I don't think it's risky."

He finally slid the fork between his lips and my eyes watched the rhythmic tick of his jaw as he chewed.

"Risky why?"

"Because we're married and a lot of women don't understand what that means when we say we want to date them."

Unease took up residence in the pit of my stomach. He wasn't wrong. And maybe it was delusion because something stronger than optimism told me Goldyn would get it.

"Goldy is beautiful and seems very nice, but we have to be honest with ourselves and remember that some women aren't cut out for our lifestyle. Dating two men at once, especially two who are already married, can be a lot."

"We can't approach it with all the negatives in mind."

"I'm being realistic, not negative, baby," he pointed

out, his voice gentling as he dropped his fork to look at me. "I don't want you to get your hopes up."

"I think she'd be open to it. She was sweet. Didn't you think she was sweet?"

He nodded and wiped his mouth with the napkin I put on his tray. "She *was* sweet. But that's the bare minimum when it comes to what we require from people. We haven't pursued a woman since we've been in Bliss Peak and the last woman we dated in King's Town got overwhelmed after three months. Even though she was very *sweet* too."

Anika had been perfect…until the reality of what we were started getting to her. She said she didn't feel like a part of our relationship, more like a temporary accessory. The note she left us said she had to leave before her already complicated feelings got more confusing and hard to ignore. And we hadn't heard from her since. That had been a few months before we packed up everything and moved to Bliss Peak.

So…over two years now.

It wasn't like I'd been oblivious to other women since we moved here. But none of them had called to me in any way. Until I met the woman who broke into our house.

And while I'd been happy with our family while we got adjusted to a new city, I couldn't deny my body's natural reaction to Goldyn. She intrigued me and made me so damn hyperaware when I was in her presence that I ran away by the end of breakfast to clear my head. I'd been so close to saying something then, but I was happy I hadn't.

I couldn't even fully articulate my fascination with her, but she was enchanting and I wanted to know everything there was to know about her. But only if Enzo was on board. Our dynamic only worked if we were both on the same page.

"So what if we tell her it's only for three months? Just for the summer?"

"So you want to begin a relationship with the end in mind? Instead of letting her feel temporary on her own, we establish that out the gate?"

That made me wince. Maybe I hadn't worded that right. I exhaled, trying to make it sound better in my mind. "I just don't want to overwhelm her. Maybe thinking of it as a ninety-day commitment will make it easier for her."

"For her? What about for us? Especially you. You don't know how to not get attached, Sin. I love that about you. You're all in. But we can't ignore our own needs to try and make her comfortable, either. I say let's see what unfolds naturally."

"But we've been here two years and I've never seen her. Not once. How is anything gonna unfold if we don't *naturally* cross paths?"

Enzo took another forkful of food and gave me a speculative glance. A wicked twinkle entered his dark eyes. "Maybe she'll break into our house again."

"You're not interested in her," I surmised. "Is that it?"

Something had to be the reason for his detached approach to this. Or maybe I really was being too much of a lover boy to see this from his pragmatic point of view.

"Sin," he sighed and the sound sent a dreadful tendril of angst through me. "That's not it, I always want you to have—"

His landline rang and clipped that sentence. We both stared at the phone as it rang a second time.

"I can ignore it," he offered, but he was already spinning in his chair to get closer to it.

"It's fine," I excused, rising to my feet. "Take it. I'm gonna go for a drive."

The phone rang again and Enzo split his gaze between me and the black device. "Are we okay?"

"Of course." I smiled, bracing my hands on the desk to lean closer to him. "Kiss me before I go."

Relief seemed to wash over him at my request and he obliged me, letting our lips meet in a quick kiss before I pulled away.

"I love you," I said over my shoulder.

His response came before I could pull the door closed behind me. "I love you too, Sin. More than you'll ever know."

"Ms. Ruby, I can't take all these nectarines."

"'Course you can, honeybee. There's plenty where that came from and we'll have even more next week," she told me with a proud smile, not caring that my arms were weighed down with her offering.

I visited Ruby's fruit stand at least twice a week, and she never failed to send me away with enough produce to feed a small family, even though she knew it was just me.

But today took the cake. It was officially nectarine season and she took one look at me when I got out of my van and shoved two baskets in my arms.

"You're too sweet."

"We take care of each other here. You ain't used to it yet?" Her smile deepened as she fisted her hands at her chunky waist.

She reminded me of my grandmother, down to her aggressively kind demeanor and full figure. She was everything I wanted to be as I aged: firm, kind and someone who cared deeply for people even if they were strangers.

And that made me remember my run in from two days ago...

"Ms. Ruby, I have a question."

"I got an answer, honeybee."

I smiled at the pet name she'd given me right out the gate. She said my blonde hair reminded her of a bee and hadn't stopped calling me that since. I wasn't sure she actually knew my real name and I was okay with that.

"I met three men the other day and I was wondering if you've heard of them." Of course, I knew she'd heard of them. Ruby knew everyone in Bliss Peak. She even knew of *me* before I ever made my first visit to her roadside fruit stand.

The other woman looked down the bridge of her nose at me, waiting for me to go on.

"Sincere, Lorenzo and Romeo. I don't know their last names, but they live near the lake—"

"In a house straight out of a magazine?" Ruby finished for me, nodding vigorously. She swatted a few flies away from her inventory and looked at me with a curious tilt of her head. "Yea, I know them. They keep to themselves out there in the woods. What you want with 'em?"

Her question made me giggle and I fought to readjust the fruit in my arms without spilling anything. "I don't *want* anything with them, I've never seen them before and I guess I was feeling nosy."

"They're good men," Ruby said, reverence coating her words. "They don't bother a soul and they help me with anything I need during the wintertime since Pauly's back has been messed up."

The mention of her husband made me smile. I'd

never seen the man without a tobacco pipe hanging precariously from the corner of his mouth or a smile on his face.

"Good boys," she added fondly, rocking back and forth on her heels.

I nodded, not at all surprised Sincere, Lorenzo and Rome were good in Ruby's book. Everybody in Bliss Peak was so damn nice it still gave me pause from time to time. Not that people were inherently cruel where I came from in New Hope, but they weren't like this.

Then again, I guess Bliss Peak hadn't earned its reputation as the safest place in the state for nothing, either. Before I arrived, the idea of a quaint, all-Black mountain town blew my mind. Especially since it was only five hours away from my hometown.

But life here felt like I'd been transported to another world.

I saw why my grandmother couldn't shut up about the place my whole life. So much so that I thought it was some fictional land she thought up to keep me entertained with her countless bedtime tales. But it was very much real and the place was so enchanting I wanted to bottle some of its essence and keep it for a rainy day. In case I didn't always live here. In case I ever forgot what it was like to be surrounded by love no matter what.

When I was growing up, money had been too tight for my grandmother and I to ever make the roadtrip to visit. And now that I had the money to travel wherever I wanted, she wasn't here to enjoy it with me…

Funny how life worked.

"You a'ight, honeybee? Look like you thinking about something mighty serious," Ruby called, breaking me out of my thoughts.

Her sweet, weathered voice broke my reverie and I looked around, remembering I was on the side of the road. I took a minute to recenter myself, taking in the familiar surroundings. The mountains served as a perfect backdrop for Ruby's yellow pickup truck and a smile tugged at my lips.

"I'm okay," I assured her. "I have a meeting to get to, so I'll see you later."

"You come around the house later if you want a plate. Pauly been waiting all year to pull out his grill and he ain't stopped all week. And I'm thinking about making a cobbler with some of these nectarines."

My mouth watered at the thought.

"Yes ma'am. I'll come by." I was fully aware she invited me over so often because she knew I didn't have many friends here yet.

And as much as I loved my own company, I couldn't resist basking in the older couple's wisdom and friendship. There was something addicting and comforting about their presence and I made a mental note to pick up a bottle of wine or something after my meeting to bring to dinner with me.

"Good luck at your meeting, honeybee," Ruby called as I climbed into my van. "I'm praying for you."

I'd known Ruby long enough to know that her saying that *was* the extent of the prayer. And something about that made me happier than it should have. With my fruit haul secured on the passenger seat,

I smiled out of the windshield at her until she was out of view.

Instead of heading straight to my appointment, I took a detour through the town square, intent on scoping out my dream storefront for good luck before going to the bank.

I slowed my van to a stop and perked up when I saw the empty commercial unit. It'd been my dream to convert it to a bookstore lounge since I moved here, and the fact that it was still empty made me feel like it'd been purposely set aside for me.

As always, I imagined the awning I would put up, the flower boxes I'd install and the little bistro table for two I'd place just outside the door on the sidewalk.

Before I could zone out too long, a now familiar violet BMW parallel parked in front of a shop, half a block up and caught my attention.

Romeo.

Had I conjured him up by asking Ms. Ruby about him? As many times as I'd been to his shop, I never saw him coming or going. And now…

Before I could second-guess myself, I threw my van in park, checked my reflection in the visor mirror and grabbed a basket of nectarines from the passenger seat before hopping down.

I still had half an hour before my meeting, and I knew how I was spending it.

I walked in Soulstice and immediately calmed when I inhaled the aromatherapy blend of the day. The calming scents of sandalwood, jasmine and lavender bathed the small shop.

Aside from the attendant at the register, I was the only person inside, and even though Romeo was at the forefront of my mind, he was mysteriously out of sight.

"Hi, Lottie," I said to the pretty dark-skinned woman up front.

Her face split into a welcoming grin, putting all her teeth on display. "Hey, pretty girl. Weren't you just here a few days ago? What you need?"

"Romeo," I answered simply, smirking at the way her eyes swelled with my reply. I gestured toward my peace offering. "I have something for him."

"Oop. I didn't know you knew him. Hold on." She pressed a few keys on her keyboard before an answering *ping* sounded a few seconds later. "He'll be right out."

"Thanks," I exhaled, turning away from the counter to study the minimalistic aesthetic of the shop.

Wood flutes piped in through hidden speakers, a spotlight table for their herbal remedy of the week and a few shelves stocked with their signature tea blends, healing balms and smell goods.

"How do you two know each other?" Lottie asked when I spun back around.

"Um we—"

"She robbed me," Romeo's deep voice cut in. He materialized from the back, dressed in all black with an unreadable look on his face.

I pursed my lips and fought an eye roll. "He's exaggerating."

"Am I, *Goldy*?" He cocked his head, a barely there smirk teasing the corner of his mouth. I didn't know what to make of this playful side of him, so I just gulped. Then the glint of diamonds caught my eye and I moved closer, transfixed by the jewelry adorning his smile.

"You didn't have that the last time I saw you," I pointed out.

Romeo didn't blink. "I told you, you threw off my routine. Forgot to put it in."

I didn't miss the way Lottie's eyes danced between the two of us, questions evident on her face.

"Right. Sorry. I brought a peace offering." Scooping up the overflowing basket of nectarines, I held it over the counter. I'd even been generous enough to give him the basket with the most fruit.

Instead of taking it right away, he eyed my gift suspiciously.

"Why are you looking at them like that? I'm not the one out here concocting teas that put people in a coma."

His eyes flickered up to mine and the piercing intensity of his dark orbs made my breath catch.

In the time since he'd walked out front, I'd become

too aware of my heartbeat and the blood rushing in my ears.

Getting riled up was the last thing I needed before heading to the bank.

When Romeo continued to stare at me unflinchingly, I placed a hand over my erratic heart and opened and closed my mouth several times.

Got damn it, why did he get to walk around looking like that? I'd never met a man more infuriatingly attractive than the one looking at me right now.

Something about the all black attire against his already inky skin was sending my whole body into a panic.

When the words stuck in my throat saw fit to untangle themselves, I announced, "I'm leaving, see you around."

Lottie said something to my back, but I was too focused on vacating the premises that I didn't catch it.

Somehow, I still heard the low rumble of Romeo's voice when he said, "Let me know the next time she comes in."

THE BEST THING ABOUT LIVING IN BLISS PEAK WAS THAT every part of it looked like a damn post card. The low hanging clouds hovering over mountain peaks. The grassy slopes. The random animal sightings. All of it was straight out of an outdoor magazine and I wouldn't even believe a place like this existed if I didn't witness it every day.

Our house was nestled in a valley, mostly surrounded by trees. But it only took going a quarter mile in either direction to find other homes tucked away like ours. I was biased, but I knew for a fact that ours had the best views all around.

The back of the house faced the lake. The side facing east had the best forest view. And the west had an unobstructed view of the summit. Our deck wrapped around three-fourths of our property, so depending on our moods, we could bask in every picturesque angle.

After customizing everything to our individual tastes, it made sense that we spent most of our time at home. But I was still aware of how much we probably missed out on too.

The balmy, summer breeze flowing in through my

open windows was enough to make me keep driving with no destination in mind.

I was only supposed to drive a few laps around the base of the mountain, possibly stop by Rome's shop to see if he would make it home for dinner, then go home. But on my third lap, a flickering yellow sign with Lucky's Tavern written on it caught my eye from the other side of the road. Lured by the charm of the small building, I steered my Bronco into the gravel parking lot and studied the restaurant with a frown.

How many times had I driven past this place and never noticed it? Was it a local hangout? When I cut my engine and checked my watch, I realized it was only a little after one in the afternoon. The few cars in the lot had to be the lunchtime crowd.

Between Lorenzo's workaholic tendencies and Rome's preference for being in the house, it was rare that we ever went out. Dinner a couple nights ago was the first time we'd gone out since Enzo's birthday in February.

And I was suddenly aware of how problematic that was. We had a pretty social life back home in King's Town. And now we were probably known as the town's recluses. Maybe it was time for us to change that. And maybe this bar was the perfect place to start.

Shaking my head with a small smile, I snatched my key out of the ignition and flung my door open to hop down.

Parked on my right was a white Audi with blacked out windows. On my left was an old pale blue and white Volkswagen bus. I smirked because those two cars were the perfect representation of Bliss Peak's demographic.

Inside, my prediction about this place being a local favorite was confirmed when I saw the amount of people cramped around the bar, baskets of food and cold beer sitting in front of them. Deciding not to add to the mayhem, I walked over to the far right wall and started looking for an empty table. I wasn't that hungry anyway, I just wanted to people watch.

I made it about five steps over the creaking wooden floors before golden blonde curls stole my attention and left me standing a few feet away from her booth.

The woman didn't notice me, she was too busy fucking up a burger and cheese fries while tapping periodically on her phone screen. She was completely caught up in her own world and I stood there for a second admiring the abandon on her face as she wiggled in her seat with every bite.

And I would have stood right there, admiring the stranger God had placed in my path for the second time in as many days, but someone bumped my shoulder and startled me out of my trance.

"My bad, man. It's tight in here," a deep voice said before moving around me.

I didn't acknowledge him as I inched closer to Goldyn. She sat alone in a booth big enough for five people and looked content to keep it that way.

Clearing my throat, I ignored the persistent thumping behind my ribcage. "Is this seat taken?"

"Hmm?" Goldyn replied absently, grabbing a

bunched up napkin to clean her fingertips before she went back to tapping her phone screen.

"Goldyn," I called.

Her head snapped up and recognition shone in her sultry, amber gaze.

"Oh! Hi. *Hi*! Sit down," she nodded to the section of the booth facing her.

After I took my seat, I stared at her for another beat and didn't bother hiding the smile on my face.

"Hi, Sincere."

"Hi, *Goldyn*." There was a natural inflection on her name and her smile brightened when she noticed.

Fuck me.

How was she this pretty? So effortlessly?

She pushed her hair away from her eyes and then propped her chin up on her hands, leaning in to me. I bit my lip, not trusting what I would say if I gave in to my instincts right now.

I'd spent the last two days obsessing about seeing this woman again and a random sign on the side of the road led me to her.

"Why do you look so distracted? Is everything okay?" She grabbed a new napkin from the dispenser and wiped at her hand diligently.

I wasn't distracted, I was *awestruck*.

With her attention split between me and her task, I took the time to get my shit together and smiled at her.

"What were you doing when I got here? Did I interrupt something?" I asked after a quick glance at her phone, realizing the screen was now black. Even though I knew she might have been busy, I was still selfish enough to hope she didn't send me away because of it.

"Oh, I was reading," she answered, her voice airy. "I usually eat alone so I always bring entertainment."

"Why do you usually eat alone?" I asked, frowning on instinct.

Her face softened at my question, but she didn't answer it. She asked a question of her own instead. "How are you, Sincere?"

"Better now." God, I sounded like a middle schooler stammering in front of my crush. But if she noticed, she didn't let on and sent me a beaming grin.

"I was just asking someone about you and then I saw Romeo earlier."

I sat forward at that information. Why was I jealous of my best friend when I was sitting here in front of Goldyn now? "You saw Rome?"

"Yea, I went by his shop." Her voice was light and airy, giving nothing away about their visit.

For a while, I sat there watching her pick at the cheese fries before I found my voice again. "I can't believe I ran into you here."

Goldyn's warm smile was still in place when she picked up her drink and took a long sip through her straw. "Well I'm here every Friday. So now you know where to find me."

I paused for a minute to take in her lightly made up face and the silk button up and slacks she had on. When she'd asked us what we did for a living, I'd failed to do the same in return. Now I tried to imagine a career that fit her carefree demeanor and was coming up short.

So I just asked. "Where are you coming from?"

"The bank," she replied in a glum tone. For the first time since I'd walked in, her smile slipped. "I went to check on a business loan and they basically turned me away, saying I wasn't their *ideal* borrower."

"Shit." The dejected look on her face made my heart sink. "I'm sorry, Goldyn."

"It is what it is." She pushed her plate away from her. "But the crazy part is that I spent the past three years paying off debt and saving money and it still doesn't matter. My business isn't old enough and my personal credit report doesn't have enough open accounts to make them trust me. They said I'd need a guarantor or something..." Her voice trailed and I could tell she was trying to keep it light, but it was impossible to miss the disappointment clinging to everything she did.

The subtle slump of her shoulders, the downturn of her pouty lips at the corner, and the faraway look in her eyes. She looked sad and that fucked with me more than it should. I wasn't responsible for the sadness, and yet, I wanted to play a part in fixing it.

"What was the loan for? If you want to talk about it..." I tried cautiously.

Luckily, Goldyn latched on to the question and launched into an explanation of her dream.

In a matter of minutes, I was swept up in her world and the way she spun words to tell her story. The crowd in the bar thinned out and the quiet that followed allowed me to hear every word falling from those pretty lips.

"I didn't graduate college until I was twenty-four," she divulged, sighing. "It took me a while to even want to go after my grandma passed right after I graduated highschool. I deferred my admission as long as they would let me, but when I finally went, it was worth it.

"All through college, I was a bottle girl. Then a bartender. I stayed in the dorms until junior year because I didn't want to spend money on rent." A laugh bubbled out of her and just like that I was addicted to the sound. "But by then, I was three to four years older than everybody else, so I got an apartment. When I graduated, I spent the summer using the money I saved from the club to convert a van that had been sitting in my grandma's backyard for ages."

Goldyn paused, a fond glint entering her eyes.

"She left it to me and I thought it would be perfect for what I wanted to do. So after I converted it, I hit the road and traveled around the States for two years. I danced for cash at clubs that allowed visitors and then I moved on to the next place. Bliss Peak was the last stop on my "tour." I had no idea where I was going once I left here, but it's been a year so I guess I'm here for a while. Not just passing through…"

Looking away, she heaved a sigh that let me know she was done talking for now.

We sat in silence. Me processing everything she'd told me, and Goldyn surveying the bar like it was the first time she was really seeing it.

I knew nostalgia and grief had a unique effect on everyone so I let the moment linger as long as it needed to.

When she finally met my eyes again, I didn't hide the smile that bloomed on my face.

Lorenzo's words from a few days ago rang true. Goldy definitely had some self-preservation skills.

"You're the most fascinating woman I've ever met. I love how brave you are."

"Thank you." I loved that she didn't shy away from the compliment. Even if she looked shy accepting it, she *accepted* it.

Somehow in the time she'd been talking, we'd inched closer and closer to each other until we were sitting side by side. Elbows and shoulders brushing as we fell deeper into the conversation. "So, your van…do you sleep in it during the winter too?" Winters were cold in Bliss Peak. We got a lot of snow and thinking about her shivering in a van didn't sit right with me.

Goldyn shook her head, mindlessly pressing the home button on her iPhone 8 screen over and over.

Snapped out of her trance, she turned her head to look at me, and notes of cherry and vanilla plagued my senses.

The more I breathed her in, the harder I got and I hoped against hope she didn't make the wrong move and notice that shit.

"When I was on the road, I stayed in places with warm winters. But last year was my first winter here and luckily I got a seasonal gig at the new resort on the other side of the mountain. Came with meals and a single room."

Another brief silence passed before I changed the subject.

"What was her name?" I asked, knowing I didn't need to elaborate.

A tender smile touched her lips, love apparent in the way her eyes softened. "Benita. But everybody called her Bennie. Grandma Bennie."

"I know she's proud of you."

Goldyn's smile turned rueful. "She'd be more proud if I could do what I said I was going to do. The funny part is that I have plenty of money. I've always spent way less than I make, but I know it looks better when a bank is backing me. This isn't exactly a cash economy."

"Tell me what you want to do," I prompted, not wanting her to stop talking.

She reached in her bag, opened a notebook and took me through her plans for Read the Room, a bookstore reading lounge. She told me every detail about the layout, the book and coffee pairings she wanted to curate, and the different seating options she would set up throughout the shop. It sounded exactly like something I would expect from a woman like Goldyn. And now I knew why I couldn't place her at any other jobs earlier. Because she wasn't doing the one she was obviously put on this earth to do.

Her breath tickled my forearm when she gave a long exhale. "I just wanna do something that means something." She met my gaze again. "You know?"

All I could give her was a nod. Because I had yet to find anything outside of my partners that made me light up the way she did talking about her goals. I was still happy she confided in me. It meant everything that she trusted me enough to talk to me for hours about it.

"I want people to have a safe place to just *be*. Get lost in a book, eat too many pastries and drink too much coffee," she laughed, the breathy sound making goosebumps dot my skin. "Hey, you never know, maybe one day I'll be bugging you to make a custom batch of cookies just for my store."

Icy tendrils of doubt tried to freeze me in place. "W-what?"

"You heard me. You're an amazing baker. I'd have the best book selection and sweets in town. Now I just have to find a coffee plug. Know anybody?" she asked, not understanding the gravity of her words.

No one had ever wanted to hire me for anything. Mostly because I didn't put myself out there. I was too scared of rejection to even try.

"I'll ask around for you," I said instead of telling her how much her confidence in me shook me sideways. It was one thing to have Enzo and Rome rave about the stuff I made. But Goldyn had no reason to placate me.

"Hmph. I might fail. I might lose all my money and have no customers. But I have to try. I won't know unless I try, right?"

I won't know unless I try.

Those words hit me right in the chest.

"What are you thinking?" Goldyn wanted to know.

I didn't hesitate, knowing a dreamy look was probably plastered on my face. I couldn't help it if I tried. "I'm thinking I could listen to you talk about your dreams all night."

Bells chiming above the entrance broke the spell my

words had cast and when Goldyn tore her eyes away from the new arrival, the moment had passed.

She stared down at her hands. "It can't be a vision that only lives inside my head anymore. I know it sounds frivolous to some people, but it's the only thing I've wanted consistently my entire life."

"So fuck what other people think."

She gasped, surprised by the force of my words and looked at me with a bemused smile.

"Isn't that what you told me? *Fuck how it looks to other people and do it anyway.*"

For the hundredth time, she batted her curls out of her face and smiled bright enough to rival the sun. "Yea, I guess I did say that. But I like how it sounds coming from you instead. I'm gonna buy you a drink."

Before I could protest and insist on paying for it, she slid out of the booth and walked over to the bar.

AN HOUR LATER, I EYED SINCERE OVER THE RIM OF MY second drink and saw his first old-fashioned was still half-full. Maybe I shouldn't have asked the bartender for his 'best middle-shelf' liquor on that first order?

"Don't like the drink? I can get you another one…" I offered.

"No." He shook his head and my brows fell. "I mean, the drink is fine. I'm just a lightweight and I don't want to be drunk when I get the courage to say what I want to say."

He sounded nervous and that made me nervous. Sweat pricked my palm and I try to play it off by collecting the cool condensation on my cocktail glass.

A few minutes ago, his knee started jumping under the table and I wrote it off as a natural reaction to sitting for a while. We'd been huddled in this booth for *hours* and he didn't seem like a man who stayed idle for long. "Oh?"

Sincere met my eyes, the kindness in them striking me for the hundredth time since he walked into the bar. I'd never met another person with such a vulnerable gaze. His brown eyes said so much even though he'd revealed very little up until this point.

My nonstop chatter probably didn't help. It was just that today hadn't gone anywhere near the way I thought it would.

Showing up at Romeo's shop earlier wasn't very *I'll never see these three fine ass men again* of me, but I couldn't bear the thought of someone being mad at me. Even though Romeo and I had ended our exchange amicably two mornings ago, I couldn't shake the way he'd looked at me. That look was missing in action when I popped up on him today, so I was counting it as a win. And now, here I was with Sincere.

I was failing the mission. Successfully. All I needed now was a Lorenzo sighting and I'd probably—definitely—lose my mind.

Sincere pulled his bottom lip into his mouth, and the dimple in his left cheek sent my stomach into a fit of flutters.

God, I would never get over that. I could see *exactly* what Lorenzo saw in this man. Too damn fine for words. Everybody in that house of theirs was just attractive beyond anything my brain could comprehend. In three uniquely different ways too.

And they're *taken*.

The men in that house are off-limits, Goldyn. Stop being a bird because one of them gave you some attention.

"Are you dating anyone?"

The chirping in my head kicked up a notch at his question and I tossed back the rest of my drink before staring at him with a teasing smile.

"Why? You wanna set me up with somebody?"

He hedged, rubbing his fingers over his bottom lip as he looked at me.

Oh, god. I was joking but he looked serious.

"Well…no. Not really." His eyes darted to mine before he quickly tore them away.

Goodness, he was killing me now. I could understand nerves, but the anxious energy rolling off of him was infecting me.

"I meant it when I said you're the most fascinating person I ever met. You're beautiful and your energy speaks for itself. I'm *really* glad we met. I'm interested in you, Goldyn."

That had to be the most respectful way anyone had ever expressed their interest in me. It was direct. And yet, I was still confused.

This man was married. I'd heard him say it with my own two ears. I'd *seen* it at that breakfast. He and Enzo couldn't keep their hands off each other.

So, what was happening?

"I'm sure that's confusing for you to hear."

I knew the smile on my face was awkward, but I couldn't help it. "A bit."

He adjusted against the booth, a little away from me so he could look me in my eyes directly. "Enzo and I are non-monogamous."

I nodded. That much had been clear when I put the pieces together about the platonic romance he and Lorenzo shared with Rome. It was refreshing and intriguing and I loved that for them.

"Okay." I sat up straighter, ignoring my bladder's

plea to break the seal. I couldn't ruin this moment and get up just yet.

"As much as we love each other, we're both still open to giving and receiving love from other people."

I nodded again, my eyes trained on his as he peered into my soul.

Sincere paused to lick his lips and I couldn't help but track the movement of his tongue.

"I'm gonna be honest with you, I haven't been able to stop thinking about you since the night we met. I talked to Enzo about it and he told me to see what unfolded naturally. And then I randomly run into you after I took a drive to clear my mind. I can't help but see that as a sign."

He'd talked to his husband about his interest in me?

"You…" I didn't know how to form the question I wanted to ask, so I let it go.

Thankfully, Sincere read my confusion and spoke up. "If I leave this bar without telling you, I may never see you again. Or it may be another two years before our paths cross again, and that possibility will never be okay with me. I want the chance to know you. And if you tell me you're even a little bit interested, I'll answer any question you have. But if you tell me this isn't your thing and you couldn't see yourself being loved and spoiled by two men who ar already in love, I wouldn't blame you either." He scrubbed his hand down the side of his boyishly handsome face. "I know it's unusual because you'd be agreeing to the both of us. But I just want a chance and I have to put myself out there even if it means you never want to see me again. Shit. I'm nervous and fucking this up. If Enzo was here, I'm sure this would come out a lot smoother. But…"

"Sin, it's okay. I hear exactly what you're saying." I placed my hand on his and my heart melted at the slight tremor in his fingers. Oh, my god. This sweetheart of a man wasn't kidding about being nervous. "First of all, I want you to know that there is no timeline where I'd never want to see you again. I wouldn't have spent the last however many hours talking to you about my dreams if that was the case."

He smiled and the timid lift of his lips endeared me to him even more.

"You are one of the nicest people I've ever met, and I say that in a town like Bliss Peak where *everybody* is nice."

Calmer now, Sincere slid his hand from under mine and started toying with the pearl button on the cuff of my sleeve. "Will you come home with me tonight? I'll cook you dinner and me and Enzo can explain everything to you." His unyielding eye contact was like being trapped in sinking sand, the longer I looked at him, the deeper I sank without realizing it. And the problem was I didn't want anyone but him to save me.

"Goldy?"

Goldy.

I'd heard some variation of that nickname for years, but he breathed new life into it. Shivers erupted on my sensitive skin and I tried not to hyper-fixate on the way his fingers felt against my wrist while he continued to fidget with my button.

"Hmm?"

"Will you come home with me? You can sleep in the same room as before after dinner. We won't touch you, but it would be easier for us to discuss everything if we're all in one place."

"I—"

My phone started buzzing on the table in front of us, shattering the moment as I snatched up the device at the sight of Ms. Ruby's name on my screen.

Shit. Dinner. I forgot I said I would come by.

"Ms. Ruby," I answered breathlessly. I had no reason to be out of breath, but it felt like I'd just sprinted up the mountain with a fifty-pound hiking sack on my back.

"Why you sound so winded, child? Did I catch you in the middle of something?" She sounded more amused than anything and I shook my head even though she couldn't see me. Her voice took a mischievous dip. "Is he nice-looking?"

My face flushed at her question because while I wasn't doing anything with Sincere, he was more than nice-looking. And he was still touching me. He'd moved on from the button on my cuff and was now mindlessly caressing the tattoo at my wrist that read *Be Good.*

I was seated, but still a little dizzy from the uninterrupted contact. If his touch alone could do this to me, then what the hell was I gonna do with Lorenzo in the equation?

"Pauly wants to know if you want hot sausage or franks for dinner. He grilled ribs, corn, and a few—"

"Ms. Ruby, can I have a raincheck for dinner?"

"Aww *sookie sookie,* now! You *are* with somebody."

Sincere's laugh let me know her carrying on was loud enough for him to hear and my face flushed again. I didn't want to know what I looked like right now.

"Why would your mind automatically go to male company?"

"It's the best case scenario, honeybee. You know I gotta live vicariously through you."

Sighing, I shook my head with a faint smile.

"Well, I'll leave you to it. But I want to hear about it. Call me on *What's Up* tomorrow so we can debrief."

It didn't matter how many times I told this woman it was *WhatsApp,* she called it whatever she felt like that day and it brought a giggle out of me every time.

When I hung up, I purposely avoided Sincere's eyes, but I didn't miss the smirk on his lips.

How did I explain that my best friend was a woman in her seventies who *really* wanted me to have a dating life? "Sorry about that."

"Don't be. Ms. Ruby is something else. I love that woman."

Funny how she'd said the same thing about him but we'd never crossed paths before this week.

A silent beat passed before Sincere's fingers stopped moving. "So…what do you say to dinner? No pressure. Just let us feed you again and have a conversation. After that, you're free to do whatever you want, but I hope you still stay the night. We have all that extra space that no one ever uses."

It would be nice to take another shower in that bathroom and actually remember it. Last time was a bit fuzzy. But I distinctly remembered a gigantic walk-in shower, the best smelling body wash and a towel warmer. It was tempting. Still…the unknown made me pause. He said no pressure, but how would things really go? Would I be able to resist him when Lorenzo was around? Did I *want* to?

"One dinner, love." His voice was quiet, almost pleading in its rawness. The soft timbre sent tingles throughout my body and made me clench in places that hadn't been touched in too long.

"Okay," I breathed. "I'll go home with you."

"SHE'S NOT GOING ANYWHERE, SIN. YOU DON'T HAVE TO stare at her to make sure," I whispered against the shell of my husband's ear. I stood beside him at the island and followed his gaze to the living room where Goldyn was reading, oblivious to anything but words on the page.

Turning to face Sincere, I cupped his nape and kissed his temple. "Stop worrying," I urged before going back to the stove to check on dinner. I'd already been cooking when he called me on his way home to tell me he was bringing company.

How he'd gone out for a drive to clear his mind and returned with Goldyn was still a mystery. But when they filed into the house, whispering and laughing together, the *how* was forgotten while I watched them interact. I was just happy she'd agreed to come because I hadn't seen Sincere this taken with another person in forever.

It took me standing at the entry of the foyer for five minutes before he noticed I was there. And when he did, he turned to me with a sheepish smile. That made my heart melt on its own, but then I glimpsed the joy shining in his eyes and knew everything hinged on this impromptu dinner.

An hour later, we were putting the finishing touches on the steaks, vegetables, and a last-minute dessert when the back door connected to the kitchen opened to reveal a frowning Romeo.

He barely spared us a glance before he walked to the edge of the room, sought out Goldyn like he knew exactly where she'd be and then turned around to face us.

"What is she doing here?"

"We invited her for dinner," Sincere said, shoving his hand in an oven mitt. He pulled a tray of brown butter blueberry cookies out of the top part of the double oven and set them on the island.

"And what else?" Romeo deadpanned, knowing there was more. There was *always* more with us.

He kept cutting his eyes to the living room like Goldyn would spawn a new head and if I wasn't already so amused by the way Sincere was fussing over dessert, I would have had time to pick apart Romeo's reaction to our houseguest.

Romeo didn't get flustered. Ever. But apparently Goldyn possessed the ability to get under his skin just by existing.

"Go speak to her, maybe she could tell you."

He cut his dark eyes at Sincere's suggestion before he said under his breath, "Yea, aight."

Then he walked out of the kitchen and down the hall toward the gym instead of going upstairs to his room. When he reappeared less than a minute later with two bottles in his hand, my jaw unhinged.

"Did you just steal the body wash out of her bathroom?" I asked in a loud whisper, making sure Goldyn didn't hear any part of our conversation. Romeo didn't take the same precaution. And even if he had, the way he spoke in an almost constant roar didn't help shit.

His eyes narrowed on us. "You just called it *her* room. Is she moving in here?"

"I hope so."

"We don't know yet."

Sin and I spoke at the same time, and Rome threw his head back and gave a soundless laugh. "I knew it."

"If you knew it, why are you stealing the body wash out of her bathroom?" Sin wanted to know.

"Because it's mine. I don't want her walking around smelling like me. I'll replace it." That was the last thing he said before he disappeared up the stairs.

I shared a long look with Sin.

Worry dimmed some of the earlier excitement in his eyes and I fixed a reassuring smile on my face. We'd just started getting the plates out for dinner when Rome reappeared, dressed down in sweats, and started setting the table.

"See?" I said, facing Sin. "Nothing to worry about. Everything is going to be fine."

I could see why Sincere was so enamored with this woman. Goldyn was sweet, funny, and could carry on a conversation about almost anything. We'd been hopping from topic to topic since we sat down to eat and she hadn't missed a beat yet. I didn't miss the way she pulled Rome into the conversations when he was quiet for too long. And I didn't miss the way he gradually softened every time she did it.

Before coming to the dinner table, Goldyn changed out of her slacks and blouse and came back with black cut off shorts and another crop top like the one she'd been wearing the first night we met.

My eyes had been glued to her stomach when I noticed the belly ring I missed the first night. Tattoos covered her toned legs and Sin hadn't stopped shifting in his seat the whole dinner.

Fighting a smirk, I dropped my hand under the table and placed it on his leg.

"You good?" I asked, low enough for only us to hear.

He nodded, but kept his eyes steady on Goldyn while she went on a tangent about the book she was reading.

The excitement in her voice had his rapt attention and I used that to my advantage, letting my hand inch closer and closer to his zipper.

When my fingers brushed over the bulge pressed against his thigh, I paused there, enjoying the feel against my palm and the way Sincere's breath hitched in the middle of his sentence.

"You okay?" I asked, innocent enough for everyone else at the table to remain oblivious. But Sin refused to back down and nodded. Then he relaxed in his chair, spreading his legs wider, and giving me more room to do what I wanted under the table.

Eyes pinned on Goldyn, he placed his hand over mine while I teased him and held me in place, letting me feel how much harder he got with each passing second.

Shit, now I was hard.

I hadn't thought this stunt through. I was supposed to be teasing him about how much Goldyn turned him on, but now *I* was getting turned on from how much she turned *him* on.

Sincere's dick twitched again and I yanked my hand away. I was smart enough to know when I was playing with fire. I had a problem when it came to Sin. I couldn't know he was hard and do nothing about it. Another minute of that and I would have blown our cover.

"We should talk about why you're here," he said a minute later, his raspy voice coming out strong and clear.

"Right." Goldyn cleared her throat, her eyes ping-ponging between the two of us from her spot directly across the table.

Sincere hadn't tapped me in, but I used that

opening as my cue to speak up. "I don't know how much Sincere told you, but if you came back with him then I'm assuming you at least know a part of it. We want you to be ours. And being ours means we want to take care of you. Spoil you. Give you whatever you want."

An imaginary wheel spun above Goldyn's head as she tried to process what I said. A flicker of doubt entered her warm eyes. "And what do you get out of this?"

"You," Sincere answered right away.

Goldyn gulped, her gaze stuck on Sin. "For how long?"

As long as it works was on the tip of my tongue, but my husband beat me to the punch.

"Three months." *Three months?* I thought we agreed not to start out with an expiration date in mind.

"Oh." One word and the change in octave was noticeable enough to make my stomach flip.

Giving Sin a sidelong glance, I waited for him to elaborate because we were already off-script and I didn't know what he was thinking, which I wasn't used to.

Rome picked up his wine glass, taking half of its contents in a single pull. "I should give y'all some privacy."

Goldyn's eyes widened when he cleared the plates from the table and walked into the kitchen without another word.

Then she turned her attention back on us. "So, you only want to date me for three months?"

Sincere nodded. "Give us the summer and we'll give you everything."

"And after? I just leave and never talk to you again?"

"We could stay friends. Right, Sin?" I tossed him a look and he nodded almost robotically. I could tell from the way he was chewing the inside of his cheek that he was rethinking his approach to this.

"Does that really work? Are you friends with the other women you've dated together?"

No. But I also knew letting her go cold turkey wouldn't be an option. Not with the way Sincere was already attached and not with the way I loved having her around. "We haven't done this in a while. But every situation is unique. We wouldn't just kick you out of our lives, Goldyn."

"Good to know," she replied dryly.

Silence dominated the room and she took the time to tie her hair up with the scrunchie on her wrist.

Still staring at both of us warily, she crossed and uncrossed her arms in silent contemplation.

When she finally spoke again, I released a breath I'd been holding too long.

"So…" She let out a heavy sigh. "The summer. And then we go our separate ways."

She sounded like she was warming up to the idea, little by little, and I wanted to do whatever I could to keep things moving in that direction. Especially since my husband was mimicking a statue beside me.

"Just think about it. And give us your answer when you're ready. No pressure."

"Does that mean you want me to leave tonight?"

"No!"

Oh, now he found his voice?

"We don't want you to go anywhere. And if you agree to this, I'd feel better if you lived with us."

Before any of us could say anything, a loud bang sounded from the kitchen before we heard Romeo clearing his throat. "My bad!"

Goldyn's lips twitched and I silently thanked Rome's eavesdropping ass for breaking the tension.

"Okay, then I'll sleep on it." She shot a brief look toward the kitchen. "And Romeo? How does he fit into all of this?"

"He doesn't. Not anymore than he already has anyway. He's not interested in the women we date." I picked up my wine glass. "At least he hasn't been up until this point," I quickly amended because with the way he'd been acting toward Goldyn, I wouldn't call it *disinterest*. "But if anything were to happen between you two, it's up to y'all how you wanna—"

"Oh, that's not why I asked," she rushed to say, her cheeks turning pink. "I was just making sure I understood everything."

"Of course," I said with a slight nod, a smile forming on my lips. "Ask us any other questions that pop up."

Goldyn nodded and Sincere relaxed in his seat beside me, and all I could wonder was what the fuck we'd just gotten ourselves into.

Whether she said yes or no, I knew the outcome

would turn our world on its head. And while that excited a part of me, another part of me was terrified.

Women like Goldyn Ambrose didn't move through this world without leaving a mark on people. And something told me the mark she left on us would be hard to forget. It already was.

"YOU WANNA TALK ABOUT WHAT HAPPENED DOWN there?" Enzo closed our bedroom door after dessert and a movie marathon with Goldyn.

He pressed his back against it while I walked over to my nightstand and started stripping my jewelry. I tugged at the white gold ring hugging my index finger and hesitantly met his eyes.

There was no explanation I could give him other than, "I panicked."

My husband released a low chuckle and closed the space between us. "I can see that. So we're back on this ninety-day deadline?"

"Yea," I sighed. "Unless she says no to everything." Because that was still a very real possibility. Goldyn could wake up tomorrow morning, say thanks for dinner and dip. The thought made my chest ache and I forced myself to sit down on the edge of the bed before my mind could run off in that direction. I was really good at thinking up the worst-case scenarios and tonight was no different.

Why did I think inviting her to dinner at the last minute was a good idea?

Enzo stood in front of me, a soft smile on his lips

and understanding in his eyes. "I know how much you obsess over things when they're important to you."

He sat down beside me and his hands found my shoulders, kneading away some of the tension.

"She's gonna say yes." He paused even though his hands kept working. I leaned into his touch and felt myself fully relaxing for the first time since I got home. "And if she doesn't, it won't be the end of the world."

I knew him saying that was supposed to be comforting, but all it did was make me sit up straighter. The more I thought about it, the more I could see her slipping through my fingertips.

It felt like missing somebody who was never mine. Grieving something that never got a chance to exist.

Shaking my head to clear the thought, I looked over at Enzo. He was already looking at me, his crooked smile still in place while his eyes crinkled at the side. When he did that, it always reminded me of the first time he gave me his undivided attention.

The first time he smiled at me and introduced himself to me as my Statistics tutor, I knew I was gonna fail that class. I was already in trouble which was why I needed his help in the first place. But when he showed up to our first session, looking like he'd just stepped out of a fashion spread, I knew it was over for me. I showed up to every tutoring session early and didn't retain shit. Somehow, I still passed the class by the skin of my teeth, and the best part was that I got to keep him. We became inseparable and the rest was history.

It was so rare to find somebody who spoke the same language as you that we didn't think twice about getting married four years after graduation. We were ten years deep and six years in to a marriage I never questioned. I never questioned *anything* when it came to Lorenzo because I knew we could do anything together.

Later, when I climbed in bed beside him after my shower, I let Enzo pull me against his chest, our limbs tangling on instinct. With his heart thumping out a familiar beat against my chest, I sighed and allowed my thoughts to wander back to Goldyn. Not that they had strayed far.

I was so tempted to go downstairs and check on her, but I knew if she needed anything she would come find us. Or Rome who was in the gym down the hall from her room. I honestly just wanted to see her again, but I was forcing myself to chill. We'd spent the better part of the day together and while I didn't tire of people I liked easily, I knew it wasn't the same for everybody else.

Lorenzo's breathing evened out and instead of welcoming sleep, I stared up at the ceiling and replayed our conversation.

She's gonna say yes…and if she doesn't, it won't be the end of the world.

I wasn't proud of it, but the only thing I could think about was the card I didn't pull. One I knew would work just based on the conversation we had today.

Goldyn wanted that bookstore more than she wanted a lot of things. But using that as a pawn to cement my chance with her didn't feel right.

It would cheapen what I wanted with her and I wasn't ready to make that move.

Besides, I already told her we would give her

everything. That came with making sure her bookstore became a reality. I couldn't be involved with someone and not do everything I could to make their life better. It was wired into who I was at this point.

All I needed was for her to agree to being ours and I'd figure out the timeline and everything else later.

GOLDYN

It didn't matter that it was the weekend, I woke up the next morning at six o'clock on the dot. My body was programmed after years of van living to get up early, go to the gym to shower and get out the way before things got crowded.

And even though I didn't have to do that today, I got up anyway, found the book I fell asleep reading buried in the sheets and settled in to read it after I brushed my teeth.

Stretched across the bed with my feet in the air, I had to stop myself an hour later when I realized I was literally giggling and kicking my feet over words on a page at 7 o'clock in the morning.

But nobody would blame me if they read what I just read. Kimber hooking up with her husband's best friend while he watched it all with a smile on his face had me flushed.

"Damn," I heard from the door, startling me out of my reading trance. I snapped the book shut and rolled over on my side to see Sincere staring at me from the door. Shirtless and wearing low slung black pajama pants.

From the angle of his gaze, I knew he was staring at my ass in these sleep shorts. My ears grew hot at the thought and desire pulsed in my core.

"Hi." Every time he was anywhere near me I lost my ability to play it cool. Not that I was very good at that anyway, but it evaporated whenever Sincere so much as looked at me. It filled me with warmth and something else. Maybe it was lust. *Maybe it was delusion.*

"Morning, Goldyn."

Abandoning my book, I hopped off the bed and walked over to him, stopping a few inches in front of him. "I didn't expect anyone else to be up this early."

My heart was never going to recover from the way Sincere's face softened the closer I got to him. It filled my head with too many possibilities and made me forget what logic was.

"You look pretty." He licked his lips and ran his eyes over me from top to bottom. "Did you sleep okay?"

"Mhm," was all I got past the knot in my throat.

We stood there, lost in each other's eyes for a beat before Sincere's long lashes fell against his cheek and broke the spell.

"I was just coming to check on you. I didn't know you were up." He tilted his head and ran a hand over the faint stubble on his sharp jaw. "Do you drink coffee? I'm about to make some."

"No, but I'll come with you." I was just happy to have another human to do something with. I didn't care if that was obvious from the way I stayed up last night watching movies with him and Lorenzo. Human companionship was something I spent too many of my days craving for me to pass up the chance.

In the kitchen, Sincere pulled out a high-back stool at the island and told me to sit.

Knees pulled to my chest, I watched him go through the steps to make a single shot of espresso and grinned at the contented look on his face when he took the first sip.

"You laughing at me, Goldy?"

Sincere cut his eyes at me but all it did was make me laugh harder.

"Never." My words came out on a breathless giggle and when I blinked, he was no longer halfway across the kitchen but standing right beside me.

Setting his coffee on the island, he spun my chair until I was facing him. On instinct, I dropped my legs. And on instinct, he seemed to fill the space between them, bracing his hands on the cushion on either side of my hips.

Timid, sweet Sincere from the night before was gone, and he'd been replaced by a man with nothing but confidence and intensity shining in his eyes.

We got locked in another staring contest, but this time neither of us looked away.

"I'm really trying to take your lead on this, Goldyn. But I've wanted to kiss you since the second I found you on our couch." His breath fanned over my freckles with how close he was and I was tempted to move closer. I wanted him to want me. I wanted him to kiss me. "Your lips are so fucking pretty. *You're* so fucking pretty."

My pussy was weeping now, completely overstimulated by the way he said every word and inched closer and closer to me.

"So kiss me," I breathed. And that was all it took. All I had to say before he had me swept up in a kiss that felt like home.

I wasn't a coffee drinker, but I could get used to the taste of it on his lips.

He broke the kiss before I could memorize the softness of his mouth and the urgency of his tongue against mine.

"Sincere," I whimpered, cupping the side of his face and letting my forehead rest against his.

"Fuck. Don't do that, Goldy. I'm already fucking this up."

I frowned, some of the haze lifted as I searched his face. "Why do you say that? That you're fucking something up when you're just being yourself?"

He'd said it at Lucky's yesterday, and now he was doing it again. But he wasn't fucking anything up. Didn't he know how beautiful it was when people showed up as exactly who they were?

Sincere tried to move away from me, but I held fast to his face, making it harder for him to retreat. "Stay right here and answer me."

He tucked his bottom lip into his mouth and shook his head.

"Please," I added in a softer tone.

"My fault, Goldy. I wasn't trying to come on strong and persuade you to stay. That's all. I want you to make the choice on your own. Not because I couldn't keep my hands off you."

"I told you to kiss me," I reminded him, still holding his face. "And I think you want to do it again."

His eyes slid shut. "Goldyn."

"Do you want to kiss me, Sincere?"

"You know I do." Those four words came out rough and desperate. I felt every syllable in my soul and spoke my next words directly against his lips.

"Then what are you waiting for?"

Sincere accepted the challenge in my question and gripped my hips, lifting me against him in one smooth motion. My legs hooked around his waist, my arms locked around his shoulders and my lips met his.

His tongue stroked mine with so much finesse, I could feel phantom strokes against my clit. The deeper he kissed me, the closer I tried to get to him. I was already wrapped around him, my limbs acting as his second skin, but it wasn't close enough.

Moaning into my mouth, he pressed my back to the island and used his hips to pin me in place. The bulge in his pants pressed directly against my clit from this angle and now it felt like I was drowning.

"Sin—" I gasped, trying so hard to catch my breath. Every breath in left me before it could settle in my lungs. I'd never been kissed like this. Never knew I *needed* to be kissed like this.

Another kiss silenced anything I wanted to say and he rocked his hardness into me.

I was too sensitive for this. It'd been too long since

I'd been touched. Too long since I'd come. If he didn't stop, I was going to fall apart in this kitchen.

Strong arms snaked around my middle, abandoning my hips for a tighter hold on me. And again, Sincere ground against me, stimulating my clit through my shorts with the pressure of his thick dick.

Oh, fuck.

"Sincere, you're gonna make me come. I can't…"

"Why can't you?" He asked, voice hoarse and full of wanting. "Why can't you come for me, Goldy?"

"I don't know," I whimpered as his tongue left my mouth and trailed against my neck, leaving hot kisses against my throat.

He pushed against my sex, the rhythm of his movements doing exactly what I needed. I couldn't see his dick, but I knew it was fucking perfect if it could make me feel like this through layers of clothes.

Sincere's pace increased, pressing his erection into me over and over. Until my legs began to shake and I threw my head back as tremors began to ripple through me.

My clit pulsed and arousal leaked out of me to the point that I knew my shorts would have a wet spot. And yet…I didn't care. I wanted this. I wanted this so bad my voice broke on a scream when my orgasm finally hit me and sent me into a shaking, stammering, panting mess of limbs.

I fell apart while Sincere held me in place against the counter, not caring to keep my voice down while sensations robbed me of my ability to do anything but come…and come…and come.

Sincere's hips didn't stop moving. He kept grinding against me through my orgasm and that made my second one hit me without warning.

My walls clamped around absolutely nothing, desperate for the fullness his hard length promised. When I finally calmed down, all I wanted was his mouth back on me, and he obliged me when I lifted my head, letting our tongues lazily move against each other.

His kiss was different now.

More urgent.

More possessive.

He was perfect. I wanted to tell him that, but then I'd have to break the kiss.

So many thoughts filtered through my head and the most dominant one was how much I wanted to tell him I accepted his offer. I would be theirs for the summer if it meant I got to experience even a fraction of that again. *And he hadn't even been inside of me.*

Still dizzy from the aftershocks of my back-to-back orgasms, I gasped when Sincere sat me back on the barstool and took a step back.

"Fuck, I need to make you come every day if this is what you look like after." He kissed my temple and shook his head. "Let me make you breakfast."

IT WOULD HAVE BEEN SO EASY TO GET WRAPPED UP IN Sincere and Enzo after breakfast, but I had to force myself away. I needed to think about what they asked me and I needed to do it away from their distracting energy.

Especially when Lorenzo came downstairs shortly after Sincere started cooking with a sinful smirk on his face. Like he knew what happened before his arrival. After he hugged Sincere from behind and dropped a kiss on his shoulder, he walked over to me, kissed the corner of my mouth and said, "Good morning, Goldy" in a throaty voice still thick with sleep. That had been enough to make me want to hop up on that counter and go for round two. This time with Sincere watching as his husband made me come. Would that turn him on? Would he watch if he knew it turned *me* on?

What would it be like to be shared by two men?

I'd read enough romance books and Reddit posts not to be scandalized by the idea, but reading it and living it were two different things.

Just the thought made heat pool at my center and I was thankful I'd put on panties today. I usually went commando unless I was on my period, but something about the way today started told me I needed an extra barrier between me and my favorite sundress.

Shivers skittered over my skin and palpitations had me clutching my chest.

I needed to remember I was in public and anybody could walk by and see me squirming right now. Mortified by the idea alone, I fanned my face and stared out of the window at my van in the parking lot.

If you agree to this, I'd feel better if you lived with us.

Sincere wanted me to move in with them. And Lorenzo hadn't objected.

Could I move in with a house full of men for ninety days?

The better question was: could I endure ninety days knowing it was coming to an end?

On the one hand, I could agree to being theirs and have the best summer of my life.

On the other, I could keep existing as I was and never know what could have been.

So what if they only wanted three months? Wasn't it better to experience something great briefly than not at all?

Because I had a feeling it would be great. There was no doubt in my mind actually. The way Sincere and Lorenzo catered to each other let me know I would be well taken care of. Didn't I deserve that too? At least for a little while?

It'd been so long since I'd opened myself up to the possibility of dating anyone that I didn't know how to do it anymore.

The two years I traveled and danced on the road, I'd

stayed single because life was easier that way. I didn't have to consider anybody's feelings when I dropped off the map for days or think about how they'd feel about me dancing for a room full of strangers every other night. It kept life simple, but lonely as hell.

And now I could dip my toe back into the dating pool with two of the finest men I'd ever seen. Maybe that would be enough to revive my desire to make it work with someone else in the future.

My phone buzzed and I smiled when I saw Sincere's name.

He'd saved his number for me before I left, making me promise to call him for anything I needed. I mostly suspected it was so he could have a way to contact me if I ghosted them.

Tapping the message notification, I read his text.

SIN:

> You left your book here. Does that mean you're coming back to get it?

He sent a picture of himself laying on one pillow in the guest room with the paperback for *Nobody to Love You Better* on the one beside him.

ME:

> What are you doing? Do you always nap in that room?

SIN:

Before today? No. But now I'm going to. The sheets still smell like you.

Three texts in and my cheeks were already hurting from the goofy ass grin stretching my face. This man was dangerous.

SIN:

I can't wait to see you again. And selfishly, I hope that's tonight.

ME:

upside down smiling face emoji

Sincere laughed at my message and then the gray bubbles appeared.

SIN:

I can't stop thinking about the way your face looked after I made you come.

I've never seen a woman look that sexy because of something I did.

I need to do it again

Heat rose to my cheeks. He wasn't playing fair. My fingers flew to my neck recalling the way his lips had felt there, and my throat worked in a swallow as my eyes became unfocused. I needed to get out of here. Grabbing up my purse, I tossed my phone inside and speed-walked to the front of the library, through the vestibule and out to my van. I wasn't going back to Sincere's house, I just needed some privacy before I did something embarrassing in public.

But as I drove away from my parking spot, I wondered how long it would be before I showed up on his doorstep.

Because I needed him to do it again too.

Thankfully, that *"What's Up"* catch up session with Ms. Ruby turned into another dinner invitation. And I was all too ready for the distraction. Because if I was left to my own devices, I would have been back at the lake house after an hour of trying to focus on alternate funding for my bookstore. Nothing made me feel more defeated than sitting down and working through the numbers for the millionth time knowing nothing had changed. My dejection made me crave the comfort of Sincere's presence and Lorenzo's teasing smile to make me feel better. Hell, even Rome's lukewarm reception would be better than sitting with the fact that my dream may never see the light of day.

But here I was, hours later, on my third 'modest' pour of moonshine Pauly made under their porch, feeling…warm and fuzzy. That had a lot to do with Ruby's gray Pit bull, Lady, snuggled against my lap. She hadn't left my side since I drove up and I smiled softly, cupping her sweet face with one hand.

"Hi, pretty girl," I cooed when she just blinked up at me.

I'd barely hopped down from my van when Ms. Ruby walked up to me, fussing about her being pregnant.

"The vet said there's five of them in there. What am I supposed to do with six dogs?"

While she looked flustered, I couldn't help but notice how happy her husband, Pauly, looked at the prospect. *"I told you not to worry yourself with all that, Ruby Jean. I'll take care of them."*

He came up and kissed her cheek before giving me a toothy grin. *"Hey there, sunbeam. We missed you last night."*

Like his wife, he'd seen me once and gifted me with a nickname that made me smile every time I heard it.

After hugging them both, I let them lead me to their back porch, where the grill was fired up and the oldies were blasting. A few people I didn't know filtered in and out the house, but I didn't get up whenever new faces arrived. Mostly because I didn't want to disturb the dog nestled against my legs. And partly because I was feeling every ounce of this moonshine coursing through my bloodstream. I was stuck, blissfully mellowed out and enjoying the nighttime air while the chatter of people faded in and out.

"You aight out here, honeybee?"

I turned my head toward the sound of Ruby's voice and she gave a wheezy laugh when we made eye contact. "Oh, girl. No wonder you so quiet out here."

She pulled up a patio chair beside me, angling it so her body faced my legs and created the perfect lounging spot for Lady. The dog settled between us, her head on her owner's shins while she draped her lower body over me.

"Ms. Ruby, can I ask you something?"

"Anything, honeybee." I loved the way she effortlessly held space for me, whether we were standing on the side of the road or gathered around her firepit. Whenever I needed to say something, she gave me her undivided attention.

Carefully, I filtered through the word vomit in my head and asked, "Would you take an offer knowing it would end in three months if you knew it was a once in a lifetime experience?"

"Probably. My life is the result of choices just like that," she answered, patting Lady's back.

"How do you detach yourself from the dread of having to say goodbye when you know it's going to hurt?"

"I don't." She shrugged, but the gesture wasn't dismissive. It was simply a reflex to accompany her words. "We can't avoid goodbyes no matter how hard we try, honeybee. Life is unpredictable, so even that person you think you got forever with could be gone in the blink of an eye."

"I guess you're right."

"I *know* I'm right," she huffed with another scratchy laugh. "But ain't that the beauty in it? Wouldn't you rather have something good for a while than to always wonder about it?"

Chills erupted and multiplied on my skin at how eerily similar her words were to my earlier thoughts.

I guess I just needed to hear someone say it aloud. And coming from this woman, whose wisdom I trusted the most, was as clear of a sign as I was going to get.

I could be Sincere and Enzo's for the summer. Maybe the end wouldn't be so bad so long as I knew it was coming. Besides, I could get to the end of the summer and decide I wanted to move back to New Hope if I didn't figure something out here. Maybe a summer with them was just what I needed before I said goodbye to this beautiful town.

Ms. Ruby went quiet beside me, her eyes fixed on the trees lining her backyard while she rubbed absently behind Lady's ear. She looked so pretty and peaceful.

Angling my phone just right, I snapped a quick picture and sent it to her, knowing she'd see it sometime tomorrow since she barely touched her phone when she was home.

Pauly walked outside, gave me a wink and another splash of moonshine in my mason jar. "How you feelin', sunbeam?"

"Good. *Warm.*"

Ruby grinned at my reply, shaking her head. "Lord, we done got this child tore up."

"That's what the guest room is for," Pauly reminded her, kissing the top of her hair before disappearing inside.

After that, I spent the next few minutes enamored with the lightning bugs flashing in the distance and sipped at my drink, my head full and empty at the same time.

I didn't know how much time passed before I started swiping around my phone screen, not understanding why everything was so damn blurry until I glimpsed the empty mason jar on the glass table beside me.

Hmm. That would explain why my fingertips were tingling and why my chest felt so warm. And now I was overcome with the urge to tell Sincere and Lorenzo I accepted their offer.

Somehow, I stumbled through my app icons until I saw a green blob and pushed it.

Sincere's message thread was still at the top and I opened it and typed out a message.

ME:

Cme hear, Sin

The gray bubbles popped up immediately.

SIN:

What the hell, Goldyn? *crying laughing emoji* Where are you?

ME:

Y ru laughin'

SIN:

Goldy, are you drunk?

ME:

Mayb

My vision blurred and his text turned into five until I squeezed my eyes shut and tried again. This time when I looked at the screen, I only saw two messages.

SIN:

Where are you, my love?

ME:

Rubyyyyy

SIN:

Ms. Ruby's house?

I nodded at his message and dropped the phone in my lap.

A second later, it vibrated against my thigh. Something that looked like Sincere's name appeared on the screen and the best etiquette I could muster was an answering, "Huh?"

"Goldyn." My name came out in a relieved whoosh. "Are you safe, love?"

"Yeah. So safe." I nodded again, my chin hitting the top of my chest with each bow of my head. "I just miss you. Can you come here?"

"I'm already on my way," he said, voice even. "I just needed to make sure you were good until I got there."

"I'm good. So good," I assured him, my words coming slower and slower. "I'm with my best friend, Ruby. Do you want to speak to her?"

A quiet laugh filled the line. "I don't need to speak to her, love. Just stay on the phone with me until I get there. Can you do that?"

"Mhmm." I closed my eyes and listened to the faint rustling coming from the other side of the receiver. Just when I felt like I was going to fall asleep, Sincere's voice cut in.

"What did you do today, Goldy?"

"Think about you."

Another quiet laugh and an even quieter sigh touched my ears. "And what else?"

"I worked on stuff for the bookstore and then I came to Ruby's house. Did you know she has a dog? She's so sweet. And she's pregnant. I want a dog so bad, Sincere. But I can't live in my van with it. I know some people do it, but I'm not made for that life."

"I hear you, love."

"Mr. Pauly gave me some moonshine."

"Did he?"

"Yes."

"How much did you have, beautiful?"

"Three fingers."

"Is that why you're calling me?"

"No. I was gonna call you anyway. I wanted to see you. All I did was think about you today. Did you think about me?"

"You have no idea, Goldy." God, I really loved his voice. It sounded so good when he said my name.

"I love it when you call me Goldy." My head lolled against the back of my chair. "I love it when you call me anything."

We talked—well, I talked and he listened until he pulled up on the side of the house and walked right up to us on the back deck.

I couldn't wipe the lazy smile off my face if I tried when he dipped his head to greet Ms. Ruby first and kiss her cheek.

"You taking my girl away from me?"

Sincere nodded, looking at me before fixing his eyes back on Ruby. "Is it okay if we leave her van here for the night? I'll bring her back to get it tomorrow."

"It don't make me no never mind. She can leave it as long as she wants. Whole summer if need be," Ruby said and I swore I saw a mischievous twinkle in her eyes. But I was drunk, so *everything* looked like a twinkle.

My heavy eyes moved from her to Sincere and stayed on him because he looked so damn good. He had a casually preppy style he pulled off so easily.

The few times I'd seen him, he was wearing a pastel button up, cuffed to show off his forearms, unbuttoned to the center of his chest and showcasing a few gold chains around his neck. Yesterday at Lucky's he'd been wearing navy shorts and white sneakers with a mint green one. Today he had on a peach shirt with light-wash jeans and brown leather shoes.

"Hey, love," he said, appearing in front of me. When his fingers grazed the side of my cheek, I closed my eyes on instinct.

"You came."

"Of course, I did." His lips slanted in a half smile. "Ready to go?"

"Yes." That's all I got to say before he had me scooped up in his arms, carrying me bridal style to his Bronco. When Sincere reached over me to fasten my seatbelt, I remembered. "We have to say goodbye to Ms. Ruby."

"We already did, love."

Oh.

"I'm really glad you called me." Then he kissed my forehead, gave me another smile and closed the passenger door.

"Should we be worried?" Lorenzo tossed me an apprehensive glance.

"She's breathing," I reported dryly. This moment felt a little too much like déjà vu. Except this time Sincere was holding on to our thief like she was the missing piece of him.

Sincere always woke up before everybody in the house no matter how late he went to sleep. It took him forever to fall asleep at night and he was allergic to sleeping in. *He* was the reason I'd been workshopping an insomnia tea for the past two months.

And here he was, sitting damn near upright and still knocked out at 9 o'clock.

"What the hell was in that moonshine?" Enzo whispered, tilting his head to study Goldyn.

"*Moonshine*, nigga."

"I know but *damn*." He paused, shaking his head. "Sin texted me saying he was staying down here until she fell asleep after her shower, but that was nine hours ago. Do you think this means she agrees to be our girlfriend?"

"Look at them and you tell me," I said, ignoring the tug in my chest.

Between Sin's infatuation and Enzo's fascination with Goldyn, I swore I was the only sane one left.

It wasn't like I was blindsided though. The talk we had at dinner last night made sure of it. The talk where they told me that even though they wanted Goldyn, they'd pull back if I wasn't comfortable with having someone new around after all this time of it just being the three of us. The talk where they told me no matter how awkward it was, they'd call off this thing with Goldyn if I didn't feel comfortable. The same talk where I lied and told them I was fine and that she didn't make me uncomfortable.

It wasn't a complete lie. Goldyn didn't make me uncomfortable, but she did disrupt my equilibrium and I was still trying to figure out exactly *why* that was.

Luckily, now that she'd obviously accepted their offer, it would be easier to ignore the random jolts I felt whenever she was near. Every time she got close to me, it was like a static shock of awareness assaulted my senses. I didn't like that shit.

But I knew her dating Sin and Enzo would be the cure. The women they dated were automatically off-limits to me. It was an unwritten rule I'd always forced myself to abide by. My indifference was just taking longer than usual to set in.

When I snapped out of my thoughts, I caught Lorenzo holding up his phone to get a picture of them from above.

I scoffed at him when he put it back in his pocket. "Why are you taking pictures of them?"

Enzo gave a nonchalant shrug but the smile on his

face told me everything I needed to know. "I don't know. It's kinda cute. I haven't seen Sin like this with anybody but me in a long time."

"Y'all *just* met her. And am I the only one who remembers she broke into our house?" I whispered.

Lorenzo tossed me a scathing look, but playfulness lit his eyes. "Sometimes I forget how much of a fucking brat you are."

I wasn't a brat. I just liked structure and I could already see that flying out the window if she stuck around.

"And it doesn't matter if we remember because you're gonna remind us every other hour," He followed up, his tone unfazed. "It's been six days, by the way. We met her on Tuesday and it's Sunday now. And you know we did a thorough check on her. You're the one who helped me with that."

He was right.

And everything she'd told Sincere voluntarily had shown up in her report.

No parents.

Raised by her grandmother.

Degree in Hospitality.

Two years traveling and dancing on the road.

She wasn't a criminal. People around town loved her. There was no reason for me to be this apprehensive. And yet…

I forced the retort on the tip of my tongue away. If I didn't leave soon, I was gonna be late getting to the farmer's market to set up. For the first time in two years, neither Lottie nor my back up could make it, so I had to man the booth all day.

It was like Goldyn jinxed me by saying she never saw me at my booth.

"Y'all can't whisper for shit. And why are you watching me sleep?"

Lorenzo flinched at the sound of Sincere's groggy voice and both our heads snapped in that direction.

Instead of justifying his question with an answer, I left his husband to do it and announced my departure. "I'll be at the farmer's market if anybody needs me."

In my car, I pressed play on the audiobook Sin and I were reading together and reversed out of our driveway. I was three chapters behind and now was the perfect time to distract myself with catching up. Hopefully by the time I got to my stall at the farmer's market, my mind would be caught up in the fantasy the narrator was weaving and not the woman with the perfect face I left on my couch.

Three hours later

NOW THAT I THOUGHT ABOUT IT, MAYBE MY OFFICE WASN'T the best place for this conversation. It was too formal and the wide-eyed stare on Goldy's face confirmed that.

She sat in front of me, staring at me expectantly with Sincere right beside her, his arm thrown over the back of her chair while his fingers idly toyed with the curls at her nape.

She was miraculously hangover free after the greasy breakfast Sin made for her and the Ibuprofen she downed as soon as she woke up.

A smile tried to take over my face. The contented expression on Sin's face always had a way of mellowing me out. Seeing him happy made me happy. And seeing the loving touches he shared with Goldyn reminded me of how lucky I was to fall in love with someone who had so much love to give.

"Last night you told Sincere you'd be ours for the summer and we just wanted to make sure you still felt the same way now that you're sober."

I didn't miss the relief that claimed her features as she blew out a breath and nodded her head. "I'm sure."

Sincere's smirk said *I told you so* without him having to utter a word and another smile touched my lips.

"Cool. So let's go over what that means for us and make sure we're on the same page."

Just yesterday, I'd been ready to tell Sincere I was bowing out. I didn't want to overwhelm Goldyn with dating two men if she'd never done it before. But I also didn't want to be the reason she and Sin didn't get to explore whatever was building between them. For the first time since we started doing this, I'd been ready to watch from the sidelines.

And now that I didn't have to, relief morphed into an insatiable hunger for the woman in front of me.

Goldyn was breathtaking. More than that, she stole my attention every time she walked into a room. There was something so captivating about her presence that made me want to soak up every ounce of attention she was willing to give me. I knew she'd spent more time with Sincere up until this point, but I didn't want her to think I wasn't just as ready to spoil her with attention and orgasms and whatever else she wanted from me.

When I broke out of my thoughts, Sincere's hand had abandoned her hair in favor of holding her hand in his lap.

God, they looked fucking perfect together. I wanted to give them whatever they wanted.

A voice at the back of my head reminded me of why we were in here and I cleared my throat.

"For the next three months, we won't be dating or sleeping with anybody but you. To keep things as uncomplicated as possible, we want that in return. We know that just because you've agreed to this, it doesn't mean we have ownership of you. You're grown and can do whatever you want at the end of the day." I clasped my hands in front of me, noting the way Sincere bit his lip when I said that. "All we ask is if you meet someone and want to explore it, just end it with us first."

"Ow!" Goldyn winced and snatched her hand free from Sincere's hold the second those words left my lips.

My husband rushed to comfort her. "Fuck, I'm sorry, Goldyn."

The tightness in his voice created a strange pull in my gut. He clearly still wasn't okay with the thought of this ending before it could get too deep, but until he wanted to speak on it and change the terms he'd set, I'd be quiet. Even if that meant I had to watch him fumble through his body's involuntary response to Goldyn potentially belonging to someone else.

Goldyn's face softened when he pulled her chair as close as it could get to his and tugged her hand up to pepper kisses along her knuckles.

"I'm sorry, love. I didn't mean to hurt you."

Her voice was just as gentle as his when she said, "It's okay. You just caught me off guard. It doesn't hurt that bad."

"Are you sure?" His eyes lingered on her face, searching for the truth.

"Positive." She gave a slight nod, welcoming his kiss when he leaned over to cover her lips with his.

The soft moan that escaped Goldyn's throat went straight to my dick, and I knew if watching them kiss got to me this much, the next three months were going to be something.

Leaning back in my chair, I tried to adjust my dick in my pants without anyone noticing, but Sincere looked up just in time and a knowing glint entered his eyes.

"We can both show you our recent STD and STI results. When's the last time you were tested, Goldyn?"

She gulped. "Two weeks ago, at my annual. Everything is negative. I'm on birth control and I haven't slept with anyone. I mean, I haven't been with—"

Her words trailed and pink tinged her cheeks before she averted her eyes.

Trying again, she cleared her throat and said, "I can show you the results. I don't know where my phone is right now, but I'm not lying."

"We don't think you're lying, sweetheart," I offered, my voice softer than it usually was.

Sincere's gaze snagged on mine before his eyes shifted to take in Goldyn's profile. His fascination with her unlocked a dormant desire in me. It'd been so long since we shared anyone that just the thought of doing it again sent a thrill of anticipation through me. I needed to make sure Goldyn knew what she was getting herself into. Especially if it had been a while since she'd been with someone.

"Come here, Goldyn," I commanded without preamble.

Sincere quirked his brow, but Goldyn stood to her feet immediately.

When she looked at me for further instructions, I patted my thigh and spread my legs to give her room to sit.

To my surprise, she sat on my lap without hesitation, her body angled so she could see both me and Sin with a simple turn of her head.

I took a minute to take her in. A soft, flowery scent met my nose while I looked her up and down. Another one of Sin's student gov T-shirts swallowed her frame, and his boxer briefs peeked from beneath the hem.

My hand went to her waist, holding her in place. "Look at me, Goldy."

When her eyes were pinned on me, I said, "I need you to know that you agreeing to this doesn't mean we expect you to give us your body on demand. We won't take anything you don't willingly give us. Do you understand?"

"Yes."

"But don't get it confused, sweetheart, we're two men who get pleasure out of pleasing others. So when we do take it there, just know that orgasms are one of the many ways we will spoil you."

Goldyn bit down on her bottom lip, her eyes shining with understanding and lust. "Okay."

Taking advantage of her undivided attention, I added, "There will be dates. There will be communication. We have to be able to trust you to tell us what's working and what's not. If we don't have that, we don't have anything. Okay?"

She nodded for the second time, her slender throat

working in a swallow. If I had any doubt she was only attracted to Sin, that died with the way her pupils expanded and all her attention stayed focused on me.

Another jolt of lust and longing surged through me. I lifted my other hand to her thigh, mindlessly massaging her soft skin.

"Do you have any questions for us, Goldyn?"

She finally tore her eyes away from mine and looked over her shoulder at Sin who was watching us with a hypnotized look on his face.

"Um, Sin said something about me living here for the summer."

He nodded. "The guest room you've slept in before will be yours for the nights when you aren't in our bed."

"Okay, I can do that."

I didn't know if she'd done it on purpose, but she shifted closer to me. The hand I had on her thigh continued to massage lazily as I looked over at Sin.

"You got anything you want to add, baby?"

A mix of emotions flickered in his eyes before he shook his head and adjusted in his seat, his hand moving over his zipper. His dick print was visible from across the room and made me hold tighter to Goldyn.

"No," he said, voice hoarse while he watched us.

With every passing second, Goldyn melted into my embrace a little more. And with every passing second, my fingers inched higher up her thigh, my eyes locked on Sincere the whole time.

"Are you okay with me touching you, Goldy?"

"Mhmm."

Sincere's eyes darkened at the slight hitch in her voice and I smiled.

"Do you want me to stop?"

"No."

My fingers crept higher, past the hem of the T-shirt and under the leg of the briefs she had on. Heat greeted me and I sucked in a breath.

"Fuck, Goldy. I don't think I want to stop either."

Sincere made a noise deep in his throat and Goldyn leaned into me, her thighs parting to give me access I hadn't asked for yet.

Shit, this woman was going to be trouble.

"Touch me, please."

"You want me to touch you while Sincere watches us?"

She didn't hesitate. "Yes. Please."

"You want him to watch me make you come, sweetheart?"

"Yes."

Goldyn's eyes fell shut as my fingertips skimmed her bare pussy. Euphoria flashed against her pretty face and I watched in awe at how affected she was when I hadn't done anything yet.

I leaned up to kiss her neck at the same time I collected the wetness dripping out of her with two fingers.

She released a tortured moan. "Lorenzo."

"Fuck," Sincere hissed.

I didn't tear my eyes away from Goldyn, but I knew

he was probably sitting there, stroking himself while he watched me take care of Goldyn. The thought was enough to make my aching dick throb harder. I didn't care if I came in my pants as long as Goldyn kept rutting against me like this.

"Can I kiss you, Goldyn?"

Instead of answering, Goldyn slammed her lips to mine and released a moan so erotic, I pushed my fingers past her lips and massaged her clit in time with the way she kissed me.

In seconds, we were both so lost in the kiss that nothing mattered except the way she moved to straddle my hips and the way her tongue snaked around mine. She raised up on her knees in her new position, making sure there was still enough room for my fingers to stroke her clit.

Her hips undulated against my touch, the intensity increasing until she was riding my hand.

"Lorenzo, oh my god," she moaned between kisses.

"You don't know how fucking beautiful you are," I said against her lips, biting at the bottom one while she continued to rock her hips against my hand. My fingers were drenched now, soaked with her arousal and I couldn't wait to feel her body shake with her release.

I knew it was close because she kept stopping to prolong the inevitable, edging herself with me and Sin as a captive audience.

That shit was so fucking sexy. I loved a woman who knew how to use me to get herself off. Watching her face contort with pleasure every time she moved her hips pushed me to give her more. My fingers slid against her swollen clit, moving back and forth until Goldyn dropped her head on my shoulder and released a strangled cry.

A string of whimpers left her throat as the orgasm worked through her, shaking her small frame with tremors.

My chest heaved like I'd been the one to climax, but watching her fall apart did that to me. I could get used to that. Feeling left out, my dick begged for release, pressing against my zipper and leaking precum in my boxers while she shook in my arms. I pulled my hand from between her legs.

With my index and middle fingers glistening from her release, I resisted the urge to taste her and called to Sincere instead.

"Come here, Sin."

As soon as I uttered the command, Sin was in front of me, leaning against the desk so the bulge in his pants was visible from my seated position.

I licked my lips and stared up at him.

Goldyn had finally stilled against me, her ragged breaths less shallow.

"Can I show him how good you taste when I make you come for us?"

She lifted her head from my shoulder and whispered, "Yes."

That was all I needed to hear before I lifted my hand in Sin's direction, silently summoning him to lick them clean.

He held my wrist in a tight grip as he wrapped his lips around my fingers and sucked every drop of

Goldyn's release off of them. His eyes slid shut and he moaned before letting me go.

"How does she taste, Sin?"

"Perfect."

"You hear that, Goldyn? You taste perfect."

Of all the ways I could have died, I didn't expect this to be the way I met my maker.

Sitting here on the lap of the man who'd just made me come while his husband licked the taste of me off his fingers.

I wasn't complaining. It was a good way to go. Just unexpected. And as my heart hammered in my chest, surely on its way to a full blown heart attack, I found myself relaxing into the inevitable, happy I at least got a glimpse of bliss before I went.

Except I didn't die. I kept right on living. And thank God, because when Sin lifted me in his arms and kissed me, I was gifted with a glimpse of heaven.

"You have no idea how sexy it was watching you come for him, Goldyn," Sincere panted between sloppy kisses.

My lips were no doubt still swollen from Lorenzo's demanding kisses and now Sincere had me locked in another one, his hungry tongue twisting around mine. The more I thought about it, the wetter I got. Never in my life had I thought being shared by two men would feel like this. My body was overwhelmed from the attention and the pleasure coursing through me.

Once my arms were wrapped around his neck, he grabbed my legs, pulling them around his waist.

Tasting myself on his tongue, feeling his hardness pressed against my center and hearing the way he moaned deep in his throat had me ascending. Every new thing I noticed was more intoxicating than the last.

How was it possible I missed his kiss when it'd only been twenty-four hours?

I didn't have an answer, but the moment his lips crashed into mine again, I knew I didn't want to pull away until his taste was branded against my tongue.

When he started walking away from Lorenzo's desk, I didn't even question where he was taking me. *Couldn't* question where he was taking me.

As long as it was somewhere we were going to be together, I didn't care.

A few seconds later, I was lowered onto the softest bed I'd ever felt, the mattress molding to hug my body the second Sin released me. The bed in the guest room was amazing, but this was on another level. And the man above me just made it better. Sincere climbed between my legs, his eyes trained on me.

He must have taken his jeans off while I was daydreaming about the bed because the only thing separating us now were our matching briefs.

I smiled up at him, unable to help the way my mood transformed whenever he was around me. Even with my clit throbbing and my pussy begging for another orgasm, I fixated on him and the way adoration shone in his eyes when he looked down at me.

"Hi, Sin."

"*Hi*, love."

He returned my smile with a soft one of his own before placing kisses against my nose and forehead.

"I want to fuck you so bad, but I won't if you tell me it's too soon."

"Sin, I just came on your husband's lap and watched you lick my cum off his fingers. How would you fucking me be *too soon*?"

Releasing a dry chuckle, he nodded, his forehead pressed against mine. "I know. I just need you to know that you're in control. We'll do as much or as little as you want. If you tell me we've already done too much, I'll—"

I lifted my head just enough to swallow his next words with my kiss. "I want you to fuck me, Sin."

When he smiled against my lips, I relaxed against the bed even more and spread my legs wider, giving him the space he needed to make a home between them.

He paused to look down at me, a million emotions swirling in his pretty brown eyes. "As long as you're sure."

"So fucking sure." I punctuated my words by swiveling my hips up to meet his and gasped when his dick twitched against my center.

Yea, I wanted that inside of me. *Right now.*

Sincere read my mind and pulled his briefs down, freeing himself completely and kicking his underwear off the bed.

Propped up on my elbows, I watched in awe as his dick bobbed against his thigh. He was thick and long, with pretty veins along the side. More wetness soaked my core and I knew if he tried to enter me right now, he'd meet no resistance. I was so ready for him, my pussy ached from the lack of his presence inside of me.

Biting my lip, I instinctively lifted my hips when he pulled his briefs off of me.

He paused after tossing them on the floor, his gazed fixed on my center. I knew I was leaking and a mess from the way Lorenzo finger fucked me earlier, but I couldn't bring myself to be self-conscious about it when Sincere looked at me like I was something exquisite he'd been waiting to sample his whole life.

"I'm gonna be so good to you," he whispered hoarsely. "So fucking good."

The rawness in his words made my nipples form stiff peaks, and the heat of his stare made more of my sticky arousal trickle out of me.

Sincere took over when all I could do was stare at him in wonder. "Lift your arms for me, love."

With my arms above my head, he easily pulled his student gov t-shirt off of me and stared at my naked body with so much tender appreciation in his eyes.

"You're so pretty. Do you know that?" His words hung in the air when he dipped his head to circle my left nipple with his tongue.

"Sincere," I moaned, falling against the mattress because I couldn't hold myself up when his mouth was on me.

He followed me, his warm body covering mine while he sucked. And sucked. And sucked some more.

Between the wetness of his tongue against my

nipples and the hard length of his dick pressed against my sex, I was gone. He didn't have to enter me for me to feel overstimulated and overcome with pleasure.

"Ah, fuck, Sin. You're gonna make me come." I held his head in place, pushing his mouth harder against my flesh.

"Shit, that's so sexy," he said against my right nipple, and the rough vibration of his words sent me toppling into a quiet orgasm. I shook from the tremors working their way through me and clutched at Sincere's muscular shoulders to anchor me in this moment and this feeling.

When he realized what was happening, his mouth abandoned my nipples and he kissed me hard on the mouth, groaning and rocking against me until tears wet my face.

"Sincerrrreee," I sobbed.

He didn't respond to my cries, but he did shove my legs apart, pressing them against the mattress while the head of his dick nudged at my weeping entrance. He rubbed up and down just once, collecting enough wetting to lubricate his length.

Sincere entered me in one languid stroke, seating himself inside of me to the hilt while my pussy spasmed around him, the last of my orgasm still making my walls contract.

Oh, God.

"You feel so good," we said together. If it were possible, his voice was even more strained than mine and that turned me on even more. I loved knowing the effect I had on him. And I loved showing him the effect he had on me. It was dizzying and empowering and so damn addictive that I knew I would never get enough.

Sincere reached beneath me, cupping my ass and pulling me against him so there wasn't room for anything but sweat between us. I was so close, I could feel his pelvis rub against my clit every time he pushed inside of me. He fucked me deep and slow. Every inch of his dick stretched me and massaged my walls so perfectly, I clamped around him like a vise, not wanting to let him retreat.

A vein appeared in his neck from the effort it took to hold himself inside of me and I leaned up, greedily licking his throat and enjoying the salty taste of the sweat slicking his skin.

"You're fucking me so good, Sin. I never want it to stop."

"Fuck, Goldy, you can't say that if you want me to last."

Smiling against his neck, I pulled back and stared up at him. It was so easy to get lost in his eyes and I did it happily, my hips bucking while he fucked into me. The slight burn in my thighs was overshadowed by the pleasure creeping into every cell in my body. I felt like I was floating somewhere in space and every stroke Sincere gave me momentarily tethered me back to earth.

"Shit, Goldyn. You should have never let me have you. Because now I'll always want to fuck you just like this."

"You can," I whimpered. "I want the same thing. I always want you to fuck me just like this."

He slammed into me then, and a gasp tore out of

me. Not because I cared that he'd gotten rough but because I didn't know he could. But he slammed into me repeatedly, so hard my tits bounced and all I could do was hold onto him.

"Please don't let me go," Sincere begged. His hips slowed and he stared down at me with renewed emotion dancing in his eyes. "God, I need you so fucking bad and you don't even know it. Just know I'm not letting you go. Not without a damn fight."

A frown tried to claim my features at his cryptic words. Because we both knew in three months he'd be letting me go, but I didn't get the chance to linger on it because he pushed into me again, grinding against my clit until my toes curled into the sheets and my mouth fell open on a scream.

LORENZO

I left my office a few minutes behind Sincere and Goldyn, giving them time to get lost in each other by the time I got to our wide-open bedroom door.

Still reeling from the way Goldyn rode my hand, I massaged my dick through my pants and leaned against the doorjamb, watching them writhe on the bed.

Goldyn was pinned beneath Sin's athletic body, her pretty tattooed thighs wide open and pressed into the mattress while Sincere fucked into her.

The wet sound of her pussy every time he moved so much as an inch was music to my ears and I took my time, working my zipper down as I gave them my undivided attention. They weren't aware of my presence yet, and I took advantage of that. My hand shoved past the waist of my boxers and finally closed around my engorged dick, tugging to relieve some of the pressure.

I hissed out a sigh of relief and Sincere's head turned toward the door at the familiar sound.

We locked eyes as he continued to rock his hips, fucking into her with unhurried strokes. The mix of passion and lust burning in his gaze made me jerk my dick harder, desperately seeking out relief. Blood roared in my ears and I used the precum beading at the tip as lubricant for my greedy palm.

He snatched his gaze away from me and went back to staring into Goldyn's soul. Sin swallowed her whimpers and groans by kissing her and another jolt of desire washed over me.

"Fuck," I whimpered lowly, desperately fucking my hand because it was all I could do as I watched how perfect they were together.

The way Sincere's ass and thighs clenched with every forward thrust held me spellbound. My husband's body was a work of art I was all too familiar with, but getting to watch from the sidelines was a treat I hadn't experienced in too long.

Sincere always bottomed for me, so seeing him buck into Goldyn with such controlled, languid strokes had me matching his strokes with my hand fisted along my dick. I loved seeing him like this. I loved hearing Goldyn sob from the pleasure he gave her. And I loved hearing the way their skin collided, the slapping sound echoing in the room while I watched with my mouth falling open into a perfect O.

I wasn't going to last long, but I didn't want to come before they did. Even though I wasn't with them on the bed, I still felt just as much a part of their rhythm as if it were me deep inside one of them.

Goldyn cried out, announcing her orgasm on a teary whimper while her body shook beneath Sin's, pushing him into his own release. He pumped inside of her one last time and pulled out to spray his cum along her toned abs, coming in spurts that depleted him until his chest heaved and he bit down on his bottom lip to mute his own whimper.

"You're amazing," he praised, bending down to kiss Goldy's parted lips.

I watched him brush tangled curls from her face and bite his bottom lip before he turned his attention to me. Well, to my dick. His eyes went straight to the hand fisted around my erection and he bit his lip.

"Come here and give me your mouth, baby."

Goldyn's head turned to watch him, but she didn't lift up to look. I didn't think she could. Her little body was too spent from the multiple orgasms Sincere gave her so she followed him with her eyes instead.

As soon as he was in front of me, Sincere dropped to his knees and stared up at me. He was so fucking beautiful and the way he so naturally obeyed my commands...if I wasn't already close to coming, I would have from that alone.

"Open your mouth."

He did and his perfect pink tongue came into view

before I palmed my dick and placed myself on the tip. Right away, he relaxed his jaw and let me in. "Fuck, your mouth is perfect, Sin."

His eyes watered as I shoved myself inside his mouth. I was gonna come and I didn't care that it was so fast. All I needed was the warmth of his mouth on me and everything felt like bliss. Sincere moaned around my length and that was all it took for me to explode against his tongue, my cum coming out in ropes. My hips jerked as I emptied myself completely, spilling against the back of his throat. I didn't move until every last thing I had to give was in his mouth and I ran my thumb along his cheek while he took it all like the good boy he was. When I pulled my dick out of his mouth, he held his jaw open so I could see my cum on his tongue.

"Swallow every last drop, baby. Show Goldy how good you can be for me."

I heard Goldy gasp on the bed in front of us and flashed her a crooked smile before I refocused my attention on the man on his knees in front of me. He closed his mouth, swallowed, and opened it again to show me that all traces of my completion were gone.

Fuck. I loved him. I loved him. I loved him.

A shudder ran through me as the weight of what he'd just done hit me. Reaching down, I twined our fingers and pulled him to his feet.

One day, I would tell him to let Goldyn taste me on his lips. But we'd get there eventually. She'd already taken so much on her first day with us, I didn't want to overwhelm her. For now, I would enjoy the taste of my cum on my favorite man's tongue.

Without hesitation, I claimed his lips with mine, kissing him until my lungs burned with the need for more air.

"I love you," we panted at the same time.

I stepped back, caressing his jaw before looking over at Goldyn. A subdued expression was on her face, but her attention was pinned solely on us and the way we interacted.

The desire glazing her orbs wasn't lost on me. Neither was the way she bit her lip as her eyes danced between me and Sin. And I knew then I was going to have so much fun corrupting her.

Seeming to snap out of his own haze, Sincere spun and bent to scoop Goldyn into his arms. I noticed how much he liked carrying her, cradling her like she was the most precious thing in the world.

He carried her to the bathroom, kissing the side of her head while he murmured, "Let's get you clean so we can go get your van."

The Next Day

AFTER BREAKFAST THIS MORNING, LORENZO HAD LOOKED at me and told me to be ready to go at noon. When I asked him why, all he did was kiss the corner of my mouth and mutter, "You'll see."

Now, I knew exactly why he hadn't told me.

Twenty minutes ago, we climbed into his G-Wagon and didn't stop driving until we pulled up in a rare parking space directly in front of the bank that had rejected me last week.

I squinted at the building through Lorenzo's tinted windshield, confusion and a little panic warring inside of me. "Enzo, what are we doing here?"

Putting the truck in park, he killed the engine and cast a glance my way. "Getting you a bookstore."

"What?" Why had he said that so casually? And why was my heart trying to claw its way out of my ass right now? When had Sincere even had the time to tell him about my little setback?

But Lorenzo didn't stick around to give me an answer. Instead, he walked around the front of his truck, slid his sunglasses in place and opened the passenger door for me.

"Enzo."

"C'mon, mamas. We have an appointment in ten minutes."

"*What*?" I repeated, this time my voice sharper as panic won the internal war. "Enzo, I don't want to go back in there."

I didn't care that my voice broke and he could hear it clear as day. All I cared about was not reopening a wound that hadn't really began to heal.

It took Lorenzo a while to react at all, but he cocked his head as he stared up at me and bit his lip. "Don't ever give someone this much power over you again, Goldy."

His delivery wasn't harsh, but I still flinched.

"Fuck this bank and fuck anybody who tells you you can't do what the hell you want to do just because you're not doing it the way they want. The other night Sincere told me about your business idea and I think it's as brilliant as you are. All you need is funding, and now you have me, so funding is what you're going to get. But not before we let this bank know you don't need them for shit."

"Can't we skip to the part where I have the funding?" I asked, the slight squeak in my voice making him smile.

His fingers grazed my cheek and I was reminded of the way he'd caressed Sincere's face when he had him on his knees in front of him yesterday. The thought sent a shiver through me, but at least the trepidation trying to whoop my ass earlier was gone.

"Let's go, Goldy. We'll be in and out in five minutes."

"And then?" I followed up, placing my hand in his so he could help me down. But he didn't pull me down just yet.

Instead, he held onto my hand and said, "And then we go to my family's bank and get you what you want."

My family's bank?

Get you what you want.

What the hell?

Why did he say these things like they meant nothing?

"Can we pause on that? Please?"

"Which part?" His lips quirked and even though I couldn't see his eyes, I knew amusement was swimming in them.

"Your family has a bank?"

He nodded.

"Who *are* you?" And I realized it was a little late to ask that question after everything I'd already let him do to me, but I needed to know.

"Lorenzo Wyatt Davenport."

"You're a *Wyatt*?!" My voice was close to a screech at this point, and he took it all in stride, pulling his glasses away from his eyes so he could stare at me as we talked.

"Technically, yes. Even though I've been a Davenport for the past six years." A proud smile lit his face and my heart soared at how happy he was to have Sincere's last name.

"I had no idea." The Wyatts were one of the wealthiest families in the state. Mostly contained between New Hope and King's Town, they'd been running their Black-owned financial empire for decades.

Private banks. Private equity. Private wealth. Period.

"Most people don't unless I tell them. I like that."

Why had he chosen to take Sin's last name?

Seeming to read my mind, he said, "It's a long story, but I'll save you the time and tell you that homophobia had a lot to do with it. At the time, my family didn't understand why I was marrying a man if I claimed I was bi. Couldn't I just marry a woman and save face? They didn't care that I was in love and didn't want me to tarnish the family name. So I dropped the family name," he finished with a shrug, his voice indifferent.

Why wasn't I surprised?

I'd only been around Lorenzo for brief stretches of time in the past week, but everything I'd learned about him backed up the decision he just shared. He was direct and a little bossy, so it came as no surprise that he hadn't let his family win when it came to how he lived his life.

I was just surprised that it came to that. Six years ago was 2018 and I could admit my naivety at being shocked that families were still against gay marriage at the time.

Then again, we *were* in North Carolina. Only small pockets of this state had a semblance of sense and New

Hope wasn't exactly one of those towns. Especially in a traditional, no doubt conservative, family like the Wyatts. But damn, if they hadn't supported his marriage to Sincere, how the hell would they react to his poly lifestyle?

From the slight tick in his jaw, I knew this conversation was hitting a sore spot and decided to steer it in another direction.

All you need is funding, and now you have me, so funding is what you're going to get.

The words played on a loop in my head. I wasn't dense enough to turn down the help, but questions still plagued my mind. "Why are you helping me?"

"Why wouldn't I?"

"Because we just met." I was a virtual stranger. "My mind can't comprehend someone being this nice and expecting nothing in return."

"I never said I didn't want anything in return, Goldyn. I want you happy in return." Lorenzo winked at me. "You agreed to be mine, and I take care of what's mine. Why do you think Sin gets whatever the fuck he wants? The thought of you spending my money and it making you happy turns me on. That's the beginning and end of it."

He leaned in and kissed me so softly I had to touch my lips after to make sure it was real.

"I have more money and resources than I'll ever be able to use in my lifetime, and I don't believe in watching somebody I deal with suffer when I can easily fix it. I know you don't technically need my money, but my name can still help. And I'm not letting you come up off a dime either. Keep whatever you saved up for yourself. Just know your bookstore is taken care of."

"Lorenzo…" I wanted to protest, but again, I was shocked not dense. I knew my bookstore was just a drop in the bucket compared to how much this man had. And no part of me wanted to turn down his offer, but I still didn't know how to articulate what I wanted to say.

Keep whatever you saved up for yourself. Just know your bookstore is taken care of.

My nipples budded at the memory of how those words rolled off his tongue. He'd said it like he was giving me the weather report and my senses were in overdrive because of it. What the hell kind of fairytale had I walked into?

"My family might not agree with all my decisions, but I still have my trust fund and access to everything I could ever need to live a life that's better than most. What's the point in having all that if I can't share it?"

I swallowed past the questions trying to claw up my throat.

"If you're sleeping in my bed and I'm not doing anything to make sure you have everything you want and need, then I give you permission to call me a deadbeat."

A bark of laughter rose in my throat, disrupting the quiet street we were on. "I don't think anyone would ever call you a deadbeat, Enzo."

"That's the goal. I try not to make promises I can't keep. And I never get involved with someone I'm not ready to fully support. Just because you think this is casual doesn't mean I didn't do my homework on you and make my decision based on that. I know exactly who you are, Goldyn. And soon enough you'll know exactly who I am."

I bit the inside of my cheek as I stared at him, at a loss for words that would measure up to the mouthful he'd just said.

Lorenzo stared at me, the same bemused look I was growing used to painting his features.

The longer I talked to him, the more I understood why he and Sincere worked so well. They were opposite sides of the same coin and it was clear they'd struck a perfect balance over the years.

His gaze was unwavering and I think I was too stunned to speak or look away, so we stayed like that, staring at each other until he gave a dry laugh. "Let's go inside, mamas."

Of all the nicknames he'd given me, I was partial to that one and an involuntary smile curved my lips.

"Shit, has it been ten minutes already?" I asked, hopping down. It wasn't like me to lose track of time unless I was buried in a book, but apparently talking to Lorenzo had the same effect. I wanted to dig deeper, but I had all summer to do that. The thin cotton of my sundress did nothing to protect me from the hard planes of his body as I brushed against him. And he didn't move when I was standing in front of him, almost like he enjoyed having me this deep into his personal bubble.

He placed his hand at the small of my back and led

me into the bank. "Remember, you don't need shit from these people."

An hour later, I crossed and uncrossed my legs as Enzo drove us to the next city over. There wasn't a Wyatt Financial Group branch in Bliss Peak and although I would be able to do everything online after the account was opened, I needed to open it in person.

"How does this work? Am I going to be an authorized user on your account or something?"

Lorenzo shook his head, lowering the volume on the radio. "No, you'll get two accounts and everything is in your name and your business's name. All I'm doing is endorsing you to open an account because this bank is invite-only."

My mouth ran dry. This conversation was out of my tax bracket. Nodding, I slid my poker face in place and tried my best to act unaffected by what he'd just said.

I was still riding the high of watching the people at my last bank trip over their feet when I walked in with Lorenzo on my arm.

All of a sudden, that loan I couldn't get approved for last week turned into double the funding and double the personalized care after my loan was serviced.

"And after my three months with you and Sin is up, what happens?"

"Nothing." Lorenzo kept his eyes on the road. "Whether you leave us today or in three months, your account still stands and you can use whatever benefits come with it."

We pulled up to the nondescript building, and for the second time today, Lorenzo donned his sunglasses and got out of his truck to help me down.

We walked into the bank hand in hand, and the only thought I had when we entered was how much it *didn't* look like a bank. There was no line leading to tellers. No receptionist in the front asking why we were here.

It was quiet, and as I looked around at the closed office doors, I couldn't help but wonder about their occupants.

A petite middle aged woman appeared in front of us with a saccharine smile.

"Mr. Wyatt, to what do we owe the pleasure?"

Lorenzo intwined his fingers with mine and said, "It's Davenport now. But you know that already, don't you, Gwen?"

I had to squint but the inconspicuous nameplate pinned to her blouse said "Glenda" not Gwen. It took everything in me to bite back a smile at his pettiness. This man did not play when it came to Sincere and everything about that made me happy on a level I couldn't explain.

"I need to speak to Killian. He knows why I'm here."

Glenda pursed her lips, her eyes narrowing at the sight of our intwined hands before she schooled her features into a tight smile and said, "Of course."

"Maybe we shouldn't show PDA?" I whispered as we waited. I didn't want to stir up any more confusion for him when it came to his family and the way Glenda studied me before turning on her heels told me that was exactly what we'd done. He was proudly touting Sincere's last name, but walked in with me? I didn't—

"PDA?" Lorenzo scoffed, moving to stand in front of me and blocking my view of the rest of the office. "It's not like my tongue is down your throat, Goldy. We're holding hands. And even if I *did* want to shove my tongue down your throat, it would be none of their damn business. The threat of gossip has never moved me."

"Okay," I gulped, nodding up at him.

Yesterday, I'd been sitting on this man's lap while he made me come, thinking I'd just agreed to a fun summer fling. Less than twenty-four hours later and I was realizing how wrong I was. There was nothing fun or casual about what he was setting me up to be able to do. Nobody in my life had ever poured into me just because. But Sincere and Lorenzo weren't like anybody I'd ever met either.

It'd barely been a week and I knew without a doubt that by the end of this summer, my life as I knew it would be different in every way. And I didn't know whether to be excited or terrified by that.

But as I settled against the soft leather of his seats on the drive home, I had to remind myself this was *exactly* what I spent months hoping for. I just didn't know it would play out like this. And maybe that was the point.

Maybe I needed to be open to things working out in ways I hadn't expected.

JULY

"We're gonna be neighbors!"

I looked up to see Goldyn damn near galloping through my door with a grin on her face. If she was fazed by the blank look I gave her, she hid it and kept skipping until she reached the service counter.

She paused and waited for me to acknowledge her, the sunny smile on her lips never wavering. Why was she like this? And why did it feel like my soul was thawing by proximity to her warmth?

"What?" I deadpanned.

"I just met with my realtor. We have to get one more signature and I'll be the owner of the shop on the corner."

Goldyn watched me with an expectant tilt of her head, eyes brimming with excitement.

"Aren't you gonna congratulate me?"

I blinked at her. "Does it mean anything when you have to ask for it?"

"Of course it does." Her long lashes fluttered against her cheeks. "I can excuse you for not having manners."

"Congratulations, Goldyn."

She leaned against the counter, her arms folded in front of her as she looked up at me with her mouth twisted wryly.

"You know, one day, you're gonna miss me and I'm not gonna be anywhere to be found."

"I doubt that," I replied dryly. Even after she left in September, she'd be down the block from me for good now. A few steps away. Too damn close for comfort.

Goldyn's next question was enough to pull me out my thoughts before I could think too long about what having her around all the time meant.

"Do you want to have lunch with me?"

"No."

"Why not?" A small frown formed on her face.

I wasn't used to people asking me follow-up questions. And she clearly wasn't used to people telling her no.

She propped a hand against her cheek, drawing my attention to the tiny freckles dotting her scrunched face.

Twenty-four on her right cheek. Twenty-two on the left. And ten across the bridge of her button nose. Fifty-six total. I didn't know *why* I knew that, but I did and it made me question everything about myself. This woman I wasn't supposed to be paying attention to took up too much space in my head.

"Lottie's gone. I need to stay here and—"

"I'm back!" My cashier's sing-songy announcement broke my sentence in half and brightened the smile on Goldyn's face.

Her eyes traced Lottie's path around the counter.

"Perfect timing. Romeo was trying to get out of lunch with me. And now you're here."

Questions burned in Lottie's eyes, but she only smiled. "You're going *out* for lunch?"

Ten times out of ten, I ate in the back, hunched over my notebook trying to brainstorm new ideas. Even on the days Sincere brought me lunch, we ate together in the back until he got bored and dipped.

"Yes, we're going to celebrate good news. We'll be back in an hour," Goldyn shared, the gold flecks in her eyes sparkling extra bright.

An unwelcome pull in my chest made me frown. She was going to send me into cardiac arrest with a smile on her face.

"I never take an hour for lunch," I explained.

"Why not?"

I swallowed hard, forcing myself to sit with her question. "I just don't. An hour is too long away from work."

"An *hour* is too much time away from your desk? That's only sixty minutes, Rome."

"I'm aware of how time works, Goldy. I got twenty minutes, tops." I gave her a pointed stare and waited for her rebuttal. I couldn't believe I was bargaining with this woman. How had she flipped my rejection into a negotiation?

"Make it thirty." She said, her voice firm as she fixed me with the most determined stare.

My jaw flexed and I averted my eyes. Not because I didn't want to look at Goldyn, but because Lottie's gaze was burning a hole in the side of my face and I didn't know what to tell her. "Fine."

A triumphant smile dominated her pretty features. "I know the perfect spot. Come on."

She didn't wait for me before she turned around and headed for the door of the shop.

Making sure I had my phone and keys, I headed out after her.

"Enjoy your lunch date, *boss*," Lottie called, her voice a little too chipper.

"It's not a date," I pointed out, pushing the door open before Goldyn could lift her hand to touch it.

She bounced out onto the sidewalk and her floral scent hit my nose, sparking twin flames of desire and frustration within me.

"Hmph. Don't hurry back." I didn't look at her, but I could *hear* Lottie's smug expression and I knew a matching smile sat on her face as she watched me follow behind the woman I was supposed to ignore.

Outside, Goldyn walked right past my car. And she didn't stop until she got to that death trap she called a vehicle. She tossed me a look over her shoulder from the driver's side until I closed the space between us, hating myself a little more every time I gave in. I did not want to have lunch with this woman. But my feet had a mind of their own, carrying me to her while my heart knocked out a rhythm that made me too aware of my proximity to her.

"I'm supposed to trust you to take me somewhere in this van?"

"Would you rather I drive *your* car?"

'Why do you have to drive at all?"

"Because I'm the only one who knows where we're going."

Instead of verbally admitting defeat, I walked over to the passenger side, squinting against the sun. When I tried the handle, nothing happened.

"Hold on, that door only opens from the inside." Her voice was muffled as she climbed into the driver's seat.

"Jesus Christ."

She stretched across the seat and popped the handle from the inside. "Okay, now try it!"

Thirty minutes and this would be over. That was just ten minutes three times. I could do that. And then I could go back to pretending this woman didn't turn my world on its axis every time she walked in the room.

Thirty minutes came and went while we were waiting for our food. But it happened so quickly, I didn't notice. Goldyn brought me to Lucky's Tavern, claiming the burgers and fries would change my life. And here I was, five minutes past the cutoff I gave her, not really giving a fuck. We'd talked about everything in the past half hour and I still didn't know how she'd gotten so much out of me. It was a gift. Or a curse.

"Are you dating anyone?" She asked, her eyes intense as the question hung in the space between us.

"Why do you care?"

"Because it matters."

"Does it? This whole conversation won't really matter in three months, will it?"

She bit her lip and a somber look flickered in her eyes before she cleared her throat. "Fine. We won't talk about your love life."

A few minutes passed before she broke the silence again.

"What was it like being raised by your grandfather?" She smiled at me for the millionth time today, and every time she did it, my defenses weakened just a little bit more. I didn't have to ask how she knew I was raised by him because it was one of those things that Sincere brought up at the dinner table to prove Goldyn and I had more in common than we thought, and she latched onto it, taking the bait.

"It was…structured. He didn't fuck around when it came to order. He was ex-military and raised me like I was headed to boot camp."

Goldyn giggled and sipped her root beer. "Did you ever enlist?"

"Nah," I replied with a shake of my head. "I went to King's Town A&M for pre-med."

Her eyes ballooned at that before she probed for more information. I didn't know why, but talking to her like this, one on one, instead of with Sincere and Enzo around, felt different. It felt like I had all her attention and that was addicting.

"Did you go to med school after?"

"No. But I got in. I was burnt out after undergrad. I

worked my ass off to make Dean's List every semester. Graduated top of my class. And when it was time for med school, I just crashed."

"I'm sorry."

My lips turned down in a show of acceptance. "I'm not. It led me to what I'm doing now. And I love what I'm doing now. Sincere has a lot to do with that."

Curiosity flickered in her eyes. "How so?"

"He just wouldn't give up on me. Even when I thought I hit rock bottom and swore I didn't have direction, he stayed in my ear about what I used to tell him freshman year. That's when we met. We shared a dorm and we became best friends. I used to tell him about all the herbal remedies my grandma taught me before she passed and he kept telling me to explore that. Until I finally did. He's always been my biggest fan. Even before I knew what the fuck I was doing."

"Wow." Awe clung to that syllable as she smiled softly at me. "I love that. I love the way you and Enzo speak about him."

I swallowed and looked over at the bar. Would it be reckless to get a shot of bourbon at one o'clock in the afternoon? Goldyn's undivided attention was dizzying and something told me a shot would balance things out. But before I could decide what to do, a waitress walked over with four baskets overflowing with greasy food.

"Two roadkill burgers, all the way. And two cheese fries with jalapeños on the side."

"Thanks, Trinity."

"You're welcome, sugar." She scanned the table to

make sure we had ketchup and napkins then turned away with a smile.

"I can't wait for you to try this."

When we made it back to my shop, it was an hour and a half after we left.

Goldyn pulled up directly in front of my door and shifted in her seat to smile at me.

"Same time tomorrow?"

I cut my eyes at her.

"Okay. Okay. I won't push it." She looked me up and down. "Have a good rest of your day, Rome."

I hopped down from her van with a grunt and tossed up a two-finger salute before going inside.

Thankfully, Lottie was on the phone with a customer when I walked in.

When I got back to my workstation in the back of the shop, it took too long for me to get my mind back in work mode.

All I could think about was Goldyn's contagious energy, the way she smiled at everyone, and the inflections in her voice when she got excited.

She may have tricked me into a long lunch break, but I didn't hate it.

And when she showed up the next day and the day after that, I didn't hate that either.

I PULLED MY BLOUSE OVER MY HEAD, TOSSING IT ASIDE ON the rug in Sincere and Lorenzo's room. Out of the two weeks I'd been here, I'd slept in the guest room once. And that was only because I'd stayed up on the couch, reading a novella all night and was too lazy to climb the stairs after.

But I had zero regrets. Reading about Vino, Nas and Bash's little triad was worth every wink of sleep I lost and missing Sincere's embrace as I slept that night.

I adored the way that man held me tight every night, snug against his chest like he was afraid to let me go. His arms were heavy enough to hold me in place and the rhythm of his heart pounding in my ear was enough to lull me to sleep . I loved every second of everything with Sincere. He was gentle and sweet and attentive. The best lover I'd ever had just based off the fact that he cared how I felt about *everything*.

Tugging on a sports bra, my mind detoured to his husband. Lorenzo had been just as sweet as Sincere, but I couldn't shake the feeling that something was off. Or missing, for that matter.

He hadn't touched me since that day in his office. Every time Sincere and I fucked, he stayed conveniently tucked away on the sidelines, watching us with a mix of emotions I couldn't decipher.

I was starting to think he wasn't attracted to me. Which was fine. He didn't owe me attraction or attention, but it was…odd after the way he'd made me feel that first day.

I'd shown him my negative STI results, so he couldn't be wary about that. Now every time I racked my brain about it, I gave myself a headache.

Because whenever Sin and I inevitably got lost in each other, he didn't play a part. Sometimes I'd see him stroking his dick through his pants while he watched us with hooded eyes. Other times, I'd be coming down from a toe-curling orgasm just to open my eyes and find him studying me like I was an exhibit in a museum. That was probably the wrong word for it, but it was the best I could do after a long day of calling designers and cleaning my shop.

I'd officially closed on the store a week ago and next week I was supposed to have a designer come out to view the space. The problem was, I hadn't found a designer yet and the clock was steady ticking.

"Hey, mamas." Lorenzo's voice startled me out of my preoccupied state and I turned around to look at him with an easy smile.

Regardless of whether he was attracted to me or not, *I* was attracted to *him*. And even more than that, I liked him. He was easy on the eyes and the soul, his presence soothing and reassuring. I wanted—

"What're you thinking?" he asked, leaning down to kiss my forehead. I hadn't realized he'd walked over to me until he was doing that and a rush of giddiness washed over me at his nearness.

Amber and leather wafted off of him and the masculine scent went straight to my core.

"About you," I answered honestly.

Lorenzo lifted his brows and paused undoing his belt. We'd both come in here to change into something comfortable before dinner and the intimacy of that hit me in the gut.

Just two weeks and we'd already settled into a routine that felt like breathing.

Except…

"Can I ask you something?"

"Anything, sweetheart." He tugged at his belt again, freeing it from the loops and set it down on the bench at the foot of the King-sized bed.

My semi-exhausted state helped me throw pretense to the wind and let the question roll off my tongue.

"Are you not sexually attracted to me?"

Lorenzo stilled, his hands stuck at the button near his throat while he stared at me with confusion and… exasperation?

"What makes you think I'm not attracted to you?"

"You've barely touched me since I got here. You only watch me and Sin and…." *And what?* It makes me uncomfortable? That would be a lie. It didn't make me uncomfortable. Knowing we were fucking in front of a captive audience always made it hotter. But I just didn't understand why he never joined in.

Now that I thought about it, what the hell was I saying? Maybe today had just fried my brain. This was a non-issue… "Actually, forget I brought it up. It's been a long day."

"No," Lorenzo followed up immediately. "We're gonna talk about it."

He hooked his arms around my middle, pulling me flush against him so I couldn't flee in the middle of the conversation. I wasn't a runner, but it still tickled me that he wanted to hold me in place.

The muscles bunched under his shirt and pressed against my stomach distracted me from the topic at hand. Lorenzo had the most tempting physique I'd ever seen. He wasn't even undressed right now and my mind ran rampant with all the ways I wanted to lick up his muscles and see his abs flexing while he pounded into me—

"You think I'm not attracted to you because I haven't fucked you yet," he surmised, getting right to the point.

Caught off guard by his candor, I cleared my throat and met his eyes. "Yes. I've been here for two weeks and you've barely touched me."

"What am I doing right now?" He asked, pulling me tighter into his body.

Heat flushed my skin and I rolled my eyes playfully. "You know what I meant, Enzo. It's not a complaint, just an observation. I just thought our summer together would be…different."

Lorenzo nodded, licking his lips as his dark gaze roved over my face. "You said it yourself, it's only been two weeks, sweetheart. We still have all summer."

"Okay."

"But just so we're clear, I am so fucking attracted to you. It's the *reason* I haven't touched you yet. But it looks like we need to change that."

"Enzo…"

"Nah, I can't have your pretty ass walking around this house or this town thinking I don't want you when wanting you is all I do. I wake up hard every morning you're in my bed, Goldyn. I've fucked my hand countless times after watching you and Sin together. There's no part of me that isn't attracted to you."

As if to prove his point, his hardening length pressed against my center and pulled a gasp out of me.

"I want you so damn bad it hurts. But I didn't want to overwhelm you, baby. I know this is your first time having two lovers and I wanted you and Sin to have your moment. That doesn't mean I don't plan to fuck you every chance I get when you're ready."

"When *you're* ready," I corrected, my lips downturned in a pout I couldn't help. I'd been ready for him since the second I rode his hand. I wanted him so bad my chest hurt at the thought of him not wanting me too. Forget everything I said about it not being a complaint.

Lorenzo's kiss suspended my next thought and a sigh slipped past my lips before I knew it was happening. Full lips covered mine, teasing and sucking at my mouth until I opened and let him in. Then his tongue wrapped around mine, turning the rest of my thoughts to mush.

I didn't know anything except the man kissing me

and the bulge pressed against my lower stomach, a very present reminder of what he wouldn't let me have.

"Lorenzo, we should go downstairs."

"Why?" He nipped at the corner of my mouth then kissed my neck before letting his tongue lap at the cleavage peeking out of my sports bra.

His mouth felt so damn good on me I lost my train of thought four times before I finally gathered enough words. "Because you said I'm not ready."

"I think I was wrong," he hummed against my throat, kissing and sucking until I slumped against him.

My pussy thrummed with a pulse of her own and I didn't know how to do anything but let him have his way with me.

Lorenzo pushed his hand into my unbuttoned slacks and cupped my leaking pussy.

"Fuck, I forgot you don't wear panties." Another kiss against my neck and I was ready to fall to my knees.

My breath stuttered as sensations assailed me and glued me to the spot. Even with Lorenzo's other arm now loosened around my waist, I couldn't move if I wanted to.

I wanted him to do everything he wanted to me.

His middle and ring fingers pushed past my folds and massaged my clit. Back and forth. Kissing me the whole time. Until I was slick enough that his fingertips got closer to my leaking entrance with every pump. Until my nails dug into his forearm. Until my breath came out in pants. Until I came all over his hand and realized my throat was raw when I tried to scream.

"Fuck, Enzo. I'm coming," I sobbed.

"And look how pretty you are doing it."

That was it. Those words threw me into another realm of pleasure and I collapsed against him, thankful for his quick reflexes because I would have been a puddle at his feet if he hadn't caught me.

My knees shook.

My head spun.

And my body wouldn't stop spasming around his hand.

It was so bad, I buried my face in his shirt, inhaling his scent to try and come down.

But Enzo wasn't a man who played fair. The second I felt a semblance of peace, he shoved his fingers into my drenched pussy and drove them in and out, over and over. The heel of his hand stimulated my clit with every movement and then I was coming again, spurred on by the soundtrack of his fingers pumping in and out of me. And this time, tears did fall, and I didn't give a fuck.

How the fuck did he do that with his hands? And why did I already want him to do it again?

"Look at me, Goldyn."

I forced my eyes open and fought to meet his hooded gaze. Slowly, he pulled his hand away from my center, keeping his other arm around me for support. "Give me your hand."

I obeyed, raising my palm for him.

Lorenzo tenderly grasped my smaller hand in his and brought it to his pants. He pulled my hand against his semi-hard dick and held it there, his eyes pinned on me the whole time. "Unbutton my pants, Goldy."

With shaky hands, I did what he told me to, pausing to look up at him when his black briefs were in view.

He grabbed my wrist, holding my hand against his softening erection. I frowned until understanding dawned and the look in his eyes confirmed it. "The next time you think I don't want you, I want you to remember that making *you* come just made me come in my pants."

My mouth fell open, but before I could gasp, he kissed me, the sloppy tangling of our tongues getting me caught up all over again. My whole body felt like jelly, but somehow I found the strength to keep kissing him. My tongue wrapped around his could say more than me in this moment.

How had I missed him coming for me? He had me so lost in my own pleasure that I didn't notice anything but his fingers fucking in and out of me.

Lorenzo hissed at the featherlight touch of my hand against his dick, and I bit my lip at the evidence of his release sticking to my fingers even through the material of his briefs.

I didn't think I'd ever experienced anything sexier than this. Knowing my pleasure got him off wrecked me in the best way. My body twitched, tremors steadily ebbing through me as I looked in his eyes.

"I just came all over myself from the thought of you coming, baby. Don't ever think I don't want you," he said harshly against my swollen lips. My eyes fell shut when his mouth reclaimed mine.

We didn't stop kissing until the sound of a throat clearing tore us out of our haze and we looked up to find Sincere leaned against the door.

Lorenzo smirked. "Hey, baby."

"Hey," he answered softly, a loving look on his face before his eyes jumped to me. A tender smile claimed his lips as he backed out of the door, his eyes still pinned on us. "Dinner will be ready in fifteen."

I TURNED IN A SLOW CIRCLE AND LOOKED AT THE SPACE I'D dreamed about owning for a year. Completely gutted, nothing remained except exposed red brick walls and weathered wood floors.

There was a lot to be done and it was both terrifying and exciting.

Every time I felt myself getting overwhelmed by how much there was to do, I talked myself off the ledge and reminded myself there wasn't a deadline I had to reach. I could do this as quickly or as slowly as I wanted. Nobody knew my little dream was in progress and until I announced a grand opening date, there was no pressure.

I fell into a squat with a heavy sigh, looking out of the windows facing the street. My van was the only car parked on this end of the block, but I knew if I walked out and turned to the left, I'd see Rome's car and it brought me peace I didn't know I needed. His quiet proximity for the past two weeks had been my saving grace, even if he acted put off every time I showed up to take him to lunch.

Having more than one familiar face in this town after years of being on my own was...nice. And I was sure Ms. Ruby was grateful for the break from being the only person I knew.

Sighing, I dropped out of my squat and sat on the dusty floor. The contractor I hired would start at the beginning of next week, building everything I'd doodled in my notebook ages ago. Then once I passed inspections, my designer would come in and make everything pretty.

It was happening. And yet, some part of me was still questioning everything.

Mainly because my original plan of this space being a bookstore bakery cafe would have to be revised. The business license I applied for before I knew what I was doing only allowed me to operate as a bookshop. If I wanted to change that I'd have to get a food vendor license and the health department involved.

When I told Lorenzo about my little hiccup a few nights ago, he'd shrugged while flipping a lamb chop in the skillet and said,

"So we'll buy the empty space next door and get you the right licenses. Problem solved."

"But then I'd be responsible for two separate businesses. With two sets of different employees. Two sets of bills. I can't—"

"Watch what you say you can't do, Goldy," he interrupted coolly.

Chastised, I clamped my mouth shut and stared at him basting the meat with a spoon. He did it so effortlessly, juggling our conversation and what he was doing like it was nothing.

"So what you're telling me is that it would be hard. Not impossible."

"I guess so." I shifted from foot to foot, avoiding his eyes.

"It seems like you want me to tell you you can't do it. And I'm never gonna do that, sweetheart. I don't care what we have to do, we'll figure it out."

When I just stared at him, my heart pounding faster than I could form thoughts, Lorenzo reduced the heat on the stove and set his spoon down. "Come here."

I fell into his embrace without a fight, soaking up the warmth of his touch as I dropped my head back to look up at him.

"You can do hard, Goldy. You wouldn't be where you are if that wasn't true. So what's the difference now?"

"I don't know, maybe it was just ambitious to think I could pull off both on my first try."

"Your ambition has never been the problem." He kissed me, his lips whispering across the bridge of my nose in the sweetest caress. "What you need is to believe you can do it. You and Sin have that in common. It doesn't matter how many people around you tell you you can do something, if you don't believe it, it'll never get done. Is that what you want? For it to never get done?"

When he put it like that...

"No," I answered, shaking my head as I met his intense gaze.

"Then make up your mind and do it, Goldy. I'll be here when you're ready. Money has never been the issue. But I won't jump unless you tell me to, pretty girl."

Tears had brimmed in my eyes at the gentle

reassurance in his tone. He was so *good* at speaking life into me and I wondered if he knew that.

My heart felt at home whenever I was around him and I wasn't sure how it happened so fast, but I knew it had a lot to do with the safe space he held for me without me having to ask.

Every time I needed him, he appeared with a lazy smile on his face and nothing but patience shining in his eyes. No matter what else he had going on with work or Sin or Rome, he *always* paused to be present for me, and it broke my heart a little to know it would be over in less than three months.

This temporary solace I'd found would be gone and I'd have to learn how to be everything to myself all over again.

Before I could spiral too deep into the pits of dispair, my door opened and the old bell above it chimed, announcing a visitor.

Expecting to see Rome or Sincere, I frowned when my realtor walked in.

Chance Summers was a contact from Lorenzo who made the buying and closing process as seamless as possible. He answered any questions I had and told me he would always be reachable if I decided to expand my portfolio.

Scrambling to my feet, I smoothed my palms over my baggy overalls to clean the dust from them and smiled as he extended his hand.

"Ms. Ambrose. Good to see you." He shook my hand, holding onto it a little longer than necessary as he studied my face with a mix of curiosity and confusion.

"Hi, Chance." He was still holding my hand and I had to look down pointedly for him to free me from his grip.

I flexed my clammy fingers and shoved both fists into my deep pockets while he looked me over.

The first time he'd done it when Lorenzo made introductions, I brushed it off. Everyone always told me I had a familiar face and I never cared to help them place where they knew me from.

But every time Chance and I were in the same room, he looked at me like he was seeing *through* me, and it unsettled something deep within me.

"Can I help you? Or were you just passing by?"

My question seemed to snap him out of his fog, and his light brown eyes focused on me, a smile crinkling his face. "I was just in the neighborhood. But I stopped by because Mr. Davenport tells me you might be interested in the shop next door."

"Uh…yea, maybe."

"Just let me know what you need and we'll get an offer drawn up in no time, just like we did with this place."

"Thanks," I answered feebly, still a little put off by the attention he was giving me. Every other time we met, Sincere or Lorenzo or a lawyer was present, acting as a buffer. It wasn't that I was scared for my safety, it was that I didn't know why he was so keen on staring at me like I had four heads.

"Where did you say you were from again?" He asked, and it didn't come out as off-handed as he attempted.

"New Hope."

He shook his head, a sad smile claiming his features and I relaxed for the first time since he'd walked in. He didn't look like a threat like this. He looked…morose?

Reaching up to scratch his balding head, he spared me another glance. "Man, you look just like somebody I knew. But I can't remember where she told me she was from. I swear she could be your twin."

"I get that a lot," I chimed in, hoping the words comforted him. "People say I look like somebody they know everywhere I go. I must have at least ten twins walking around out there," I added with a forced laugh.

Chance nodded, a weary look settling on his face before he rocked back on his heels and sighed. He looked around the gutted shop and I took the opportunity to study him.

He couldn't have been more than fifty years old. He was on the shorter side, about five-six with a salt and pepper beard and a slim build. He was polished and the Jaguar he pulled up in every time we met told me real estate had been good to him. That and the fact he was a close contact with Lorenzo told me everything I needed to know. The man was well-connected in every sense of the word which made his odd fascination with me even more confusing.

"I'm excited to see what you do with the place," he said, breaking me out of my thoughts. "I'll get out your hair, but you have my number if you decide you want to expand next door. Don't hesitate to use it."

"I won't."

When he left a few minutes later, I pulled my phone out of my pocket to check the time.

Shit. It was five-thirty. I was supposed to be dressed and ready for a date with Sincere at six.

I ran around the shop, grabbing up my purse and checking my phone. Happy to see I still had five percent of my battery left, I typed out a quick message to Sincere and locked up the store.

ME:

Don't kill me. I lost track of time. I'll be home in 15. I just need to shower and change clothes.

SINCERE:

I could never kill you, love. Drive safe.
I'll be waiting when you get here.

When I pulled out of my parallel parking spot, it was with a smile on my face and my encounter with Chance forgotten.

This had to be the most peaceful date I'd ever been on. We sat in the back of Sincere's open Bronco, the lake a few feet away from us. The view of the mountains and sunset reflected on the surface of the water was hard to pull my eyes away from, but when Sincere grasped my chin and extended a fork in my direction, I made an exception.

The cinnamon roll melted on my tongue, the cream cheese frosting making my eyes roll to the back of my head.

"God, Sincere. I need you to open a bakery so I can have this every day of my life."

A smile softened his handsome face as he lowered the fork. "I've been thinking about that honestly."

I swallowed and stared at him wide-eyed. "Wait, really?"

He gave a sheepish nod and looked out at the water, releasing a contemplative sigh.

"Yea, really. Being around you for the past few weeks has got me thinking about a lot."

I leaned into him, scooting closer to him in the back of the truck. "Thinking about what?"

My head found the perfect resting place on his shoulder and when he dropped his head on top of mine, a smile stretched my lips.

"About finally doing something about my baking. I don't know, Goldy. Just listening to you talk about your bookstore and everything you want to do with it…I'd kill to be that passionate about something. I know I'm good at things, but I never see them through. I never try because if I don't try, I can't fail. And I think it's finally getting to me."

"I hear you."

He drew in a breath, the soft timbre of his voice pulling me in. "I love Lorenzo with everything in me. I know he'd do anything for me. And he has. For years. Everything I want, I get. And I love making sure he's good. But I've always been the only one in our group without something outside of *us* to occupy my time. He's a consultant and he loves it. Rome has his shop and he loves it. What can I say I love other than them?"

His voice dipped and the sadness clinging to his words hurt my heart. I hated hearing him like this, but at the same time I was so happy he trusted me enough to speak his truth.

"I'm not complaining. I swear I'm not."

"I know you're not," I offered, my voice quiet as I ran my hand down his forearm until our fingers threaded in a loose grip. "I can see how much you love them. You could never say it and I see it, every day. And your feelings are still valid. You want something that's just for you and that's more than fair. I'm sure they'd want the same for you."

He went quiet, gripping my hand tighter.

"I'm really glad you're here, Goldy."

Words caught in my throat, but I nodded against his shoulder, my eyes unfocused as I watched the water with a contented sigh.

"Ready to paint some plates?" Sincere asked after a few beats of silence. His voice was lighter now, the heavy emotion from earlier nowhere to be found.

So, I took his lead and sat up, smiling at him. "Ready when you are."

A few minutes later, our laughter replaced all the quiet from the first half of the date.

After Sincere laid out an old sheet for us to sit on while we hand painted ceramic saucers and mugs, we got lost in the creative process, racing the waning sun to see who could make the best set.

"I didn't know you were so competitive, love." Sincere's voice had a teasing lilt and I cut my eyes up at him.

"You started it," I reminded him. "I was perfectly fine making mediocre art in the back of this truck with you and then you had to add in a prize for the winner."

"Nothing you make could ever be mediocre, Goldy."

My hand stilled, the paintbrush between my fingers suspended above my saucer, the cute little cherries I was painting forgotten.

"You're not playing fair when you say things like that. It's like you want me to be flustered and mess up."

Sincere threw his head back and laughed. "Damn, that's what you think of me, Goldy?"

I wanted to answer, but I was stuck. Just sitting there with a goofy grin on my face because he looked so damn good like this. The golden glow of sunset washing over his rich brown skin. His smile. His light. His everything. My heart swelled and damn near burst when he sat his supplies down and patted his lap, a silent invitation for me to come sit on it.

"Come here and kiss me."

And just that easily, I dropped everything and went to give him what he wanted. Because it was what I wanted too. And when we packed up the car later, headed back to the house, I sat in the passenger seat with a smile plastered on my face because I'd just gone on the best date of my life with a man who didn't know how much he meant to me.

THE SAME NIGHT, LORENZO WALKED INTO OUR ROOM A little after midnight. He pulled his reading glasses off the bridge of his nose and smiled at the sight of me and Goldyn cuddled up watching the reality show playing on our 70-inch screen. *Braxton Family Values.* She claimed to like it because she'd always wanted to be a part of a big family and it filled the void.

Now it was a part of our nightly routine because I was incapable of telling her no.

"How was your date?"

"Good," I said, the memory of our time together bringing a smile to my lips.

He'd been holed up in his office when we got back, so we left him alone and showered, knowing he'd eventually join us in bed.

"She sleep?" Lorenzo asked, walking to our side of the bed. He stared at her face resting on my chest then bent to kiss me and Goldyn groaned.

"I'm not sleep," she lied in a groggy voice, stretching against my side.

Enzo smiled against my lips and angled his head to kiss her too. "Hey, pretty."

My eyes wandered to the TV until a whimper from

Goldyn pulled me back to the kiss happening in front of me. Lorenzo held Goldyn's face in his hands, his tongue parting her lips as they kissed and sucked at each other. Another whimper escaped and this time I was sure it came from Enzo. That was enough to have my dick stiffening in my pajama pants while my eyes glued themselves on the two people who meant everything to me.

Grudgingly, Goldyn broke the kiss and stared up at Lorenzo with hooded eyes. "I love kissing you."

The raspy notes of her voice made my dick harder and I looked at Lorenzo just in time to catch his reaction. He licked his lips like he was trying to soak up every trace of her taste and let his eyes fall on me. Without warning, our lips clashed and I felt Goldyn free herself from my loose hold, giving Enzo room to move on top of me.

"Fuck," I gasped, welcoming the heavy weight of his body on me and the feel of his hard length sliding against mine through the thin material of our pants.

But he didn't give me time to get used to it. He propped himself up on his forearms above me, just out of reach while he stared down at me with a satisfied smirk.

"I've missed being on top of you, Sin."

My lips parted but no words came out when he reached between us and fisted my length, his fingers flexing over my pajamas while he watched desire play over my face. It *had* been too long. And now that he'd brought it up, all I wanted to do was fix that.

"Enzo, *please.*" Even as I said his name, I reached out

for Goldyn. I didn't know what I was doing, but I wanted her to be a part of this. Needed her to know that my excitement didn't exclude her. It never would. I always wanted both of them.

"What do you want, Sin?" My husband's voice clawed me out of my thoughts and I stared up at him, a knot forming in my throat.

"I want you. And Goldyn. Right now." I managed to choke out the words, desire drenching every syllable.

He stroked my dick again, this time harder and I hissed out a breath until Goldyn's lips crashed into mine and captured the last of the sound. Fuck. She tasted so sweet and Enzo felt so good, his fingers flexing and tugging at my erection.

He vacated the space on top of me, pushing my legs apart so he could settle on his knees between them. And Goldyn somehow slid in his place, straddling my waist and sitting her wet pussy directly against my stomach.

She lifted her hips like a pro, giving Enzo enough space behind her to jack my dick while she leaned down to keep kissing me.

I couldn't help but moan around her tongue, loving the way she filled the space between us. Like she'd done it a million times before. Just thinking about it made me thrust up into Enzo's hand.

Goldyn groaned at the slight jolt, gasping when she looked down at my abs. "Shit, Sin. I'm making a mess on you."

Before she could think about moving, my hands flew to her hips, holding her in place. She didn't have any panties on under the oversized t-shirt she was wearing and the heat of her arousal seared my skin in the best fucking way. Her juices could soak my torso for all I cared. Just as long as she was on top of me.

Lorenzo yanked at the waist of my pajamas and freed my dick with one tug. I didn't wear briefs to bed so my dick sprang free, smacking Goldyn's ass before Lorenzo fisted it again.

I couldn't see what he was doing behind Goldyn and that somehow made it more intense. All I had was *feeling* and the wet warmth of his mouth against my tip surprised me so much my head started thrashing against the pillows.

"Yes!" I hissed, biting down on Goldyn's plump bottom lip. She whined her hips against my waist, and I felt her wetness coating my skin while Lorenzo forced me down his throat. The sound of me hitting the back almost undid me, but then Goldy cradled my face in her hands and stared down as she kept rocking against me.

There were too many sensations to name. I didn't even know if I was feeling all of them in real time. Lorenzo sucked and Goldy's hips bucked, trapping me in a never-ending cycle of lust and need. And there was nothing I could do but lay here and take it. Lay here and *love* it.

"Fuck, you feel so good." They *both* felt so good. It took a while for my mind to let me focus on anything except enjoying this, but when it did, I reached between Goldyn's legs and pressed my thumb against her clit so that every time she drug her hips forward, she was met with the pressure of my touch.

Her face fell into that pretty ass frown that told me

pleasure was rushing through her faster than she could process it. Eyes brimming with pleasure and tears, she stared into my soul as her hands moved from holding my face to spread against my pecs. She kept her hands there, her palms innocently grazing my sensitive nipples and driving me closer to the edge.

But I talked myself down, slamming my eyes shut because I knew the longer I looked at her the faster I would come. It was working until Lorenzo released my dick with an audible pop and smacked the head of it against his wet lips.

My hips bucked again, against my will, seeking out the release they were both building within me. I'd never felt this overwhelmed in my fucking life. Never knew two people had the ability to bring me to the brink of losing my mind over and over again.

And then it happened. Lorenzo used the precum and saliva coating my dick and moved lower, pressing his finger against my tight hole. "Enzo!"

Something dark flickered in Goldyn's eyes hearing my hoarse voice and she folded herself in half to capture the taste of my scream off my tongue. Fuck, I loved this. I loved *her*.

That truth hit me the instant Lorenzo fucked his index finger into me. He didn't go past the first knuckle, giving me time to get adjusted to the intrusion while Goldyn's tongue tangled with mine.

His deep voice snapped our lust driven haze. "As much as I wanna make you come in my hand, Sin, I wanna watch you fuck our girl until she comes and then I'm gonna come inside of you."

Goldyn's breath stuttered and so did mine when Lorenzo eased his finger in another inch, pumping slowly until there was enough give for him to move faster. My fingers dug into Goldyn's thighs, locking her in place while my husband worked up to adding another finger.

"Oh, shiiiiiiit," I drew out, humping against his hand while my dick stood at full attention, ready to erupt.

Between the tightness of my balls and the painful pressure building along my shaft, I was fucking lost. I couldn't think past what I was feeling and then Enzo's hand abandoned me.

I was empty, still leaking precum until it ran down my length and so damn wound up, I couldn't open my eyes.

"Make our girl cream on this pretty dick, Sin. And then I'll give you exactly what you need."

As if on autopilot, Goldyn's hooded eyes focused on me as she reached behind her, grabbed the base of my dick and then lifted up so she was hovering over me. The insides of her toned thighs were soaked with her arousal, and I knew she wouldn't meet any resistance when she sat down, impaling herself on every thick inch of me.

"Yessss," we breathed in unison.

My dick twitched inside of her, happy to be home. And her walls clamped all around me in a welcoming grip.

She was perfect. This was perfect. Except Lorenzo

wasn't fucking me. And I really, really needed him to fuck me.

GOLDYN

Somewhere in the span of two minutes, I'd gone from riding Sincere to him grabbing me up and flipping us on the bed. When he rose up on his knees to look down at me, I let him push my knees to my chest and fuck his hips in shallow thrusts, slowly filling me up and withdrawing even slower. His dick stretched me out, opening me up to take every beautiful inch of him.

My eyes rolled back.

My mouth hung open.

Even without him falling all the way inside, I was full and so damn close to my first orgasm, my pussy ached with the need to release. I'd been edging myself too long before he was seated inside of me and now I needed it like I needed oxygen. Needed to release every pent up emotion I couldn't express with words. Because it felt like Sincere's dick had been made for me and I didn't know how I could ever go back to not having it.

He spread my legs wider, so my knees touched the comforter on either side of me instead of my chest, creating more space for him to fuck me deeper.

He bit down on his bottom lip in concentration, accentuating the dimples in his cheeks and that's when I lost control. Something so simple and I went careening off the edge of the cliff, lost in waves of pleasure and the way this man looked when he was pleasing me.

It was addicting. It was vital. It was everything I needed.

My orgasm barreled into me, my pussy gripping Sin until he couldn't move, and forced him to watch me shudder and shake through every wave of intense pleasure.

"That's it, baby. Come for me."

Oh my god.

"I'll never get over how pretty you look coming on my dick."

Before I could catch my breath and respond to his praise, the bed dipped behind us and a ghost of a smile pulled Sincere's lips up. He leaned closer to me, erasing the space between our torsos until his warm breath coasted over my freckles. He was still deep inside of me, his dick absorbing the lingering spasms of my climax.

"I got you, okay?" He whispered against my cheek. When I frowned up at him, he kissed me hard. Until his hips jerked forward and he went impossibly deeper inside of me.

"Sin."

His tongue ran over my jaw before following the same path with soft kisses that made me clench all around him. The next thing I heard was a bottle cap snapping open and I knew it was lube when Lorenzo shook something in his grip before squirting it in his palm.

Sincere tensed for a second above me and I could imagine the cool gel hitting his skin before Lorenzo worked some along his dick.

"Can I fuck you while he fucks me, Goldyn?"

I was so gone from the force of my completion that it took me forever to register what he said.

So he asked me again, adding, "If you tell me no, we won't do this. But I need you both so bad right now, I—"

"Yes," I replied, not needing to hear more. The torture twisting his face melted away before the bed dipped again and I saw Lorenzo's hand at Sincere's tatted waist.

His fingers flexed as he lined himself up behind the man on top of me.

My heart knocked out a furious rhythm.

My breath hitched in the back of my throat.

And my eyes stayed pinned to them as Lorenzo worked in the first inch, whispering in Sincere's ear the whole time. "You can take it, baby."

Pleasure and pain contorted his face before he bit down on his lip and threw his hips back to take another inch.

"Fuck, you feel good." Their groans came out in unison and my already drenched pussy flooded with even more arousal.

Sincere's dick pulsed inside of me, and even though he wasn't moving, the fullness alone sent my senses into overdrive. That and watching his husband fuck into him, inch by inch, was going to be my undoing.

Lorenzo froze, his hands still gripping Sincere's waist while he murmured something in his ear. I couldn't hear it, but the soft timbre of his voice and the gentle kisses he stamped across Sincere's neck was… everything.

"Just fuck her and I got us. Okay, baby?"

Sincere nodded, no words leaving his lips before he drove his hips forward again, blessing me with a deep thrust before he pulled out and impaled himself on Lorenzo's dick.

We fell into a slow rhythm, rocking and swaying, our limbs entangled, our pleasure intertwined.

The whole time, Lorenzo kept whispering in Sincere's ear and whatever he said must have been exactly what he needed to start fucking me with abandon again. His pace increased, knocking the wind out of me and he looked down at me with so much emotion clouding his eyes, I had to look away.

"Kiss me, Goldy," Sincere pleaded. When I gave in, his tongue met mine in a sloppy tangle.

It was familiar and necessary. Comforting and so damn nasty my toes curled into the sheets.

I wanted to write songs about the things his tongue made me feel. The way his dick made me believe in heaven. The way his body made me happy to be alive.

Lorenzo's attention zeroed in on me, his eyes burning into mine. "You're so fucking perfect for us, Goldy. Don't ever forget that. This is exactly where you belong."

A blubbering response sat on the tip of my tongue and I lost it before it could turn into something coherent.

Every time Lorenzo thrust into Sin, he drove into me and another orgasm blindsided me.

I was crying. Desperate tears slid down my face. Rawness scratched my throat. And every muscle in my body tensed until I forced Sincere into his own release, tripling the sensations until my legs shook so bad he had to let them go. Pleasure coiled low in my gut, spreading outward until it consumed me. And each time I thought I was coming down, it hit me again. And again.

Fingers grazing my cheeks, Sin held my gaze and emptied every last drop of his cum inside me.

The warm flood of his completion snapped my last shred of dignity and I cried out, "Ah, fuccccckkkk!"

Seconds later, Lorenzo stilled again. Then he bit down on Sincere's shoulder and they released a joint whimper.

It was too much. I was full of Sin and Sin was full of Lorenzo. A flutter of awareness shook me and I had to close my eyes.

There would never be anything in my life to rival what happened tonight, and I just needed a moment of silence to sit with that before I tried to deal with the aftermath.

Sincere's soft lips brushed my brow before he released a guttural groan as Lorenzo pulled out of him. He kissed the side of my head and then pulled his softening dick out of me, looking down at the mess we made as it dripped against the sheets.

"Fuck, Goldy. Look what we did."

I NEVER WENT LOOKING FOR TROUBLE, BUT IT HAD A fucked up way of finding me.

Every night, I did the same thing.

Went up to my room after dinner. Read a few pages of a book. Made a plan for what I was going to do in the gym. Then I went downstairs and worked out while the rest of the house slept.

But tonight, that plan got derailed when I opened my bedroom door and heard moans before I ever set foot in the hall.

Sincere and Enzo's room was too far away for me to be hearing Goldyn's unmistakable moans this clearly.

Our suites were on opposite sides of the staircase, giving us all enough distance for this sort of thing to never happen.

But Goldyn had disrupted every structured thing in my life since she showed up two weeks ago, so I shouldn't have been surprised this was happening.

Desperate cries ate up the space between our rooms and filled my ears with a melody I was never supposed to hear. Because now that I'd heard it, I knew it was all I would be able to think about.

The splinter in her throaty voice. Sin and Enzo's

deeper moans that followed up her high-pitched cries. And the rhythmic knocking of the bed against the wall.

All this shit was happening on the other side of the house, yet I could hear it as clearly as if I was standing right outside their door.

And I had to walk that way to get down the steps.

I heaved a sigh and questioned what I'd done to piss the universe off this much.

The past two weeks proved that we weren't as locked in as I thought and I needed to fix that shit because I couldn't take the constant torture being sent my way.

And it just kept getting worse.

The moment I took my first step toward the staircase, my dick twitched to life in my compression pants and I blew out another sigh.

Tempted to turn around and say fuck this shit, I shook my head and kept walking.

I couldn't keep walking on eggshells in my own home just because a beautiful woman had moved in.

It didn't matter how much my body responded to her cries the closer I got to their side of the house. And it didn't matter how damn good I knew she looked getting fucked, either.

I needed to get laid. That was it. As soon as I found someone else to occupy my time and mind, this little obsession with Goldyn would fade away.

That's what I told myself. Even as I made it to the top of the stairs and paused. Even as I strained to keep listening when her voice grew faint. Even when I stroked a hand over my dick when I heard her hoarse, *"Ah, fuccccckkkk!"*

Time stood still and I stood there with it, lost in the sound before snatching my hand away from my dick and forcing my feet to move. I jogged down the stairs, shaking my head the whole way.

As soon as I got back to my room after the gym, I would add 'getting laid' to my to-do list.

When I reached the bottom of the stairs, beautiful silence greeted me. But I still didn't go straight to the gym as usual. Instead, I walked into the kitchen, found the canister of pre-rolls I kept in the island drawer, and walked outside to the back deck to face a joint while listening to the crickets.

My dick was still heavy against my thigh. And my heart was still knocking in my chest like I'd been standing at the foot of the bed watching her get fucked into oblivion.

Why did the thought of my friends pounding her to the point of tears make my dick press harder against my pants? Why was she the only one of their girlfriends I couldn't ignore? Why did I want to fuck my hand to the memory of her voice as she came for them?

Letting my hand fall away from my lap, I took another pull of the jay and let the smoke fill my lungs.

The mellowing effect the weed usually gave me was taking longer to kick in. I was riled up, too fucking aware of how much I needed the woman upstairs.

I knew it wouldn't happen, but my mind kept snagging on the same outcome.

Goldyn, on top of me, full of my dick and her

tongue wrapped around mine until her screams turned into moans and her moans turned into cries.

My abs tightened, and I clenched and unclenched my fists while the joint hung from my lips.

I needed to chill the fuck out. Goldyn Ambrose was off-limits. Even in my fantasies.

Any woman who drove me this off the rails without touching me was a woman I didn't want anyway.

A week later, after a string of sleepless nights and too many hours spent at the shop distracting myself, Goldyn was the first person I saw when I walked in the house.

She was in the kitchen, inhaling the bouquet of jasmine and lavender I left there this morning. She probably thought Sincere or Lorenzo put it there. But after noticing how much she liked the combination of scents, I clipped a few stalks of lavender from my inventory at Soulstice and stopped at the florist to buy fresh jasmine before I came home last night. The vase had been waiting for her on the counter when she woke up this morning. And watching her inhale with that peaceful look on her face was almost enough for me to live with the fact that she would never know they were from me. *Almost.*

"Hey, Rome!"

Why was she always so excited to see me?

I hated how much I didn't hate it.

She was everything I usually avoided in a woman.

Bubbly. Talkative. And too damn optimistic.

Every time she opened her mouth to speak to me, it felt like the sun was shining directly on us, regardless of whether it was night or day.

I didn't understand how the novelty of her hadn't worn off. And I definitely didn't understand why I'd been straining my ears every night since last week to hear even a hint of her whimpers or moans.

On cue, my dick hardened against my thigh, making me happy with my decision to wear baggy black cargo pants today.

Oblivious to the storm her presence created, Goldyn continued to beam up at me until I spoke around the lump in my throat.

"What's up, G?" There was no point in ignoring her. She was immune to it and had a way of wearing me down without saying a word. I was done fighting it. Just like I was done fighting a lot of things when it came to her.

"We're going to the Opera tonight," she reported quietly, pivoting to look at me instead of the purple and white bouquet.

A soft smile was her default expression when looking at me and emotion fisted my stomach every time I saw the slight curve of her lips.

Was this how it felt to slowly go insane? To be addicted to something I knew wasn't good for me? To dread it and crave it at the same time? I was a walking, breathing contradiction with Goldyn and the worst part was that I didn't know how to fix it.

"Sin and I went shopping for something for me to wear, do you like it?" She turned in a slow circle, watching my expression over her shoulder the whole time. "Don't lie."

Why does it matter what I think? sat at the tip of my tongue, but I kept it bottled up because I knew she wasn't asking me for shits and giggles. She was asking because she really saw me as her friend after the past few weeks and guilt tugged at my chest every time I thought about being short with her.

I eyed the simple cocktail dress, more drawn to the glimpses of her golden-brown skin and told the truth. "You look fine."

Saying she looked fine was a cop out. Goldyn was stunning in whatever she wore. I was in awe of how she made everything look good. Would I ever tell her that? Fuck no.

"What are you going to do while we're gone?"

Breathe. Being around her and not doing anything about the pull in my gut was as close as I got to suffocating every day.

I'd tried to distract myself with other women. I downloaded the apps. Updated my profile. Did everything I was supposed to do. And yet, every time I matched with someone and got past the introductions and small talk, I disappeared. Because I wanted to talk to Goldyn instead. Or let her talk to me. She was an endless well of information and stories and never seemed to care that I just listened instead of talking back.

At first, it was because I thought it would make her stop talking. How long could someone speak without feedback from another person? The limit apparently didn't exist with Goldyn. And by the time I figured that out, I was already addicted to the sound of her voice while she told me stories about traveling in her van for two years. Or the way her grandmother had raised her on reruns of *Night Court* and *Matlock* so when people at school talked about the shows they were watching, she never knew what the fuck they were talking about.

I tried not to smile remembering the way her eyes rounded when she told the story.

God, I needed to get a fucking life.

"Do you want to come with us?" Her question pulled me out of my thoughts.

Masking how much her invitation threw me off, I followed up with a question instead of answering. "Sin and Enzo know you inviting me on y'all's date?"

She looked contemplative before lifting her shoulders in a shrug. "Technically, *I'm* the third wheel. You'd balance us out."

"Who's a third wheel?" Lorenzo wanted to know, walking into the kitchen with his tie undone. He paused directly in front of Goldyn, staring down at her with a possessive glint in his eyes I didn't even think he was aware of.

When she lifted up on her tiptoes to kiss him, his arm locked around her waist, pulling her off her feet until she giggled. "*Enzo.*"

"You're not a third wheel, Goldy."

My mind was still racing long after Sin came downstairs and they left the house.

I picked up my book, trying to block out Goldyn's voice in my head.

You'd balance us out.

If I listened to her long enough, I'd do something reckless one of these days like believe her.

I woke up in the middle of the night, spooning Sin. The warmth of his body nestled against me felt as amazing as it always did. And while I was happy he was sleeping easier these days, I still knew something was *off*. Goldyn wasn't in bed with us and her empty spot in front of Sin had me climbing out of bed to go look for her in our hotel suite.

Instead of driving two hours back to Bliss Peak after the Opera, we'd stopped at this hotel in Charlotte and booked the last available suite they had.

Making sure Sin was still sleep, I tiptoed out of the bedroom and found our girl on the couch, her knees pulled to her chest while she read something on her phone.

After a few seconds, she tossed the phone aside and sighed heavily before resting her chin atop her knees.

I leaned against the door frame and cleared my throat, quietly announcing my presence.

Goldyn didn't startle at the sound, almost like she'd expected one of us to come looking for her, and I didn't know if that made me happy or sad. Unhurriedly, she lifted her head and smiled across the room at me.

The slightly parted curtains lit her profile in beautiful moonlight.

"Hi, Enzo."

"Goldyn."

We held eye contact until I made it to the sofa and sat beside her, instantly pulling her snug against my body.

"Why are you up this late?" In the time she'd been with us, I'd never known her to have trouble sleeping. Unless she was up lost in a book, she was usually the first one asleep and stayed that way until I climbed out of bed to hit the gym in the mornings.

Goldyn huffed and I knew a lie—or at least a partial truth—was coming. Her tells were so easy to catch it made me smile against her curls.

"Ms. Ruby texted me. Lady had the puppies."

"You needed to get out of bed for that?"

She paused. "No. I guess not. But then I got to thinking about some other stuff and didn't want to wake y'all up by tossing and turning."

"I woke up anyway because I knew you weren't there."

Tilting her head, she peered up at me with a sheepish pout. "I'm sorry."

"Don't apologize." I closed the space between us and kissed her softly. Jasmine hit my nose and reminded me of the vase I saw Rome setting up when I came downstairs this morning. For some reason, he thought he was doing a good job hiding how much he liked Goldyn. And maybe if I didn't know him as well as I did, it would have worked. But I saw through that nigga and was just waiting for the day his restraint snapped and he said something to her.

"I was thinking about the book store and how much work I still have to do before it's ready. Especially since I put in an offer on the store beside it. How it'll probably take a year for me to get it where I want and how different all our lives will be by then."

"Different how?" I brought her hand to my lips and kissed her palm.

"Different as in I won't be living with you anymore. I mean, do I even send you an invite to the grand opening? Will you be with your new girlfriend? Will you bring her? Will you even want to come?"

"Oh, so you were out here stressing yourself about hypotheticals?" I laughed lowly and Goldyn scowled at me before it fell into another pout.

"It's not *all* hypothetical," she pointed out and her voice sounded too dejected for me to make another attempt at teasing her. "This summer will eventually end and I'll have to go back to existing without my new normal."

"We'll worry about that when we get to it."

"It's easy for you to say that, Lorenzo. You and Sin will still have each other after this is over. And I'll have me. You might not notice my absence, but I'll damn sure notice yours."

Without a word, I pulled Goldyn into my lap and positioned her legs so they were on either side of my hips as she faced me. "That's the second time you said something like that tonight. First, you told Rome you were a third wheel and now you think we won't notice when you're not around. Why do you keep referring to yourself like you're temporary?"

"Because I *am*," she said right away, the catch in her voice undeniable as she frowned at me. "Have you considered that maybe it's easier for me to look at it that way so I don't end up with my feelings hurt by the time I have to leave?"

I didn't know what to say. She had only agreed to three months with us. And since we hadn't had a talk about changing that, she was right. This was temporary and I hated admitting that. And unless me and Sin stopped avoiding the inevitable, the future she talked about would become a reality.

Goldyn held the side of my face, her soft fingers gliding over my skin and lingering over my frown lines.

"I'm sorry, I wasn't trying to start a fight," she apologized, her sweet voice low while she looked over my tight expression.

"We're not having a fight, mamas. I love how honest you are with me, and you're right about a lot of things. You didn't do anything wrong."

Her shoulders deflated, and the worry painting her face melted away.

Fuck, she wore her heart on her sleeve just like Sin. I wondered if she knew I could read every emotion she tried to stifle in her whiskey gaze. The lights might have been off, but anxious energy radiated off of her, giving her away.

Goldyn leaned into me, hiding her face in my neck. She inhaled and wrapped her arms tighter around my shoulders.

"You always smell good," she murmured, her soft lips grazing my skin with each word.

I moved my head until our lips aligned and pleaded against her mouth, "Kiss me, Goldy."

She did and my heart pounded in my chest at the connection. We both sighed before deepening the kiss, relief a prelude to the passion Goldyn unleashed when she pushed her tongue past my lips.

I fucking loved kissing her. I loved so much about everything that had to do with her. Before she showed up, I didn't even know I had the capacity to love anyone this *deep* other than Sincere. Puppy love? Yea. Lust? Sure. Infatuation deep enough to sustain a fling? Absolutely.

But not this…this all-consuming protectiveness, joy and peace wrapped up in one unnamed emotion every time I thought about her.

Well, it wasn't unnamed. Not really. I loved Goldyn. No, I was *in* love with her. I knew that and there wasn't shit I could do about it until me and Sin had a long talk.

Goldyn bit down on my lip when she shifted in my lap and felt my dick trying to stand at attention between her thighs.

How I'd made it almost three weeks without being inside of her was a puzzle I didn't have time to solve. Because right now, she kept grinding against me, her hips ticking until she dropped down on me and repeated the same dance all over again.

The only thing covering her body was a hotel robe and I knew for a fact she didn't have panties on under it. That didn't make resisting her any easier. Luckily, I didn't have to resist her.

"Can I sit on it?" Goldyn panted between kisses.

Fuck. Me.

I knew she wasn't a stranger to asking for exactly what she wanted, but it still left me too shocked to speak sometimes.

Instead of fumbling over my words, I lifted her against me, just enough to give me room to shove my briefs past my hips and sat her back in my lap.

"Get rid of that robe, Goldy." I watched with hooded eyes as her fingers undid her belt and she pushed the robe to the ground, exposing her hard nipples and perky tits. Her tight body and bare pussy.

Goldyn was heaven in human form. A sight I could rest my eyes on for the rest of my life. All I needed was her and Sincere, and I'd die a happy man—

That thought came crashing to a halt when a soft palm fisted my dick, and she lifted up on her knees, running the crown of my leaking dick against her glistening lips.

Goldyn shuddered, sucking in a breath at the contact.

Eyes pinned on me, she raised up, notched me at her slick entrance and slowly inched down. Her teeth sank into her bottom lip as her eyes tried to slide close, but I gripped her chin, forcing her attention back to me. "Look at me when you take this dick, pretty."

Sucking in a breath, she obeyed my command, her mouth falling as she took me all the way in.

"You're doing so great, mamas."

"Enzo, please," she whined, covering my hands with hers when they fell to her hips.

We stayed like that for a while, her staring at me with a mixture of pain and pleasure on her face before she started moving her hips back and forth.

"Fuck, Enzo. Your dick…it's—"

"It's what? Stretching this tight pussy out?"

"Yes." *Kiss.*

"Giving you exactly what you wanted?"

"Yes." *Kiss.*

"You know how good you feel squeezing my shit like this, Goldy?"

She whimpered her reply, but her hips kept jerking.

Goldyn wasn't riding me, but grinding against me instead, using my dick to fill her up and pushing her clit into my pelvis with every sensual swivel of her hips.

Back and forth. Back and forth.

I felt everything. Saw everything and my dick was just happy to be here.

Every whimper.

Every moan.

Every roll of her eyes because she was feeling too much.

Every tremor of her thighs as she tried to control her jerky movements.

"God, Enzo, you're gonna make me come."

"Then come, pretty. Show me how wet you can get this dick when you use me."

Goldyn shattered on the spot, my words driving her to an orgasm that made her clamp her hand over her mouth and ride out the wave until she could control her movements again.

I watched in awe as this unexpected gift of a woman came down from a high I supplied and leaned in to kiss her. "You make us so fucking happy, you know that?"

All I got was a shaky nod, and I was happy with that.

Smirking at her voiceless state, I moved until I was hovering over her on the couch, her back pressed into the plush cushion. I smiled at her, still fully inside of her before slamming my hips forward.

Her mouth parted on a scream that I easily intercepted with my tongue. "Do you want to wake Sin?"

She shook her head with tears brimming in her eyes.

"Take this dick and kiss me then."

And she did. Over and over. Every hard pump and deep stroke, she took it all with my tongue snaked around hers and her walls spasming all around my length. Now I knew why Sincere was so obsessed with being inside of her. He didn't let a day pass without making her come on his dick, and I was scared I'd just signed myself up for the same fate.

"Do you know how good you feel?"

Her hips bucked in response, wetting me up and letting me know I made her feel good too.

"You will always belong right here with us. Fuck everything else. You're ours. As long as you want us." I blurted out the words before my brain could filter them, and I couldn't say I regretted that shit. Sometimes the heat of the moment was the perfect time for the truth to come out.

The problem was Goldyn looked so lost in her own haze of pleasure that she barely acknowledged my words.

Still pumping into her, I fucked her until my chest hurt. Until the ball of tension at the base of my spine was too much to ignore. And then I was coming, shooting thick streams of cum against her pretty pussy as soon as I freed myself from her tight walls in the nick of time.

"Fuck," we panted together, smiling lazily at each other until our breaths came easier and I got up to get a damp towel to clean us up.

Whether she knew it or not, she'd just sealed her fate with us forever. I wasn't letting her walk away when she made me feel like this. I couldn't. And I'd do whatever I had to to make sure she knew that. Before the three months were up, Goldyn Ambrose was going to know exactly who she belonged to.

Saturdays were my easy days. I worked until two at the shop and then I went home and found something to do. Some days it was fishing. Some days it was a boat ride out on the lake. All days it ended with me relaxed and ready to enjoy my upcoming Sunday, the only day of the week I reserved for zero work.

Today, however, I'd made a detour on my way home.

And before you ask— yes, Goldyn had everything to do with it.

She'd been keeping her distance from her shop since construction started and that meant she wasn't around to have lunch with me on the regular. I only saw her for dinner if I made it home in time. That was what I wanted.

So why had I damn near caused an accident when I saw her van in the library parking lot?

Why had I swerved through two lanes of traffic in the opposite direction to get here?

Why was I walking in the building I had only visited once to get my library card last year?

I didn't know. But I *did* know breathing came easier when I found her tucked away in the back corner of the reference section, typing away at the new laptop Sin had to force her to accept.

The woman was determined to do all her business from that ancient iPhone 8 and he'd finally worn her down enough to accept the computer as a gift.

Her fingers flew over the keys, her head cocked as she stared at the screen in concentration.

I waited until her hands stilled and she took a break to pop her neck before announcing my arrival.

"G."

Her head snapped up at the sound of my voice and her face split in a smile. "Romeo! What are you doing here?"

She was speaking in a loud whisper, watching me with barely contained excitement as I slid in the seat adjacent to her. I winced when I was seated on the wood chair. It was uncomfortable as fuck. How did she sit here for hours every day?

"Saw your van and stopped by," I replied, giving nothing away. But Goldyn's brows wiggled on her forehead before she narrowed her eyes and leaned into me.

She smelled like a different flower every time I saw her, and I didn't know how that was possible.

"Did you just admit to visiting a place because you knew I would be there?"

"When did you hear me say that? Maybe I wanted to get some books." That was a lie. I used my library card to check out ebooks and audiobooks online because I had enough herbal medicine books to constitute a small library and didn't need to add to the chaos on my bookshelves.

Goldyn popped her tongue and closed her laptop with a soft thud, giving me her undivided attention.

"*You* said it when you said you saw my van and came in this library to see about me." A self-satisfied smile took up residence on her lips. And what was I gonna do? Tell her she was wrong? So I said nothing.

I stared at her, my face unaffected but I knew my eyes gave me away when she giggled and covered her face to hide her smile.

I would do a lot to keep that smile right there forever. She deserved all the happiness and smiles. And knowing I'd given her one made my heart skip a few beats.

"Romeo Wilde, it's okay to admit you like me."

A scowl claimed my features so fast she howled out a laugh, before covering her mouth with wide eyes and looking around to make sure a librarian wasn't coming to tell us to shut up.

"How long before we can go home?"

"As soon as you tell me you like me." She folded her arms across her chest. "We're friends and you like being around me. Say it."

She was wrong. I didn't like her. It was something deeper than that. Something worse that I would never say aloud.

"Fine, stay here on these uncomfortable ass chairs. I thought you wanted to learn how to wakeboard but I can teach you another time." The coolness in my voice belied my erratic pulse as I stood to leave.

"Wait!" Goldyn scrambled to grab her things and stuff them in her floppy tote bag. "I do wanna learn. Rome, wait for me. Please!" She hissed when I was back at the periodicals, using my long gait to my advantage. I slowed down when I reached the entrance and smirked when she caught up to me, out of breath.

We fell in step, walking out the entrance and back into the late-July sun.

"Don't I need special gear to wear before I can get in the water with you?"

"Already got it." I'd ordered a new board and two different life vests in her size last Friday, the day she saw me and Enzo come back from a session and asked how hard it was to learn. I'd known the second those doe eyes swelled in interest I would be the one teaching her.

"Is there anything you aren't prepared for?"

Just you.

Nothing could have prepared me for Goldyn.

We made it to the driver's side of her van and I tried to keep my face neutral. Knowing she drove this thing around the narrow cliff roads leading to our house fucked with me.

"I'll be right behind you," I told her, yanking her door open.

Goldyn tossed her bag inside and looked up at me, her eyes fixating on my mouth.

"How many of these do you have?" She pointed at my grill, her finger skimming over my chin before she lowered her hand.

Jaw flexing, I gripped her door tighter. "Lost count."

Her eyes hadn't strayed from my bottom lip since she discovered I only had in bottoms today. I focused my attention on the messy bun sitting at the top of her head. I couldn't look at her looking at me. I would lose my shit. Matter of fact, I knew I already had.

And if her hand came anywhere near my mouth again, my self control would snap and the kiss I'd dreamed up in my head too many times would be painted across those perfect fucking lips.

"Get in the car, Goldy."

"I can't tell if you're being bossy or chivalrous," she mumbled, climbing in. When I heard her seatbelt click, I shut the door and jogged to my car.

It was going to be a long afternoon.

We'd been on the water for two hours already and Goldy still hadn't stood up on the board. Every time she got close, she panicked and asked one of us to pull her out of the water.

And we did, every single time.

She'd watched me and Sincere get up out of the water and ride over and over again. And when she said she was ready, one of us made sure her bindings were tied right, gave her the handle, and dropped her in the water while Lorenzo idled the boat.

When Sin rode, I explained everything he was doing and how to mimic him when she got back in. Every time, she nodded and said she could do it. Until it was time to do it and she froze.

I fell into a squat at the back of the boat, squinting against the sun. "All you have to do is get up, Goldy. It's all in your head."

"I feel like I'm going to fall."

"You're attached to the board. Where you going, G?"

She huffed out a quiet laugh and looked at the water. Sincere and Lorenzo were at the front of the boat, talking about something we couldn't hear.

"I'm wasting everybody's time. We should just go home. I know y'all are tire—"

"We aren't tired of anything," I interrupted and her eyes flickered to mine. "We all started as beginners at some point. Nobody is rushing you. Take your time and it'll come."

"What if I don't get it?"

"Then we'll try again tomorrow. If you don't get it tomorrow, we'll try again next weekend."

Goldyn blinked against some of the water still clinging to her lashes. Tucking her bottom lip into her mouth, she looked at me. "Okay. I wanna try again."

"Sin!" I called over my shoulder.

We got her back in the water and stood there waiting for her to do her thing.

"Remember to hold the handle still," I coached.

Sin chimed in beside me. "Wait until you feel tension and keep it right in the middle of the board, love."

She nodded, her body disappearing under the water as she brought her knees to her chest.

"That's it, keep your knees just like that until the boat is moving away from you. Then let your body roll forward."

Goldyn absorbed everything we said, nervous concentration furrowing her brow before we gave Lorenzo the go ahead to speed up.

My eyes didn't leave her. I stood in place, where she could see me and waited for the ripple of blue water around her to expand.

She held tight to the handle but didn't pull it to her and I smiled at the determination lining her face. She wasn't fucking around and something told me this time would be the time she got it right. Sincere was at my side, biting his thumb nail and crossing his arms across his chest. She got farther and farther away, growing smaller until the line connected to her handle was straight instead of sagging in the water.

"Come on, Goldy. This shit is cake, you got this." She couldn't hear me, but it didn't stop me from hyping her up either. I knew she could do this shit, and I couldn't wait to see her face when she did it.

Time moved in slow motion when Goldy followed the tension and let her body roll forward. Her eyes were fixed on the handle in front of her. The water rippled in an expanding circle around her and the board slowly appeared from its resting place under the water.

Now was the time she usually caved and asked for a rescue. This time she didn't. She got up, shifted her left hip toward the handle and rode the fucking wake.

"She fucking did it," I muttered to myself.

Sincere's celebration was more vocal. He cupped his

hands around his mouth and shouted her praises until a big smile took over Goldyn's face.

She fucking did it.

And she rode for a full minute before throwing up three fingers to signal she was done.

Goldyn had wakeboarded for a full minute. Pride crowded my chest as I pulled in her line then tugged her out of the water by the shoulders of her life vest.

When I got her out of her bindings, she jumped into Sincere's open arms, soaking up his praise. "You're fucking amazing, love."

When they kissed, I busied myself with getting the board on the back of the boat so Lorenzo could steer us back to the dock. I kept my eyes off Goldyn until I *felt* her in my bubble.

"You did great, G," I mumbled without looking up.

"No, *you're* a great teacher. Thank you, Rome."

"Any time." I finally looked at her and smiled.

She let her eyes dance over my face, from my eyes to my lips and back to my eyes before she bit her lip and went back to sit on Sin's lap.

I obsessed over that look the entire ride home, dissecting every detail until it was branded in my memory as if I caught it on film.

And then after that, when we got home and everybody went their separate ways to get cleaned up before the takeout we ordered arrived, I got in the shower and stroked one out to the memory of her smile and the light in her eyes.

I was never coming back from this woman. She owned me in ways that didn't make sense for someone

I'd never even kissed, never even hugged. She'd burrowed herself so deep into my existence I couldn't remember what it was like to *not* want her.

Her name left my lips on a sigh, barely audible over the spray of water as cum shot out against my fingers and dripped to the shower floor.

"What's up with you and Rome?" Lorenzo walked up behind me, pressed kisses along my neck and then pulled me against him in a hug while I washed the pitted cherries I'd gotten from Ms. Ruby earlier today.

"Me and Rome?" I echoed, distracted by the feel of his warm lips against the shell of my ear.

"Mhmm. What's up with y'all?" He asked the question with a well-timed tilt of his hips that pressed his dick against my ass and made me forget what I was supposed to be doing.

Water rushed down the drain while I held a bunch of cherries suspended in midair, lost in the instant pull Lorenzo had on me. Snapping out of it, I turned off the faucet, turned in his arms and stared up at him. "What makes you ask that?"

"Because I got eyes. I see the way he is with you and he's never like that with anybody."

"I don't know, maybe I finally wore him down," I teased, holding a cherry up to his lips.

He opened his mouth and let me place the fruit on his tongue, his eyes snagging on mine. "You don't know or you don't *want* to know?"

My face scrunched and I tried to look away, but

Enzo held my chin, coaxing my eyes back to his. Why was he so good at seeing through me? He noticed everything and called me on it, even things I didn't realize I was doing.

"Does it matter?" I asked, finally swallowing around the uncertainty in my throat. The truth was that Rome and I had fallen into a nice…rhythm. I didn't want to jinx it by calling it something else because it had taken so long for us to get there. But today, when he walked into the library and sat down with me, I felt hope.

"Of course it matters." Enzo inclined his head, a silent request for another cherry.

I gave in, slipping another one past his lips and sighed. "I haven't cheated on you and Sin, if that's what you're worried about. I would never do that. You told me to end it with you before I started seeing someone else and I—"

Enzo smirked down at me.

"What's so funny?"

"Nothing," he lied, running the pad of his thumb over my bottom lip. "You're just cute when you're flustered."

I groaned his name and he wrapped his arms around me, pulling my head against his chest while it rumbled with laughter.

"Rome has never been off-limits," he said. "He's the exception to every rule Sin and I have. If you want to see where this is going between y'all then go for it."

He's the exception to every rule Sin and I have.

That was a mouthful and I didn't have time to

dissect it because I was too busy trying to make sense of the other part of his statement.

"You wouldn't be mad at me for dating Rome?" What was I even saying? Rome had expressed no interest in dating me.

"Not at all." He pulled back to smile down at me. "You think I'd be cool with him buying you flowers and having a standing lunch date with you if it made me upset?"

"They weren't dates," I pointed out defensively. "I just like talking to him. He barely reacts to anything I say."

"That's more than he gives most people. He doesn't do shit that he doesn't wanna do. So trust me, him showing up every day and letting you have lunch with him is enough. That nigga is whipped."

Laughter bubbled in my throat and died just as fast when I snagged on another part of his earlier question. I'd been too distracted to catch it before, but now I couldn't get past it.

You think I'd be cool with him buying you flowers?

"What did you mean by him buying me flowers? Rome has never bought me flowers."

The man above me licked his lips and laughed dryly. "Damn. Y'all are both clueless, huh?"

"Can you just tell me instead of calling me names?"

Another laugh claimed the quiet kitchen and I tried to free myself from his hold only for him to pull me in closer.

"That bouquet of jasmine and lavender you loved so much last week."

"What about it?" My heart raced because a part of me knew what was coming.

"Rome."

"Oh my god." He'd watched me gush about those flowers, inhaling them every chance I got and hadn't said a word.

"Those sunflowers on your nightstand?"

My eyes swelled and I stared at him in disbelief. "No."

"Yes. That man is obsessed with you, or didn't today on the lake prove that to you?"

Today had been…different. I didn't know Rome had it in him to be as patient or as gentle as he was with me on the water, but he hadn't batted an eye at all my failed attempts. He kept pulling me out the lake, coaching me through my anxiety, and letting me repeat that cycle as many times as I needed to.

He'd tugged at my heart in more ways than one today and now my mind was filtering through all our other interactions.

Obsessed seemed like a strong word, but Rome did *tolerate* me. And that was a win after the way he'd been when I first got here.

"Anyway," Lorenzo said, cutting into my thoughts. "I can't wait for him to stop tiptoeing around his feelings for you and do something about it."

He pressed me against the counter, leading with his hardening dick and I sucked in a breath.

Biting my lip, I slanted my gaze up at him. I didn't recognize my voice when I asked my next question.

"Does that turn you on? The thought of me being with him?"

He rocked against me again, letting me feel him through the wispy fabric of my shorts. His eyes darkened before he dropped his head to kiss my neck. "That's what you don't get. The thought of *everything* with you turns me on, Goldyn. I love the thought of you getting whatever the fuck you want, even if it doesn't come from me."

The puzzle pieces were slowly clicking into place. That made sense. So much sense I was surprised I hadn't caught on earlier.

His obsession with watching Sin and I together. His love for watching me use him to get my pleasure before he ever tried to get his. The way his eyes damn near glazed over at the thought of me spending his money. He got pleasure from giving pleasure, no matter what form that took. I'd never had someone so invested in making sure I was satiated in every facet of my life. And every day I fell a little bit more in love with him because of it.

Lorenzo sucked at my neck, pulling me up until I wrapped my legs around his waist. The pulse at my center demanded the closeness so I welcomed it.

"You want to come for me, Goldy?"

Why would he ask me that? Of course I wanted to come for him. And I didn't care that we were in this wide-open kitchen where anybody else in the house could walk in on us at any given moment.

"I *need* to come for you," I answered, loving the way he hissed at my brazen rearrangement of his words.

He wedged his hand between us, wasting no time as he pushed my shorts away from my center and stroked a finger against my throbbing clit.

"Enzoooo," I cooed, arching into the contact.

"Fuck, Goldy. You're so sensitive."

The second pass of his finger over my clit made me release a desperate cry and throw my head back.

"Look at me, mamas. The only thing I wanna see when you come for me is your pretty face."

I crashed my lips against his, my mouth urgent and demanding. And he reciprocated, giving me what I wanted while his fingers worked between my legs, pushing past my slippery lips and pumping in and out of me.

"You're so fucking wet, Goldy. I don't think I'll ever get tired of the sounds this perfect pussy makes when you're about to come for me."

Panting against his lips, I begged for release, grinding against him to speed up the inevitable. "Enzo, please—"

Footfalls on the staircase pulled us out of our reverie, and Lorenzo took his time freeing his hand from between my legs. When he did, he raised his fingers to my lips and pushed until I opened my mouth, tasting myself on his skin. Then he dropped me to my feet and stared at me like he hadn't just left me hanging over the edge. My pussy still quaked with the need for release, but I forced my ragged breathing to even out as the footsteps grew closer.

"We have all night to fix that pout on your face,

Goldy," Lorenzo promised with a smirk. "Now feed me another cherry, mamas."

ANOTHER WEEK PASSED AND INSTEAD OF SPENDING Saturday night on the couch sandwiched between Enzo and Sin watching *Braxton Family Values*, I was tucked away in the kitchen, eating cheesecake alone while they entertained guests for a dinner party.

Everyone was spread between the dining room and living room, chatting in small groups, and while I'd spent the first half of the night happily hanging off Sincere's arm while he introduced me to all of Lorenzo's business associates, I'd finally snuck away to take a breather after the tenth introduction.

There were over thirty people here, but because the house was so huge, the party barely seemed bigger than a family dinner.

Lorenzo had kept an eye on us, his gaze bright every time it landed on us before he went back to making sure his guest were good. Apparently, this was a thing they did every year, regardless of whether they were in King's Town or Bliss Peak.

Since Lorenzo was a consultant for multiple clients and not tied down to one company, he liked hosting a dinner party twice a year to show his appreciation for their business. Once in the summer and again in the winter, closer to Christmas.

And that was what my mind decided to fixate on.

The Christmas party.

The Christmas party I wouldn't be around for because my time with Sincere and Enzo would be over three months prior to that. The realization sat in the pit of my stomach like a lead weight.

I peeked out of the kitchen, catching a glimpse of Sincere near the entrance, receiving praise for the desserts he'd prepared and a smile washed away some of my unease. The dinner had been catered, but Sincere volunteered to make a few desserts at the last minute, and hearing the compliments he received made pride bloom in my chest.

His shy smile and acceptance made it that much sweeter. He deserved all the praise, even if he did look like he was searching for an escape route to get away from it.

My lips quirked when Lorenzo appeared at his side, kissing his temple before taking over the conversation with a practiced ease.

They looked so in love.

They *were* so in love.

This was their norm. Their life.

And soon, I would be a memory while they carried on with their norm.

Everything I'd eaten tonight threatened to claw up my throat and make a messy reappearance, so I bowed my head and looked away.

"'Round Midnight" filtered through hidden

speakers throughout the first level of the house, the nostalgic sounds reminding me of my grandma. Miles Davis and John Coltrane had been staples in our house. And now…

And now she wasn't here to do her word search while I sat beside her and read a book as the sound system played jazz. *Loud enough for us to enjoy and loud enough to drown out any visitors who decided to show up at our door without calling first,* as she liked to say. My grandmother took her alone time seriously, but she never minded having me in her space. We'd spend hours like that, lost in our hobbies, alone but together and I missed that so much.

Every time I thought about having to go back to being alone when this thing with Sin and Enzo was over, my heart broke a little more. I'd trained myself over the past nine years to be alone and fine with it. But apparently, it only took five weeks of consistent company to undo that.

A painful lump camped out in my throat, and annoying tears stung my eyes as I drained my whole glass of wine in one inelegant gulp.

You will always belong right here with us. Fuck everything else. You're ours. As long as you want us.

Lorenzo's words from that night in Charlotte taunted me. I wanted to believe them, but if life had taught me nothing else, it had taught me not to take anything a man said in the throes of passion as gospel.

And since he hadn't brought it up again in the two weeks since, I found no solace in that declaration, regardless of how good it made me feel in the moment.

So, I had less than two months to savor everything about this feeling before it got snatched away.

You agreed to this, Goldyn.

Yea, and past me clearly had no sense of self-preservation. This was more than a fling. I was doing more than sleeping with them. I was in love. With both of them. Fully. Irrevocably. Foolishly in love with two men who were already happily married and had no use for me beyond this summer.

God, some days it felt like I'd hopped right into one of my romance novels. Except I wasn't sure about this ending in a happily ever after.

I'd just refilled my glass of white wine when I heard a voice behind me that made all the hairs on the back of my neck stand up.

"There she is, honey. I told you I'd find her."

Chance Summers.

When I faced him, his smile was brighter than the diamonds lacing his companion's neck.

"Hi," I offered, unable to keep the agitated edge out of my voice. Why had he been looking for me? And why did the woman beside him look like she'd just placed something sour on her tongue?

Chance fidgeted with his hands, smiling up at me. Since I had on heels tonight, I had at least two inches on him.

"We're about to get out of here, but I wanted to congratulate you again on having your offer accepted for the second space. You're gonna do great things."

Well, now I felt bad for being annoyed.

"Thanks, Chance. And thanks for your help."

Because the second storefront was owned by a different company, it'd taken longer for my offer to be accepted even though the spaces were side by side. He'd sounded more excited than me when he called to congratulate me a few days ago.

"No problem." He rocked on his heels, smiling at me like a proud family member, and then seemed to remember we weren't alone. "Oh, Goldyn, this is my wife, Lilith. Honey, this is Goldyn Ambrose. The one who's going to open the best bookstore in town."

The *only* bookstore in town.

But he was right. It would be the best.

Fixing a gracious smile on my face, I extended my hand to the woman he called his wife and laughed when she just looked at it.

I was too tipsy for this shit.

The smile she gave me in return could only be described as acidic and I wished she could read my mind and understand I wasn't interested in her husband. Not in the slightest. I had enough going on with my love life. Getting involved with a married man wasn't on my to-do list.

Because you already checked it off.

Sincere and Lorenzo are married, the voice in my head taunted. *Happily too.*

Ignoring the stinging truth of my thoughts, I grabbed up the half-empty wine bottle and tried to excuse myself, but Chance's hand on my arm stopped me.

He clearly hadn't registered how cold his wife was acting—or he simply didn't care—and now he was staring at me in that way that made my skin prickle with the awareness of too much attention.

"You know, I never got a chance to ask, who are your parents?"

"Never met them." My words came out clipped. Hopefully, that would be enough to get him to leave me alone.

But, of course it didn't.

"Oh, I'm sorry to hear that."

"Don't be. My grandmother raised me." And she did a damn good job.

A strange look flickered on his face, like he was summoning the courage to ask more questions, but I'd had enough.

Between my semi-meltdown before he arrived, his wife's glacial stare, and the way he was studying me, I needed to leave.

I hastily excused myself, wine bottle still clutched in my hand and walked toward the back door.

Shivers raced over my skin at the memory of his eyes on me. Had I danced for him at a club and couldn't remember it? Was that why he was so fixated on me? Was that the reason why he kept looking at me like he knew something I didn't?

I pushed the thought away as I opened the backdoor and stepped outside onto the massive wraparound deck. The same deck I'd climbed up on to break into their house almost six weeks ago. It felt like a lifetime ago.

The first inhale of fresh mountain air settled my frayed nerves just enough for me to breathe.

Lingering near the door with my back pressed against the side of the house, I looked down at the heels I'd bought just last week and smirked at the memory of the shopping trip. The way Sincere had given me a minimum I needed to spend. The way he followed me into the dressing room and made me watch him fuck me in this dress to prove how pretty I would look in it.

Heat flooded my core at the flashback and a little bit of the tension bunching my muscles subsided. I couldn't look back on any memory with Sincere and call it a sad one, even when my chest ached at not having those moments in the future.

I loved him.

It'd only been five-and-a-half weeks. Why did the thought of leaving them already hurt this much?

Because I wasn't supposed to fall in love. I should have known from that day at Lucky's that I would fall for Sincere as hard as I had. He was the easiest person to love and I dove in, headfirst, thinking I would have time to teach my heart not to get her hopes up.

Time and time again, I tried to trick my brain into doing that. And time and time again, I failed.

The wine bottle felt heavy in my hand and I decided to do something about it.

Kicking my heels off by the door, I walked down the deck steps to get to the fire pit on the side of the house.

I was neither surprised nor disappointed when I found a fire already lit and Romeo sitting in a chair facing it, quiet contemplation etched on his beautiful face.

"Do you want to be alone?" I asked instead of a usual greeting.

Rome tore his eyes from the fire and looked up like he'd been expecting me. He shook his head, his body relaxing more into his chair and that's when I noticed the joint hanging loosely from his fingers. "Nah. You can be here. Sit down, G."

Relief washed over me at his invitation and I moved to sit in the Adirondack chair beside him before he changed his mind.

"I brought wine." I lifted my contraband to show him and his answering smirk made my stomach do somersaults.

The fire's glow lit his inky skin in the most ethereal way and I had to take a moment to drink it all in.

"How long have you been out here?"

"About an hour."

"Dinner ended an hour ago."

"Exactly."

I smiled at my lap. He'd dipped as soon as people started getting social. *Very on brand.*

He took a pull of his jay and I stared, entranced by the orange flicker at the end and how it compared to the fire burning in front of us.

When he pulled it away from his lips and extended it to me, I shook my head.

"Oh, no thanks. I don't know how to inhale."

He ashed it in a tray sitting on the arm of his chair and cut his eyes at me.

When he took another hit, I sat there watching him, forgetting time existed.

I didn't mind quiet when it came to Rome, but the wine had me feeling greedy.

"Do you wanna play a game with me?"

"What game?" It wasn't a no and I smiled setting down my now empty wine bottle.

"I don't know. Twenty-one questions or truth or dare."

"You can just ask me your questions, G. You ain't gotta call it a game."

I gulped. "But don't you want to ask me questions back?"

Rome shook his head, his eyes on the ground near my bare feet. "Not really. You talk enough for me not to have any questions for a while."

I wanted to be offended, but laughter spilled out of me. Sitting up straighter, I shifted my body toward him.

"What's your favorite color?"

"Black or purple."

"Like your car," I murmured.

"Was that a question?"

Eyes narrowed, I pursed my lips. "You know it wasn't."

Romeo smirked, but remained quiet, pulling out his lighter to relight his joint.

"Are you happy?" I wanted to know, jumping off the deep end.

"Depends on your definition of happiness."

"What's *your* definition?"

"Having everything I need and all the people I care about being happy and healthy."

"Is that true for you right now?"

He stared at me, unblinking, for a full minute before looking away. "For the most part, yes."

"Can you tell me a secret?" Did a man like Romeo Wilde have secrets? He was straightforward to a fault. But maybe there was something he kept tucked away just for him. My pulse spiked at the possibility of being the one he shared a secret with. My knee bounced while I awaited his answer, my fingers tapping idly against the arm of my chair.

"I have plenty of secrets, Goldy. But the only one on my mind right now is how much you drive me fucking crazy."

My fingers froze. My knee stopped jumping and I looked over at him with my mouth slightly agape.

Rome didn't flinch as our eyes met. In fact, he looked more relaxed now than he had a second ago.

I couldn't break my gaze away from his and fell into the magnetic pull of his lingering stare.

Again, the wine had me loose in the lips because my follow up came too easily. I didn't know who the woman borrowing my voice was but she said, "So do something about it."

Her words hung in the air between us until I scoffed and rose to my feet.

"You don't know what you're telling me to do, Goldy." I got up and made quick work of spreading the ashes around the base of the dying fire. Then I picked up the watering can I kept nearby and slowly doused the remaining embers.

Goldyn's voice called to me as I watched everything in the pit turn to ash.

"If you're scared to make a move, you can just say that, Rome."

"I'm not scared of anything." The lie came so easily because I'd rehearsed it for weeks now. I picked up the shovel after a few minutes and pushed around the ashes, making sure everything was wet.

When I turned to face Goldyn, she was watching me with an incredulous look painted on her face. With the fire gone, the only light that remained was the glow from the fairy lights hanging from the few trees in our yard.

The lights were dim, but they were enough to see the challenge still lingering in her eyes.

I stepped away from the pit and back into her bubble, standing in front of her. A smirk tipped up the corners of her lips as she reclined in her chair, staring up at me with smug satisfaction.

Eyes never leaving hers, I reached in my pocket, fished out my lighter and lit the last of my jay. I had two good hits left and I knew exactly how to use them to wipe that smirk off her pretty ass face.

Squatting in front of her, I kept my legs wide enough to bracket her crossed ones as I moved deeper into her space. "Come here, Goldyn."

The command was simple and she followed it without question, leaning forward to study me. Her languid perusal of my face had me mirroring her actions until I broke the spell and inhaled, filling my lungs.

My hand found her jaw, pulling her closer than we already were.

My thumb found her bottom lip, brushing over it until her mouth fell open in a sigh.

My lips found hers, covering them as I exhaled smoke into her mouth.

Goldyn's gasp forced an inhale and when she exhaled again, releasing the smoke through slightly parted lips, I smirked at her.

"Look at you, inhaling and shit," I praised.

Her cheeks rounded and she smiled at me like I'd just unlocked the secret to the universe.

"Again?" I asked before taking the final pull.

Eyes fixed on me, she nodded and tried to scoot

closer to me, eliminating the last bit of distance between us.

I leaned into her again, my free hand still cupping her jaw and covered her mouth with mine. I was deliberately slower at pulling back this time, enjoying the feel of her lips on mine too much to rush it.

And when I pulled back, Goldyn's eyes were hooded as she watched my retreat.

"Exhale."

She followed my command and tried leaning into my touch just as I pulled away from her.

"I'ma head back."

"You can't just kiss me and flee the scene," she snapped, irritation making her face fall into a cute scowl.

"I didn't kiss you. I blew you a shot gun."

Goldyn shot up to her feet, eyes narrowed on me. "Your lips touched mine. I'm calling it a kiss. And now you're running from me."

"Nobody's running from you, Goldy."

I wasn't prepared for the sting of her next words. "Yes, you are. You've been running from me since I got here."

"Man…" I trailed, rubbing at the back of my neck.

"Tell me I'm wrong."

Seconds ticked by and turned into minutes with me standing there, looking at everything but her.

When the silence became too much, Goldyn kissed her teeth and relented, shaking her head.

"Fine. Run. Again. I don't care. But don't say I never tried."

Run. Again.

Those two words cut deeper than the hurt on her face and the frustration lacing her tone.

"I know you bought me those flowers. I know you don't like anyone but Sin and Enzo, but for some reason you like me too. I know you go out of your way for me and try to disguise it every single day. But what I don't know is why you're trying to deny it right now." She ended her words with a huff and tried to step around me.

But I couldn't let her leave. Not when it looked like she was about to cry. Because of something *I* did.

Blocking her path, I let our bodies collide, anchoring my hands on her shoulders when she tried to turn the other way. "Now who's trying to run?" I challenged.

She rolled her eyes, but leaned into my touch when I held her face again. "You're so confusing."

"I know. I don't mean to be."

"Why don't you wanna admit you like me?"

"Because you scare the shit out of me."

"Why?" she asked on a gasp.

"Because you already have too much power. You throw me off without trying. I don't wanna know what would happen if I gave in to you. Fully."

"You think I'm going to hurt you?"

"No." I let out a dry laugh, my fingers tracing the shape of her face. "I think you're going to ruin me."

"What if I want you to ruin me too?"

"Goldy…"

"Kiss me, Rome. Kiss me again without trying to

mask it as something else." Her voice was pleading and my dick ached at the desperation in her eyes.

Nobody ever looked at me like their next breath depended on my touch, but Goldy did. She hung on every word I said. Every stolen touch I gave. And now she was asking for more.

"Fuck it," I swore, just as my lips crashed into hers.

GOLDYN

Rome's kisses were the opposite of everything I expected from him.

His lips were slow, soft, sweet and searching as they moved against mine, sipping on my sighs and sucking on my tongue.

I craned my neck, desperately trying to keep our lips connected until he grabbed me by my hips and lifted me like I weighed nothing.

Relief let my body sag against his, relishing the kiss, the closeness, and his hardness pressing up against me.

"God, you taste good," I whispered between kisses, looping my arms around his neck. "You feel good too."

His only answer was a moan from low in his throat while his fingers trailed over my spine, up to my neck and tangled in my curls.

"Goldyn. *Fuck.*" Romeo hissed, his mouth moving from my lips to my jaw and breathing me in. "We shouldn't do this."

He said that but never stopped kissing me. Never stopped clinging to me like I could supply his next breath.

"Why not?"

"Because I'm clingy, protective, and possessive."

"Hmm," was all I said before kissing his neck. He smelled like smoke and pine. And he tasted like an answered prayer. I didn't know how much I'd been craving something I'd never had until I had time to let my lips trace over every inch of smooth skin exposed above his collar. "I'm already with Enzo and Sin so you should know I don't have a problem with any of those traits. I like my men clingy. Protective. And possessive." I repeated every word back to him, punctuating each one with a sucking kiss against his neck.

Rome whimpered and my heart and pussy took that personally. I was so damn soaked, I knew my thighs would be sticky whenever he set me back on my feet.

It took everything in me to take my lips off him, but I did and stared at him. "What's your next excuse so I can tell you it doesn't matter?"

His hooded gaze was a boost for my ego, even though I knew it probably had more to do with the weed than me.

"You belong to them, not me," he answered as if he'd been waiting for the chance.

"If you hadn't noticed by now, I like being shared. And they don't have a problem with me being with you."

Eyes wide with alarm, he asked, "You talked to them about this?"

"Of course." I dropped one arm from his neck and swiped my lipstick from his lips. "Now, what's your next excuse?" I asked again.

But Rome didn't have one ready this time. Instead, he kissed me again. Deeper, rougher, and more urgent than before.

He sucked my tongue into his mouth and kneaded my hips as he held me impossibly still against him. I didn't want to be anywhere but right here with him, but I knew there was a whole party still happening yards away from us and I needed to go back inside before Sin and Enzo got worried.

"We should go back inside before they come out here looking for us."

Romeo nodded, his forehead against mine. He pecked my lips and released a shaky breath. "Everything about you is better than I expected."

He carried me back to the house, my legs wrapped around his waist and his hands anchored at my hips.

At the back door, he placed me down and I squirmed at the mess between my thighs. I was going to need to sneak away to freshen up before I could go back to this party with a straight face.

While I was lost in thought, Romeo was kneeling in front of me, lifting my foot in his palm and putting my heels back on without a word. He secured the pearl-beaded strap around my ankle like he'd done it a million times then sat my foot back on the deck, his hand brushing over my ankle and sending a shiver of awareness through me.

"Let's go back inside," he said when we were eye to eye again. His fingers threaded with mine and he led us back inside, and my only thought as the kitchen came back into view was that I would follow him anywhere.

WAKING UP WITH GOLDYN BESIDE ME WASN'T A PART OF the plan. And as I watched her chest rise and fall with each breath, I realized I didn't give a fuck about a plan. Her bare face was the picture of peace while she slept beside me as if she'd done it countless times before.

Since she was sleeping, I allowed my mind to wander and mentally go over how we ended up here.

Once most of the guests left last night, Goldyn had intwined her fingers with mine and told me she was ready for bed.

"Before you say I'm drunk and trying to jump your bones, I just wanna sleep. With you." She hesitated, *searching my face with a flicker of uncertainty entering her eyes. "If that's okay."*

It was more than okay with me. And when I looked over her shoulder to find Sincere and Lorenzo watching us with bemused looks on their faces, I knew no wouldn't be falling from my lips.

I was tired of denying myself what I wanted with her. And after kissing her I knew we'd never go back to how we were before.

So, we came to my room. She walked into my bathroom to shower and when I walked out after mine, she was already in bed, one of my T-shirts swallowing her body. She smelled like *me* because she'd showered using my soap and was wearing my clothes. Unlike the first time it happened, I didn't go into a fit of panic at the realization. I *liked* her smelling like me. Just like I liked having her here with me.

Goldyn fell asleep as soon as I got in bed. She curled into my side, threw her leg across mine, and she'd been sleep ever since.

Since I didn't want to wake her up, I used the time to stare at her uninterrupted, noting all the features I loved.

Her complexion had darkened in the last few weeks, thanks to all the time we spent out on the water, so her freckles weren't as visible as they usually were. I still tried to count them, brushing my finger over the bridge of her nose and smiling to myself when she stirred under my touch.

"How long are you gonna watch me sleep?" she whispered sometime later, peeking one eye open.

"As long as you let me," I whispered back, dipping my head to kiss her forehead. She stretched until her legs shook and looked up at me with peace softening her expression.

"Morning, Romeo."

"Morning, G."

"How long have you been awake?"

"I don't know. I haven't checked the time yet."

"Why not?"

"Had something better to do."

My eyes never left hers as I ran my hand over her

curls, happy I already used silk pillowcases because she didn't have a scarf in my room. I added that to my mental shopping list while she stretched again, this time into my embrace.

"Your bed is so comfortable. I slept like a baby." She breathed me in, her arms snaking over my waist so she could trail her nails up and down my spine.

I almost shivered at the touch. I loved her hands on me more than I loved most things, and I needed to learn how to contain that shit.

But then Goldy kissed my shoulder, and my bicep, and my chest. And suddenly, holding back my reaction to her lips on me fell to the bottom of my list of priorities.

"I've been obsessed with your skin since the first time I saw you. Even when you had that gun to my head," she confessed between kisses, her mouth moving down to my abs before she came back up and kissed along my chest. I couldn't do anything but watch her head bob as she explored my body, whispering kisses along my hot skin.

When her hand moved from my back and to the space between us, Goldyn's eyes locked with mine. I sucked in a breath, all the blood in my body rushing to my dick.

"Do you want me to stop touching you?" she checked in, her hands and mouth just out of reach, giving me time to tell her no. But I wouldn't. I couldn't. I wanted her mouth back on my skin and I needed her touch. *Wherever* she wanted it to land.

"No."

"I was hoping you'd say that," Goldyn whispered, inching closer to me until her front was pressed into my chest, and she threw her leg over mine again while I remained on my side, facing her.

Her hand fell between us again and I watched, entranced at the way she bit down on her bottom lip as her fingers grazed my erection. Her hand slipped into my shorts, cradling my length. She released a sexy moan when I grew harder against her palm.

My one-track mind bypassed every other sensation and focused on the heat spreading through my veins. Desire twisted in the pit of my gut, sending tingles up and down my spine.

"Goldy. Fuck. Please don't stop touching me."

She sucked my neck—the same spot she was obsessed with last night—and whispered something I couldn't hear because her fingers tightened around me, twisting at the base and then jacking my length.

"Ah, fuck."

"I really, *really* wanna see you come for me, Romeo."

If she kept kissing on me and moving her hand like that, she was going to get her wish granted faster than I could catch my breath.

I jerked against her, helpless to do anything but let her pump me to the brink of an orgasm before she pulled her hand away from my aching dick to caress the side of my face.

"Do you wanna come for me, Romeo?"

Swallowing the words stuck in my throat, I nodded, and unleashed a raspy sound I didn't recognize as my own voice.

Goldy watched me with wonder, studying every reaction I gave her like she wanted to commit it all to memory.

She tightened her hold on me again, stroking my dick with her left hand while the other explored my body.

"I didn't expect you to be this responsive."

Those perfect fucking lips reached the hollow of my throat and sucked. And sucked. And sucked until that alone had me bucking against her hand. My precum smeared across her small palm, and more followed it with every thrust I made against her grip.

Who the fuck was this woman? Was this *why* Enzo and Sin were so damn gone over her? Or was she only like this with me? I didn't have time to filter through any more questions before Goldyn increased her pace. She tugged and stroke, the combination of friction and pressure pulling me under.

My hips stilled.

I released a desperate whimper. "Goldy… *please*….don't stop."

She didn't. She held the same rhythm once she noticed it was getting me there and didn't stop touching me or kissing on me. Not until the first spasm of my orgasm erupted against her hand. Then she pulled her lips from my jaw and watched the pleasure play across my face while I writhed against her touch.

"You try to act so grumpy and cold, but look how well you come for me."

"*Goldyn.*" I tightened my hand over hers, doubling the pressure around my shaft until I emptied everything on our hands and my stomach. There was cum everywhere and I didn't care about anything except the way it felt like I was floating and the way Goldyn peppered kisses along my jaw until the aftershocks quieted and I could breathe again.

"What the fuck did you just do to me?"

An innocent smile was my reply as I climbed out of bed to go clean myself up. When my stomach—and chest—were free of cum, I shed my shorts, brushed my teeth and walked back into the room to find Goldy waiting for me with desire etched across her face.

Her lips were parted as she watched my approach. My knee sank into the mattress as I got on the bed from the foot of it, pulling her ankle with enough strength to make her yelp. With her legs parted, I fell between them, happy to see her glistening pussy bare and waiting for my tongue.

"Romeo," she hissed when I kissed her mound, my head nestled between her thighs while I hooked my arms under her thighs and opened her up the way I wanted.

"Nah, Goldy. You talked all that shit when you were making me come. Now I want to see how you act when I make this pussy cream for me."

Pushing my tongue past her folds, I sucked her clit into my mouth and hummed at the taste. "You taste fucking amazing, G."

I swirled my tongue against her swollen clit, groaning at how turned on she was from making me come. If I wanted to fuck her right now, I could slide right in. But since I'd fucked around and let her make me come, I needed time for my body to recover. Which was perfect because I wanted to take my time tongue fucking this pretty pussy until she made a mess on my chin.

"What? You don't have anything to say?"

"Unh," she whined, hips bucking. Her fingers threaded through the longer coils at the top of my head and I could feel more of her wetness leaking against my tongue as she tugged.

The slight pain from her pulling my hair wasn't enough to make me stop eating her pussy. I savored every drop of her arousal. Every shudder. And every moan that left her lips.

This was addicting. I wanted to spend forever like this if it meant she would always be wrapped around me, sounding this good.

"Romeo," she cried, her thighs squeezing the side of my head. "You're...fuck."

"You wanna come for me, Goldyn?" I asked, parroting her earlier question.

Now that she was on the receiving end of it, she could barely get the throaty "yes" past her throat before she was whining again, filling my ears with the sweet sound of her need for me.

My dick twitched to life against the comforter, slowly coming back to life after the way she wrung me out. I couldn't wait to be inside of her.

I licked and sucked and tongued her into a screaming orgasm. Her thighs trembled against my shoulders and her voice was hoarse from how loud she screamed. I knew Sin and Enzo would be able to hear her, no matter where they were in the house, and that made my dick harder, more desperate to be inside of her so she could scream for me again. And again.

Goldyn still shook beneath me when I pulled my mouth off her and watched the slow trickle of her arousal leak from her entrance and down to her ass.

Her release coated her asshole until it glistened, tempting me to lick up the mess.

But I had different plans for the way I wanted her to come for me next.

Plans that involved her on her stomach. The side of her face pressed into the pillow. And her pussy full of my dick.

"Fuck, you feel good," I sighed when I slid inside of her. Her walls fluttered around my erection, already trying to coax my next nut out of me.

I pushed into her, deep enough for my balls to smack her lips before pulling out and doing it again.

She moaned again, her hips undulating to create more friction. When I slammed into her, bottoming out, her eyes slid closed and she bit her lip.

"Talk to me, G."

The pillow beneath her absorbed some of her cries, so I slowed my thrusts, allowing her to speak.

"Romeo, yes, yes, oh god, yes. Please. More."

Plunging into her again, I watched the relief on her face. "Fuck. Goldy. You like it rough?"

"With you…yessss." The rest of her sentence split into a satisfied cry. She threw her hips in a slow circle, almost raising up to her knees to fuck me back with every stroke I gave her.

"*Harder*, Rome. Please."

And I gave her what she wanted, filling her up with strokes that were just as hard as they were deep. My balls tightened at the way her ass jiggled with every jolt. She looked so fucking good like this.

"Romeo."

"Yea, baby?"

"I'm coming."

That was all the warning I got before her pussy quaked around my dick, glazing my length with her release. She reached back for me, pulling me against her until my chest was flat against her back and I could speak directly in her ear.

"Tell me what you want, G."

"I want you to come for me." I fucked into her hard, my thrusts growing frenzied before I pulled out and came against her ass.

We both panted in the aftermath and then Goldyn stretched, pushing her lithe body against me.

"Oh, my god," Goldyn purred. "That was amazing. You're amazing."

I smiled at her when she folded her arms under her like a pillow and rested her head, already looking closer to sleep than awake.

Little did she know, she'd just given me a new obsession. And if fucking her to sleep was what she wanted, it was what I would do.

LORENZO

"Did you see the way Chance cornered Goldy in the kitchen last night?"

Sincere paused tucking his side of the duvet under the mattress and stared across the bed at me.

We were making the bed, about to go downstairs and clean up the leftover mess of the party.

"I saw them talking, but I didn't know he cornered her. I thought he just wanted to introduce her to his wife?" he commented with a flippant lift of his shoulder.

"Maybe. But he was on a mission trying to find her. He asked me twice where she was before he found her and his wife didn't look happy at the introduction." I had no shame admitting I'd been watching Goldy from afar all night. She'd been on Sin's arm for most of the after-dinner mingling before she withdrew, hiding in the kitchen while the rest of the guests roamed about the first level of our house.

Worry needled me from the moment I noticed, feeling guilty for asking her to basically be a gracious host when we still had so much to discuss about where she stood in our lives. And I saw the second that wave of uncertainty hit her. But every time I tried to get away to ease her mind, another guest walked up and held me up.

When I was finally free to leave the main part of the house, she was nowhere to be found. Until she reappeared an hour later with Rome by her side.

Chance had left by the time she came back, but not

before telling me to tell her to call him. His wife looked annoyed when they said their goodbyes. Now, hours later, his fascination with her still rubbed me the wrong way. What did he want with her? Had I read him wrong all these years? Was he a fucking pervert trying to lock Goldyn in to some seedy arrangement?

Sincere snapped his fingers, pulling me out of my thoughts.

"What's wrong? Why are you frowning?"

"Nothing." I bit back my words as we finished making the bed.

"She spent the night with Rome," Sin noted, fluffing the pillows on his side.

"I know, you think they're gonna be weird about it?"

He cut his eyes at the door. "You hear *that*? You tell me."

Goldy's muffled moans hit my ears through our closed door and I raised a brow. I would know those sounds from anywhere. Her voice—and cries—were too unique to mistake for anybody else's. "Oh, shit."

Sincere smirked. "Yea. I don't think Rome is coming back from Goldy. He can try, but…"

"It'll be pointless," I finished for him. There was no coming back from a woman like Goldyn. We'd known that the first day she stayed with us.

He sat down on the bed, facing me as I walked around the perimeter. The somber look on his face clued me in to what he was about to say. "I want her to *stay*, Enzo. We've never had a woman who fits this well with all of us. Who *feels* this good with all of us. We need to sit her down and tell her we changed our minds."

"Mhm," was all I said with a slight smile.

"What?"

"Nothing." I shrugged, my smile growing wider. "I've been waiting for you to say that."

Sincere's face relaxed into a smile and I joined him on top of the covers, hugging him tightly from behind. "We'll have the talk and we can forget this three-month thing ever existed."

"Okay."

I nibbled at his earlobe, driving him to inhale sharply before moaning my name.

"Lorenzo."

Another round of Goldyn's seductive moans reached our ears. My dick stiffened and I placed my hand in Sin's lap to see if he had the same reaction. His dick was harder than mine, greeting my palm with heat even through his sweats.

"Tell me how you feel hearing Romeo take care of our girl like that."

Sincere turned his head to kiss me and I let him, stroking his tongue with mine while I massaged his dick.

"Hearing her like that turns you on, doesn't it?

"Yes."

"Why?"

"Because, knowing she's coming makes me want to come."

Fuck. "You wanna come right now?"

"Enzo, stop playing with me." He rocked his hips

up into my touch, hissing when I squeezed his dick and kissed along his neck.

"Say you wanna come and you know I'll give you that. I always give you what you want."

He let his head fall back against my shoulder while my fingers worked against his length, squeezing and tugging until he was fully hard and fully ready for me to stop teasing him.

"I wanna come, Enzo. Please."

"Then you'll come."

Soon, Sin's moans eclipsed Goldyn's because I had him on his stomach, my face buried in his ass while I ate him until he whimpered that he was about to come on the bed. He reached beneath him, rubbing his dick to try and relieve the pressure. And the sight almost made me come. But before I got lost in that feeling, I flipped him over, aligned his body with mine, spit against my palm, and fisted both our dicks in my hand, stroking and pulling until we both came on his stomach.

We never got around to having that talk with Goldyn because she was occupied with Rome all day. They only came out of the room once to grab food and then disappeared into their cocoon again. Every time Sin and I heard them trying to fuck the bed through the wall, we shared a smile and promised to have that talk with her tomorrow.

AUGUST

The next morning, Goldyn entered the kitchen with a complacent smile on her face. Without speaking, she fell into my side for a lingering hug, giving me time to kiss the top of her head.

"I haven't seen you since Saturday. You okay, love?"

She nodded, that same grin glued to her lips. "Very okay."

Searching her face, I found the truth of her words in full effect. She looked happy and that made me happy. I hadn't caught Rome before he left for work this morning, but I bet he had a matching look on his face.

"I made you breakfast," I told her, squeezing her tighter and adoring the rush of warmth that touching her always gave me. "And cinnamon rolls," I added before jutting my chin toward the island where her plate was waiting.

"You're the best," she whispered, leaving my side.

Her praise made me grin as I filled my new favorite espresso mug. It was only half-covered in hand painted cherries because Goldyn and I had spent the rest of the date making out in the back of my truck. Every time she offered to finish painting it, I turned her down. Because it was perfect just like this.

A few minutes later, Enzo walked in, looking a little more distressed than usual for a Monday morning. The emergency text he received from a client this morning on his way to work out had everything to do with that. In the two hours since then he'd bought a plane ticket, showered and packed his bags.

"Why is there an extra two-hundred fifty grand in my business account, Enzo?" Goldyn quizzed in place of a greeting.

He faced her, snapping the lid on his travel mug of coffee. "There was a grant for new business accounts that opened in Q2. Applications were open all of July. Nobody else applied, so the money went to the last person to join the bank. You joined at the end of June, so it was perfect."

She screwed up her face. "That's not how grants work, Enzo."

"Hmm," he hummed noncommittally, walking over to grab the back of her neck. "Give me your lips, mamas."

On command, Goldyn inclined her head and let him cover her mouth with his.

But the moment she pulled away, she asked, "Did you really just sneak a quarter million dollars in my account?"

"I don't know what you're talking about." He glanced down at his watch and then over his shoulder at me. "And I have to go if I'm gonna make it to the airport on time. Ready, Sin?"

"You're leaving?" Goldy's voice held alarm as her eyes darted between the two of us.

"Emergency business trip. I have to go help my client clean up a mess. In person." Lorenzo smoothed the frown on her face and kissed her again. "Don't look at me like that. It's already hard enough to leave. When I get back, Sin and I wanna take you out. We need to talk to you about something."

"Why would you tell me that? Now I'm gonna obsess over it until you get back."

A quiet laugh escaped me at her crumpled expression before Enzo kissed her again and whispered something against her lips.

Whatever he said washed away her frown and turned it into a shy smile as she breathed, "Okay."

I loved glimpsing the softness he brought out of her. Goldyn was hyperindependent by default, but she melted into him, dropping her defenses enough to just...be. Because she knew Lorenzo had her. I'd been loved by him for a decade and still wasn't used to the way he made everything so easy by being his naturally dominant self. I loved her with him. I loved *her*. I was so in love with her it made me question if we'd known each other in a past life because she felt so familiar.

Goldyn fit in with us like a missing piece we never knew we needed. She felt like a part of our family even though it'd only been a little over a month and I never wanted to go back to being without her.

Quieting those thoughts, I pushed off the counter and walked over to her.

"I'll be back in a few hours, love," I told her as Enzo gathered his bags and walked to the front of the house.

"Be safe," she said against my mouth when I bent to kiss her.

As we pulled out of the driveway, my mind obsessed over how good it felt to know she would be waiting for me when I got back. Our home was exactly where Goldy belonged. For good.

Goldyn

Endometriosis, you raggedy bitch.

I hadn't dealt with this ho in nine weeks and she wanted to show up on a random Wednesday and terrorize me with cramps from the blazing pits of hell. On the day I was supposed to go kayaking with Sincere. Instead of getting my sunscreen and snacks together, I was doubled over in the bathroom with tears streaming down my face.

Sweat dotted my forehead from the intensity of the pain. It felt like someone had wrapped their fist in barbwire and was going to town with my insides. I hadn't even started bleeding yet, but I couldn't move. Couldn't do anything past wincing and gripping the bathroom sink until my hand shook and my knuckles turned white.

There was no way I was getting in a cramped kayak when I couldn't even stand up straight without wanting to faint. Grabbing my phone, I walked into the guest bedroom and curled into a ball near the foot of the bed. I couldn't be bothered to move toward the pillows. I just needed a break from being upright and I would worry about my position on the bed later.

Holding down the home button on my phone, I waited for Siri to prompt me and told her to call Sincere.

"Hey, love. Got your sna—"

"Sin, I can't go anywhere. I'm sorry, I don't feel good." Every word I spoke pushed me closer to another torrent of tears and my voice cracked on the last one.

Sincere apparently heard the tears too because a silent beat passed before I heard footsteps headed down the hall to my room.

"Can I come in?" he said into the phone when he reached my door.

"Please," I groaned.

Relief flooded me when the door opened and he rushed to my side. "Hey, love. What's wrong?"

"I have cramps and it hurts to do everything right now."

His hand landed softly against my back, rubbing in slow circles while his eyes darted over my face. He tried to mask the sadness in his eyes before I could see it, but I did and it made me sadder. I felt guilty for making him worry and more moisture coated my cheeks.

"What do you need right now?" Sin's soft voice soothed me while the soft press of his fingers under my shirt gave me a sliver of comfort. The pain wasn't the kind that could be massaged away, but having him this close felt better than being alone.

"Can you just stay here with me?"

"Of course, love." He gingerly scooped me up and

carried me to the head of the bed, placing me against a mountain of pillows before he swiped away the mess on my face.

He climbed in with me and cuddled me to his side, his soft murmurs pulling me out of my panic a little more.

Sincere stayed with me all day, brought me food when my appetite finally returned and let me nap off and on across his lap while he worked on his iPad.

"What are you working on?" I asked quietly.

"Researching vendors for if I wanted to bake on a larger scale."

"A larger scale like a bakery?" I asked, hope swelling and pushing down some of the pain.

"Mhmm," Sincere replied, using his Apple Pencil to write something on his screen.

"Does that mean I can hire you when my store opens?"

He hedged. "I don't know about that yet. I'm just seeing what's out there for now."

"I'm proud of you," I said, nuzzling deeper into his touch.

"Don't say that yet. I haven't done anything." He tried to laugh off my praise but I cut my eyes up at him as best I could in my predicament.

"You don't need to do anything for me to say I'm proud of you and mean it, Sincere. You don't have to downplay who you are until you do something you think is worthy of praise. Because I'll always find a way to remind you of how amazing you are for simply existing."

Sincere didn't speak, but he did set his iPad to the side and kiss along my hairline. "Okay."

"Now, let's try this again. Sincere, I'm so fucking proud of you."

A dry snort of laughter escaped before he followed up, "Thank you, Goldyn."

His acceptance lulled me to sleep that afternoon and when I woke up again, Sincere was knocked out on my left while Rome took up space on my right, quietly reading a book beside us.

The pain in my abdomen was at about a three right now compared to the raging ten from earlier, so when I sat up to greet him, my smile was real instead of a grimace.

"What are you reading?" His phone was in dark mode so I couldn't see much more than a white blur of words on the screen as my eyes adjusted to being awake. The only light on in the room was the little lamp on my nightstand.

"*The Fifth Season* by N.K. Jemisin."

"Hmm. I've heard good things," I muttered, wrapping my arms around his torso from the side. Rome tossed his phone on the bed and pulled me fully onto his lap, kissing my face while he breathed me in like it'd been months instead of hours since we saw each other.

"Why didn't you call me to tell me you were sick?"

His lips hovered over my neck, placing featherlike kisses there until I answered him.

"I didn't want to bother you. And I had Sin here

with me the whole day. He took care of me," I answered.

Romeo grumbled low in his throat and lifted his head to stare at my profile. The heat of his gaze compelled me to face him.

"You're not bothering me when you tell me something is wrong, G. I wanna be bothered by you. It made me feel worse to know you weren't okay all day and I never checked on you."

"You're checking on me now," I pointed out, puckering my lips for a kiss.

He relented, but he still studied me like he didn't believe I was okay when he pulled away. "Are your periods always this bad?"

Heaving a sigh, I shrugged. "Yes and no. I'm not even on my period yet, but the cramps a few days before are atrocious."

"And you're not in pain now?" The earnestness in his eyes melted my heart.

"A little. But it's nowhere near as bad as it was."

"How long as it been like this?" He followed up.

"Since I was a teenager. I've had bad periods all my life. I have endometriosis and up until two years ago, I had fibroids. But I got them removed after I graduated college. I couldn't take it anymore." Bleeding through my clothes wasn't something I'd wish on anyone, and it took me until my senior year to find a doctor who listened to me about it not being normal.

Rome's voice sounded tortured when he tried to soothe me. "I'm sorry, G. I can't imagine how much that shit hurts."

I shrugged. "I'm used to it. I know it's fucked up, but I used to see it as a silver lining that I only had to deal with my period a few times a year. But now when I do get them, the pain is so bad that I just want a consistent, normal cycle."

Rome nodded, still deep in thought as he settled his hand over my abdomen. He apologized again and again, his voice growing more faint with every repetition. "I'm sorry, Goldyn."

The helpless look on his face sparked a familiar emotion in my chest.

I didn't know how I'd gotten so lucky to stumble into their lives. Every man in this house made me feel cherished. Seen. Adored more than I ever had in my life.

They were so sweet it made me want to cry.

Too emotional to speak, I laid against his chest. The only person we were missing was Enzo. I felt his absence just as deep as I felt Sincere and Romeo's presence. And I knew if he wasn't on his business trip still, he'd be crowded on this bed with us. The thought made me smile, and that smile quickly slipped when I realized the next time this happened, they probably wouldn't be around to comfort me. And that made me want to cry a little bit too.

I was really gonna miss them. And the only thing I could do about it was soak up the present moment for what it was and be grateful that at least I had right now with them.

ASIDE FROM AUNT FLO TRYING TO SHAKE THE TABLE FOR the first few days, August started with a little rain and not too much fanfare.

Lorenzo's quick turnaround trip had turned into a fifteen-day journey, split between King's Town and Charlotte while he wrapped up negotiations for a longtime client. Thankfully, he was set to fly back in the morning. The energy in the house wasn't the same without him, no matter how much we tried to distract ourselves with each other. We *missed* him.

And when my mind selfishly obsessed over how much time he was missing during my last full month with them, I redirected my attention by creating a new routine.

I had lunch with Rome, even on the days I wasn't working on anything in my shop. I went to Ms. Ruby's house almost every day to play with the new puppies and check on Lady. I spent every night wrapped in Sincere's arms because I knew we both missed Lorenzo, and I didn't want him to be alone.

The routine was simple but peaceful. And it worked. I spent less time ruminating on what was to come and put all that energy into enjoying now.

Life was…good.

And it was better with Romeo's dick in my mouth.

Which was exactly why I was in the home gym, on my knees, taking him to the back of my throat while he sucked in pleading breaths above me.

Cornering him in the gym had been risky, but the payoff was hearing him whimper while he slid against my tongue, his fingers fisted in my hair.

Romeo had a perfect dick. It wasn't as long as Sin's or Enzo's, but it was fat and I loved every second of him inside of me. Loved when he let me fill my mouth, pussy, or hands with every inch of him until he came with a grunt that sounded like my name.

He was always so in control that I felt superhuman whenever I made him lose it.

Kinda like now.

His hips bucked, fucking his dick into my mouth until I gagged. "Goldy…your mouth. Fu—"

Words failed him and I took the opportunity to cup his balls and overwhelm him with even more sensations.

I choked on him, saliva leaking from the sides of my mouth and down my chin, but I didn't stop sucking him. I hollowed out my cheeks, holding him with a vacuum-like grip and hummed in the back of my throat. The sensations made him jerk against me, freeing his hands from my hair while he switched to moving my head back and forth along his shaft.

"Fuck…yea…just like that, G. Shit."

Pretty soon, he gave up on trying to talk. The only

sounds he made were husky and tinged with a mix of pleasure and desperation.

Desperation for me and everything I was making him feel.

That sent a heady flood of confidence coursing through my veins and I increased my pace, sucking him faster. Sloppier. My jaw was stretched so wide, my lips grazed his pelvis. If I had on mascara, it would be smeared against my cheek along with my tears. But since I didn't, I just stared up at Rome, my wet lashes sticking to my cheeks as I let him have his way with me. His sculpted abs flexed, contracting with every pump of his hips.

The sloppy sound of my mouth on him joined the muted sounds of his workout playlist because his headphones had fallen at his feet a few songs ago, forgotten while he got lost in my obsession with him.

"Get up, G. Please...get up...don't...wanna come yet."

The labored breath between each word further inflated my ego, but I freed him, my lips releasing the suction I had on him with a pop.

I stood up, just for him to immediately drag me behind him to the nearest wall. He pressed my back against it, dropped to his knees and bunched my sundress up around my hips.

"Put your legs on my shoulders, Goldyn."

"Huh?" I couldn't think past anything but his hot breath on my sex. I was pulsing and soaked with my need for him.

Instead of repeating himself, Rome grabbed my

right thigh and hoisted it on his shoulder. Then he did the same thing with my right one. A low growl left his throat when he breathed in my arousal, his nose brushing my clit til I ground into him, my hips moving on their own accord.

I didn't understand his need to have my weight pressing down on him like this while he ate me out, but then he stood up, and I went with him, my upper body suspended in the air while his face burrowed between my thighs, licking and sucking and fucking me with his tongue.

My breath hitched.

My legs shook.

My eyes rolled back.

I was going to suffocate him. I knew it. There was no way he could breathe like this. And yet, there was nothing I wanted to do about it.

His tongue lapped up my slit, swirled around my clit and sucked me into a state of delirium.

When I opened my leaking eyes again, I had an aerial view of the gym, my gaze falling on the state of the art equipment before Rome's moan against my clit hijacked my attention. The brush of his rough facial hair against the inside of my thigh was enough to fixate on, but that moan. Oh, my god that *moan*.

Both of his palms had a handful of my ass as he held me against the wall, but then he dropped his left one, pressing his fingertip against my asshole.

Rome didn't stop tongue fucking me while his finger pushed past the tight ring of muscle.

My senses heightened.

My body tingled from head to toe.

And I shed real tears as I came with a low cry against his probing tongue.

"Roooommmeo."

Rome ate me through my orgasm, his finger pumping in and out of my ass.

When my thighs stopped shaking, he lowered me from his shoulders to his waist.

He leaned in, claiming my mouth in a kiss that tasted like me, and pushed his dick inside me so smoothly, I gasped from pleasure and surprise.

"You thought I wasn't coming in this pussy, G?"

He wrapped me in his arms, so my back didn't collide with the wall while he pounded into me.

Rome smirked when my mouth fell open.

His strokes were shallow and teasing. Then deep and soul-shattering. The unpredictable rhythm knocked the little sense I had in my head loose.

I needed him as deep as he could go. Until he touched my soul and signed his name.

Romeo rotated his hips, driving into me like a man possessed.

"You like playing with me until I shut you up with this dick, huh?"

"No."

"Then what you call that stunt you just pulled?" He withdrew then reentered me with the unhurried finesse of a man who knew how much power he held over me.

And when he stilled inside of me, walked us away from the wall and then used my hips to fuck me up and down his length, I knew my fate was sealed. There was no coming back from the way he was fucking me. I was ruined.

"I wasn't playing. I just wanted…you."

His hips surged forward, stealing the rest of my vocabulary.

I was begging.

I was moaning.

I was coming.

"Fuck, G." Romeo's voice cracked and he held me against him until I felt him swell inside of me and his dick jerked against my tensing walls before filling me with cum.

I couldn't help the way I ground against him, milking him for every drop. The action prolonged my own orgasm and made Rome bite down on my shoulder.

"You something special, you know that?"

A teasing smirk curved my lips as I caught my breath. "Should I let you get back to your workout?"

"Fuck that workout," he grumbled. "You wanna take a shower with me?"

Nodding, I let him carry me down the hall to the guest room. He wasn't wearing any clothes but if he didn't care, neither did I.

We made it to the bathroom in twelve steps, his longs strides purposeful.

"You're so fucking beautiful." He cradled my face, his touch gentle after fucking me so hard.

Caressing from my thighs up to my waist, Rome set

me down on the floor and pulled my dress up over my head.

He took a step back, tipping his head to watch his cum trickle out of me, onto my inner thighs.

"And so fucking mine."

MY PROJECT LEAD, CRIS, WALKED UP TO ME THE NEXT DAY with an unreadable look on her face.

"What's wrong?" I looked at the clipboard in her hands, expecting the worst.

"Oh, nothing bad," she assured me, raking a hand over her fluffy, jet-black Afro. The hair bounced back into place the moment her fingers were gone. "I wanted to run something by you, actually."

"Oh? Go for it?" Turning away from my laptop and the open spreadsheet on the screen, I gave her my attention.

Cris was the best in the business. At least that's what Lorenzo told me. She could take a gutted shoebox and turn it into a coveted destination. And I was counting on her to do at least a fraction of that with my bookstore and cafe.

"Considering what you want to do with the space, we think it would be best to create a second floor since the ceilings are so high."

"I'm listening." I angled my head to look at the clipboard she held between us, pretending I understood even half of the plans drawn on them.

"It would more than double your square footage

since we knocked out the wall separating the bakery. The lounge area could extend in that direction without you having to sacrifice space for books. And it would give you better separation between your retail and lounge areas."

"Yea, but that can't be the only place we have seating." I imagined Ms. Ruby trying to climb the stairs with her ailing hips. Or readers in wheelchairs not being able to utilize the space and shook my head. That wouldn't work. "It's not accessible if we put all the couches upstairs. customers with mobility issues won't be able to enjoy it and that defeats the purpose."

The woman's face fell before she gave me a curt nod.

"I'm not opposed to the idea, Cris." I laid a hand on her forearm. "But I need it to make sense. For everybody. I think we can still do that by having the top and bottoms mirror each other. Of course, the top floor will just have more room."

Her smile returned and she nodded, jotting something down. "I'll draw up new plans and get those to you right away."

"And how much time would that add to my timeline?"

"Twelve weeks. But that's a conservative estimate. We need to get electric and plumbing back in here to make sure everything is good to go and then we could start."

A sharp squeeze tightened around my chest at the thought of the mounting price tag, but Lorenzo's voice filtered through my head before I can make an excuse not to do it.

The thought of you spending my money and it making you happy turns me on.

He hadn't done anything to make me second-guess it, but the ongoing tally still made my head spin. Between the cafe and bookstore, I was already half a million into the project and we hadn't even fully finished designing the space. All that money went to demolishing the old interiors, redoing electric and plumbing and pre-ordering building materials. I still needed to figure out what appliances I wanted in the cafe, what couches were the most comfortable and durable for the reading lounge, and where I was going to source all my books once my custom shelving was built. Then there was the matter of hiring employees for both sides of the operation once the doors opened to the public. It was…a lot.

An avalanche of emotions assaulted me, sudden wooziness making me sway on my feet.

"You alright, Ms. Ambrose?"

"Of course, I just need to sit down for a minute."

Giving Cris another smile, I turned to find a seat. I plopped down on an overturned bucket and released a shaky breath.

It was happening, every single dream I'd had for years was falling into place, and I needed to calm the fuck down.

I was overwhelmed. Happy. In disbelief that this was my life. And a small part—the part of me that still felt like an eighteen year old finding out her grandmother passed unexpectedly—wanted a hug from Benita to tell me I deserved this.

Deep breath, Goldy. It's happening because *you deserve it. You deserve to be here, receiving all the love and support that you are.*

If my grandmother was here, she'd gently tease me for crying, and I could hear her raspy voice as if she were standing in front of me.

"I know my grand baby ain't sitting up here with tears in her eyes." Then her rough hands, weathered from years of gardening and factory work, would wipe away the tears while she smiled at me. "See? You a'ight. Just as pretty as you wanna be." A kiss against my forehead. A squeeze against my shoulder. "You still my sunshine. I don't care how old you get."

When I came down from my episode, Cris had vacated the space in front of me and I looked around the shop with a smile on my face.

Benita Ambrose might not be here to see all my dreams come true, but I could still honor her. She'd be proud of me for getting this far. For not letting the idea die with me as a doodle in my journal.

I'd just braced my hands on my knees to stand up when the front door opened, sending the bells above it into a musical trill.

My eyes traced the new arrival with alarm.

Lilith Summers? What the hell was she doing here? And why did she look so mad about it?

Her tart expression didn't take away from how stunning she was. Her bone structure was unreal. Her gorgeous chestnut skin was unblemished. And her stride was confident and attention-grabbing.

"Mrs. Summers, what are you—"

Ignoring my greeting and everyone else in the room, she pulled to a stop in front of me in a cloud of Chanel and calculated calm.

"My husband is obsessed with you and I want to know why," she grit out, her lips barely moving as she looked me over.

Brows hiked, I narrowed my gaze on her. "I'm sorry, what?"

"Don't you fucking act clueless. Who are you? Did you bribe him with sex to get this place?" She looked around with a haughty sniff before staring icy daggers at me.

"Of course not." The words came out on a nervous laugh. What the hell was this woman talking about?

"You're lying," she snarled at me. "I went through his phone and it was *full of you.*"

"*What*?" It was the only question I could ask as my eyes zeroed in on her flared nostrils and pinched features.

She looked stricken, like a woman reliving a betrayal and she needed to know that had nothing to do with me.

"Stop playing innocent!" A sharp rise in her voice won us a few looks before the crew went back to pretending to work. I knew they couldn't focus on anything but the shit show playing out in front of them, and I was about to put an end to it.

"Look, I'm sure whatever you think you found upset you, but please understand, I never sle—"

Lilith's scoff cut me off. "What? Being shared by

three men wasn't enough for you? You had to come wreck my home too?"

"I'm not—"

"I know all about women like you."

Oh, my god, she wouldn't let me finish a fucking sentence and my blood began to simmer from the blatant disrespect.

Tucking my lips over my teeth, I stood there, letting her get her little rant off and call me a slut six different ways.

When she was done, she looked satisfied with herself and hiked her purse strap higher on her slender shoulder.

Her gorgeous features contorted into a sneer. It was a shame that a woman this pretty had let insecurities turn her this ugly.

"You don't have anything to say for yourself?"

Oh, now she was going to let me get a word in?

Another humorless laugh escaped me, and that was the wrong thing to do.

Lilith's face hardened and the look of contempt in her eyes was enough to scare Satan.

"Seems like you've said it all, Lilith," I said coolly, my voice belying the annoyance and mortification ebbing through my veins. It was one thing to call me a slut. But she brought Enzo, Rome, and Sin into this when she didn't know what the fuck she was talking about.

"He'll never love you."

"I'm counting on it," I snapped back before I could tell myself not to take her bait. "His *love* is the last thing

I want."

I finished with a suggestive wiggle of my brows and enjoyed the stricken look on her face at my retort.

Was I sleeping with her husband?

Hell no.

But I wasn't about to let this sour-faced woman talk to me any type of way in my place of business either. If she wanted to go low, we could take a bullet train to Hell for all I cared.

Lilith sputtered, looking somewhat vindicated. "I can't believe you."

When she spun on her heel to leave, I didn't bother trying to correct her baseless assumptions again.

Cris was in front of me before the bells above the door chimed with her exit. "You alright, Ms. Ambrose?"

Holding up a hand, I tried to ward off the pity I felt coming off her in waves. "I'm fine. It was just a misunderstanding, but I need to go handle something."

My eyes roamed the shop, landing on the other workers.

"Why don't you all call it a day and start fresh tomorrow morning?"

"You sure 'bout that?"

"Positive. Go get yourselves lunch on me and then go home. I'll see everyone tomorrow."

I didn't wait for her response. I grabbed up my laptop, phone and keys and hurried out to the sidewalk to get to my van.

As I pulled away from the curb with a screech of my tires, I was vaguely aware of lunch plans with Rome. I'd have to call him once I got where I was going because I wasn't going to make it. I had more important things to take care of.

There was a great possibility that the man I'd come to see was on lunch break.

There was an even greater possibility that the woman who'd just left my shop had come straight here.

But as I weighed those odds, I decided I didn't care enough not to go through with my plan.

Double parking, I hopped down and walked to the front door of his quaint real estate firm with my shoulders set in determination.

An older receptionist greeted me when I made it inside, her matronly smile easing some of the agitation coiled low in my gut.

"Ms. Ambrose. How nice to see you again. Is Mr. Summers expecting you?"

"No. But this is an emergency. Is he in?"

Her eyes widened with concern but she gave a simple nod. "Yes. Just a moment."

I didn't sit down in the small waiting room while she spoke to him, too keyed up to stay in one place. So I paced until Chance showed up in the lobby, a surprised but pleasant look on his face.

Oh, good, so he was ignorant to his wife raising hell on the other side of town.

"Goldyn, come with me."

We made it to his office in five steps. He closed the door behind me while I took the opportunity to scan for any obvious evidence of this "obsession" Lilith claimed he had.

"Have a seat." He stopped by the guest chair facing his desk and waited for me to comply.

"I'd rather not," I replied. "I won't be here long. I only came to tell you that your wife has concocted some story in her head about us and you need to check her before she shows up at my business again."

A look of horror claimed his face before he said, "I think I can explain. But I really think it's best if you sit down for what I have to say."

I took two deep breaths in and popped my neck. "Fine. You have five minutes."

Chance hurried around his desk and sat down, a grateful light entering his eyes.

"I was going to contact you later, but it's good that you're here now. I've been doing some digging and I think I finally know why you look so familiar."

He clicked around on his computer screen before turning his monitor to face me. He gave me time to soak in the image before addressing me.

In ten seconds flat, I went from angry to feeling like I was free falling from a cliff into rocky water. Thankfully, I was sitting. But even that didn't do much to soften the blow of his confession.

"WHAT HAPPENED TO YOU AT LUNCH?"

Goldyn and I stood across the island from one another, gathering everything to set the table for Lorenzo's first dinner back with us in two weeks.

She seemed startled by my presence even though I'd been in the kitchen with her for the past fifteen minutes. She dropped her glassy gaze and stopped collecting forks. "I needed to take care of something."

Her voice was lifeless and so low I had to strain to hear her follow up.

"*Alone*. I'm sorry I didn't let you know."

I frowned at the slight tremor in her hands before she could hide it by balling them into fists.

"You straight," I excused, still looking her over, searching for an answer to her shifty behavior. "Is everything okay?"

She nodded, swallowing hard. "Mhm. Everything's okay."

I showed up at her shop at noon only to find both places pitch black, no workers or Goldyn in sight. I chalked it up to her deciding to come home early to see Lorenzo, but when I texted the group chat with him and Sincere to see if she was home, they told me no.

Whenever I called her phone, it went straight to her voicemail, which was full. Which meant she'd purposely turned her phone off or it died again. Anxiety spiked not knowing she was okay until Sincere texted me an hour later saying she'd just gotten home and went to take a nap in her room.

But the bags under her eyes didn't look like they belonged to someone who'd slept for a couple hours in the middle of the day. The red rim around them didn't back that up, either.

Before I could ask another question, Lorenzo entered the kitchen and wrapped her in a hug from behind. The slight flinch she played off could have been read as surprise, but had me on high alert.

Why was she jumpy, and why did she look so sad?

"You okay, mamas? You been quiet today," Lorenzo noted, kissing her cheek.

"I'm okay. I just missed you," Goldy answered, smoothly spinning in his arms to bury her face in his chest.

He grinned, tightening the embrace. "I missed you too, Goldy."

I watched it all with a frown on my face, until they pulled apart and Goldyn went back to collecting silverware.

Something was off, and the brittle smile she flashed me when her eyes darted to mine, begged me to let it go.

So I did. For now.

Goldyn pushed her food around on her plate, passive in every conversation. But Sincere and Lorenzo were so busy catching up on the past ten days, it was easy to miss her distant mood. She didn't make eye contact. With anybody. A few times during dinner, she placed a hand over her chest like she was trying to calm her heart, and if she kept chewing on her bottom lip like that, blood would be joining the dejected look on her face.

After dinner, her mood brightened a little and she disappeared upstairs with Sincere before Lorenzo joined them.

Maybe I was tripping.

Maybe she really did just miss Lorenzo and tomorrow she'd be her usual bubbly self.

Since it was my night to clean the kitchen, I pressed play on a new audiobook and tried to push Goldyn to the back of my mind. And it was working. I made it through cleaning the kitchen and headed to the gym earlier than usual.

I was in the middle of my first set when I heard a sound at the end of the hall.

When I looked out the cracked door of the gym, light spilled out from Goldyn's room, and I stayed ducked off at the end of the hall to see if she would come back out.

But I didn't expect to see her carrying bags when she appeared. Her purse was slung over her body and her overnight bag was clutched tightly in her small fist.

She turned around, careful not to make noise and pulled the door shut with a soundless click before tiptoeing down the hall.

Just like that first day, I traced her steps from a distance, hanging back enough that she wouldn't hear me.

Still in denial, I reasoned maybe she was just taking her shit upstairs since she spent all her time in my room or with Lorenzo and Sincere. She wouldn't just leave in the middle of the night without saying anything. We were better than that.

But Goldyn proved me wrong when she ignored the staircase and kept walking toward the front door, digging around in her bag for something. When she still hadn't found what she was looking for once she got to the foyer, she dropped onto the bench near the shoe rack and heaved a shuddering breath.

From my spot by the staircase, I saw her lip tremble.

What the fuck was going on?

A single tear fell and she rushed to swat it away. Like if she didn't acknowledge it, it wasn't real.

I tried to keep my distance and watch her until something about this made sense, but then she dropped her head in her hands, shoulders shaking and I couldn't watch from the sidelines anymore.

Her soft cries filled the foyer, muting my footsteps, so I approached without notice.

Dropping to a squat in front of her, I placed a hand

on her lap and waited for her surprised gaze to clash with mine. The heartache in her stare shredded my heart into a million pieces, and I had to swallow past the painful lump crowding my throat.

Forcing a casual tone, I asked, "Going somewhere, G?"

MY HANDS WOULDN'T STOP SHAKING. IT FELT LIKE I WAS breathing through a soggy paper straw. And my head was about two seconds away from floating off my shoulders, too full of thoughts I didn't want to deal with.

Logically, I knew I was in the foyer. Sitting on something.

But my head wouldn't anchor me in reality.

All I could focus on was panic and that made me panic even more.

Breathe, Goldy, breathe. At least make it to the fucking van before you melt into a puddle of over-stimulated nerves.

The more I coached myself, the less calm I felt. I was really fucking bad at this.

Before I knew it, my shoulders were shaking with cries that had clawed up my throat and freed themselves. And I didn't stop until I felt firm pressure on my shaking shoulders, calming the tremble just a little.

My eyes flew open and collided with Rome's concerned ones. And that's how I knew I was out of it. I *always* knew when Rome was near. There was no reason I shouldn't have sensed his closeness.

"Going somewhere, G?"

That deep drawling voice was even, but the worry knitting his brows sent a flurry of dread racing through my stomach. He'd caught me when I didn't want any of them to know I was leaving.

I tried to stand on shaky legs, but he rose with me and gently pressed down on my shoulders until my knees bent on their own accord.

"Sit down, Goldyn," Rome commanded, not saying anything about me trying to sneak out.

So I sat down, my eyes fixated on his towering frame. He was shirtless, clearly fresh out of the gym even though no sweat slicked his deep mahogany skin. And then he blurred as more tears clouded my vision.

The cool wood of the bench kissed my thighs and I balled my hands into fists beside me, not knowing what else to do with them.

Quietly, Rome knelt between my parted legs and peered up at me. "What shoes do you want to wear?"

He cast a glance at the shoe rack, awaiting my response.

Guilt and shame sat heavy on my chest, stealing all my words.

"Which shoes, baby?" Rome tried again, his voice softer than before.

More guilt sank into me, weighing down my limbs.

"You're not gonna say anything about me trying to leave?"

"Not right now. If you wanna leave, you can leave." He shrugged before quickly adding, "But I'm leaving with you." His hand massaged my right calf while his imploring eyes stayed fixed on me. "So, which shoes, Goldyn?"

Nodding toward the sandals in front of the shoe rack, I bit back more words and watched him slip them on my feet, concentration clear on his face.

Then he stood, pulled on one of Lorenzo's hoodies from the coat rack and snagged his keys from the hook by the door. "Let's go."

We didn't speak again for thirty minutes.

Not when he grabbed up my overnight bag.

Not when he opened the passenger door for me.

And not when a deer jumped out in front of his car and he had to slam on the brakes, cut his lights, and wait for it to cross to the other side.

The quiet was unnerving. But it was better than being alone.

With his high beams on, he drove us over a rocky path and didn't stop until it looked like we would drive off the side of a cliff if he didn't.

"What is this place?" I asked. My voice was hoarse and embarrassment still had a chokehold on me. Why wasn't he reacting to what I'd done—well, tried to do?

"It's called Miracle Overlook, best place to watch the sunrise in town. You think you can explain to me why you were leaving before then?"

My gaze snapped to the dashboard, reading eleven p.m. The sun wouldn't be coming up for another seven hours...

"Romeo."

He reached up, flicking on the interior light so the car was bathed in warm light. "I just want to understand, Goldy. Take all the time you need as long as that time leads to some answers."

"Okay," I said around a hard swallow.

With his head resting on the back of his seat, he let it fall to his right to look at me.

"Why were you leaving, baby?" I wasn't used to his voice being so soft and my face twisted at the sound. I couldn't keep the steady stream at bay anymore and cried freely.

"I needed a second to breathe. I'm overwhelmed and I think I should take a step back."

"From what? The shop? Did something happen today? Is that why you left work early?"

"Not from what. From *who*. I don't think I can stay here with you and Sin and Enzo anymore."

The silence was loud. Louder than any words he could have spoken as his eyes fastened on the fidgeting fingers in my lap.

I rushed to explain even though he gave me no clue about what he was feeling. "It's been hitting me a lot lately. And I know the longer I stay, the more it's gonna hurt to leave. So I should just go now."

"And that just hit you in the middle of the day and made you shut down?" He didn't sound like he believed me and I didn't blame him.

"Not *just* that, but it's a part of it. I'm tired of convincing my brain this is what I want when I know it's not. I don't wanna feel like this anymore."

"And leaving in the middle of the night was the way to solve that?" He clipped out, his voice heavy and void of its earlier softness. "You weren't even gonna say shit, Goldyn. That's fucked up."

I didn't have a comeback, so I just sat there, looking at my hands because the weight of his stare was too much.

"And where were you going, G?"

"I don't know. I didn't make a plan past what I would do when I made it to my van."

A scoff filled the tight confines of the car before he shifted in his seat, adjusting the automatic lever until his legs were spread in front of him. "You're not going anywhere, Goldyn. I don't know why you thought running was something safe to do, but you got a few things fucked up between us if you think I'ma let you go that easy."

Heat flamed my face and chest at the conviction in his words.

"You belong wherever I am. I never agreed to three months with you. Remember that."

"What does that mean?"

"It means exactly what it sounds like. This little ninety-day thing is between you, Enzo and Sin. It ain't got shit to do with me and never will."

"But—"

He reached across the console and pulled my jaw until I was looking at him. Then he continued like I hadn't tried to interrupt.

"It means I don't just let go when my heart is involved. I don't fall in love easy, and you made me give a fuck. I'm not gonna just watch you walk out my life. We'll figure it out." He sounded so sure I almost believed him.

"I was *always* leaving in three months, Rome. And those three months are halfway done."

With a shake of his head, he released his hold on my face. "I don't give a fuck about any of that, G. And if you think Sin and Enzo want you to leave, then your eyes haven't been open."

"They haven't told me otherwise, so I'm not gonna assume and get my feelings hurt."

Romeo laughed dryly. "You hear yourself right now, G? You not gonna assume and get your feelings hurt, but you were just sneaking out in the middle of the night because you *assumed shit and got your feelings hurt.*"

Defiance stiffened my shoulders as I stared at him. He wasn't wrong, but I didn't want to tell him he was right, either.

Silence crawled into the cracks of our conversation, pushing down the words I needed to say.

The words about Lilith and Chance and everything he'd told me.

Staring straight ahead, I tried to make out the mountains beneath us, but all I saw was darkness now that Rome's headlights were off.

So I focused on the moon instead, drawn to the glowing orb propped up in the sky.

"I...um...I had a meeting today and it brought up all this stuff I didn't want to deal with. It felt easier just leaving..."

"A meeting with who about what?" he wanted to know, latching on to the first part of my announcement.

"With Chance. My realtor."

"What's going on?"

"He's been drawn to me since we met and it creeped me out. He would stare at me until I got goosebumps and then—"

"Did he fucking touch you, G?" Romeo cut off my rambling and I shook my head.

"No. It's worse."

"What the fuck is worse than that?"

"His wife came to the shop today and accused me of being a home-wrecker, so I went to visit him to figure out what she was talking about." As it turned out, his obsession had nothing to do with some misplaced attraction.

"What did he tell you, G?" Romeo's voice was tight with barely leashed fury. He was assuming the worst and I didn't know if what I had to tell him would fall in that category.

Ignoring the lead ball in my stomach, I replied, my voice as flimsy as my nerves. "He thinks he's my dad."

Eleven Hours Ago

IT WAS OFFICIAL. CHANCE SUMMERS HAD FINALLY CROSSED the line from oddly fascinated with me to straight up creepy. That was the only explanation for what he was showing me on his screen right now.

A digitized photo took up the display, but it had clearly been taken on film decades ago.

And the woman the picture captured was all too familiar. I shared all her features. Looked just like a carbon copy of her. Yet, I'd never met her in person. At least not while I was old enough to remember it. She made sure of that when she dropped me off on my grandmother's doorstep and disappeared without a trace.

The woman who'd gifted me with all my features. The first woman to make me feel like a burden for simply existing. The woman who chose herself over the life she created.

She wasn't smiling at the camera, more like *smizing* with a smug light in her eyes. A thick cloud of black curls framed her face. I'd dyed my hair blonde for years to look less like her.

It wasn't often that I felt anything but apathy where Veronica Ambrose was concerned, but today? Today, a symphony of rage and disdain flooded me at the sight of her.

Fighting past the storm of emotions trying to swallow me whole, I found my voice and asked, "Why are you showing me a picture of my mom?"

Chance read the rising ire in my posture and turned the screen back to face him. Smart man.

"I—I used to know her." He threaded his fingers on his desk and I had to look away. But then my eyes landed on the framed pictures lining his desk. They all featured one woman: Lilith. And suddenly, watching him fidget didn't seem so bad.

"Good for you." I couldn't keep the bitterness out of my voice and sick satisfaction trickled through me when Chance flinched.

"I've hit a sore spot."

It wasn't a sore spot. Unless my whole got damn existence could be considered a sore spot.

Just an hour ago, I was in my shop teary-eyed over my grandmother's memory. And now rage simmered in my veins at the sight of my mother. Funny how their absence in my life triggered such polarizing effects.

Shoving down my attitude, I addressed Chance. It wasn't his fault my life had panned out the way it had. He probably thought he'd made some groundbreaking discovery and wanted to share with the class.

"Look. I'm happy you finally know why I look so familiar, but I can't say I exactly care or want to talk about my mother. Like I told you, I never met her—"

"I know." He sounded contrite as he studied me with sadness in his gaze. "I'm sorry for showing you that picture. I didn't know it would stir up—" he gestured with his hands toward me "—this reaction with you. I just wanted you to understand why I always looked at you like I knew you. But I guess there could have been a better way to do that."

Mouth sealed, I stared at him, trying to filter through the past half-hour and make sense of it.

"Excuse my frankness, Goldyn." He cleared his throat. "But your mother and I had a relationship the summer before you were born. She showed up one day and said she was just passing through." He held up his hand like he was asking for more time, even though I had no plans to interject. "Maybe I shouldn't have but I wrote down your date of birth from the ID you gave me when we processed your paperwork. And you were born eight months after your mother disappeared from Bliss Peak without a trace."

My lips curved but never quite formed a smile. "She disappeared on you too? She's good at that."

Chance looked flustered, like he was growing impatient with me about something and I didn't know what to tell him.

"That's not why I brought it up, Goldyn." He softened the exasperation in his voice. "I got your birthdate and started putting puzzle pieces together. You said you were from New Hope. It's fuzzy, but now I think I can remember Roni telling me she was from there a time or two. And that's where you were born. You said you never met your parents. It all started making sense. But not in the way I wanted. If I knew…I never would have wanted you to grow up without at least one of your parents in your life."

If he knew? If he knew what? My mind finally freed the question and let it tumble from my lips.

"Goldyn, I think I'm your biological father."

A thick, disbelieving silence wedged itself between us in the wake of his declaration.

Unfortunately, I was the first to break it with a howl of laughter.

"Chance, what?"

He wasn't deterred by my reaction. In fact, he looked more earnest and determined to get me to hear his side. "I searched public records. Your mother's name is on your birth certificate. And that date. March 7, 1997."

Chance shook his head as he recited my birthday to me and that was what made me sit up straighter and listen a little closer to his words.

"She must have left here as soon as she got pregnant. I doubt she even knew when she left. Said she was headed to the beach because she was tired of the mountains. That was what I liked about her. She would just get up and go on a whim. But I didn't know she was taking a part of me with her." He stared pointedly at me and a surge of queasiness settled in my gut.

I didn't know she was taking a part of me with her.

"I won't sit up here and tell you we were in love."

I wished he wasn't telling me anything. It would really help the throbbing at my temples and the thumping in my chest.

"But I couldn't let you go through the rest of your life thinking I knew about you and decided not to be present."

I shook my head as his words soaked into my skin. "You don't even know if I'm your daughter and you're already talking about—"

"We can fix that. I know a place we can both get tested and have the results in less than a week."

"Of course you do," I huffed.

"I can see you're gonna need some time to process this."

Just as he finished the words, I shot to my feet. "Actually, I don't need time to process anything. I don't care if you're my father. I've made it twenty-seven years without knowing about you, and I wish you hadn't told me at all."

Hurt flitted over his features and a nauseating wave of realization crashed into me.

I had his eyes. Light brown. Bright. Like pools of whiskey under the summer sun.

Oh. My. God. I just taunted a woman—his wife—about sleeping with a man who could very well be my *father*.

I was gonna throw up.

"Goldyn."

Spinning on my heel, I tripped over my feet and stumbled to his closed office door. Once my hand stopped shaking long enough for me to get it open, I tossed my farewell over my shoulder. "Goodbye, Chance."

I perked up at the sound of birds singing.

My eyes popped open and the sleek dashboard came into view, all the controls and shiny chrome finishings on full display.

Ok, so this definitely wasn't my van.

Daylight had arrived and so had a slight crick in my neck from sleeping sideways in this passenger seat.

I groaned, stretching, and panic set in when I didn't see Romeo in the driver's seat beside me.

Dew kissed the windshield, making it impossible to see out.

I scrambled to open the door and hopped out to find Romeo, stopping when I saw the figure leaning against the trunk of the car, smoke billowing in front of his face.

Romeo.

"Morning, G," he spoke without turning to face me.

The scent of the herb he was smoking met my nose, and my feet carried me to him, not stopping until I was wrapped in his tight embrace.

"We slept in your car."

"Yea, you fell out after you told me Chance could go fuck himself and that paternity test he wanted you to take."

I grimaced at the reminder. Apparently, when emotions were high enough, I blacked out, no substances needed.

It wasn't the only embarrassing thing I'd done last night.

Sneaking out was number one on that list. And if Romeo hadn't caught me, I didn't know where I'd be. Because I definitely wasn't in the right frame of mind to drive last night.

I replayed the scene in the foyer over and over, burrowing my face deeper into his chest, which was still covered in Lorenzo's hoodie.

Lorenzo's cologne mixed with Romeo's earthy scent, giving me a double dose of two out of three of my favorite smells.

"I'm sorry for trying to run last night. I wasn't thinking."

Romeo's hand found the back of my neck, and he massaged out a kink without me having to tell him where it was.

"Once you told me what happened, I got it. It hurt knowing that you wanted to leave, but I understand why you did. That shit is a lot to process. Shit," he drawled before taking another hit. "Running probably would've been my first instinct too."

I rested my chin on his chest and looked up at him with a slow curve of my lips.

I loved this man.

Every inch of his grumpy, brooding, logical self.

Residual guilt assailed me and my smile dropped.

"Thank you for being here. You didn't have to stay with me last night."

Romeo cut his eyes at me the way he'd done a million times before. For someone who didn't speak a lot, his facial expressions were always loud and clear.

"Yes, I did. What did I tell you last night?"

So many things. I remembered every single one, but the thought of repeating them made emotion burn in my throat.

"You said…" My voice trailed as my thoughts scrambled. I couldn't think straight when he was looking at me like that.

He held fast to my chin, locking me in place with his piercing stare. "I don't just up and leave when my heart is involved, Goldyn. You're not a temporary fling, and I don't leave the people I love hanging just because they're having a hard time."

The people I love.

Tears stung my nose and Romeo shook his head as they welled in my eyes.

"Don't start that shit. I can't deal with you crying again."

And of course, those words flung me right over the edge.

"Sorry," I gasped, crying anyway. "I love you and it keeps hitting me at the worst times."

He smirked, running his thumb over a tear. "And when would be the best time for it to hit you, G?"

I smiled through another wave of tears and he mirrored my expression, his eyes softening around the corners as he peered down at me.

"Why am I here, Goldyn?"

"Because I made you give a fuck and you love me."

He nodded, pride claiming his face at my easy recitation. "And what else?"

"Because I belong wherever you are."

"Good. And don't ever forget that shit."

He'd just put out his jay by stepping on it and pulled me into a hug when we heard tires crunching over rocks. I looked up in time to see Sincere screech to a stop in front of us, throwing his Bronco in park before he climbed down. Lorenzo followed at a much slower pace, looking half asleep while Sincere rushed to my side.

"How the fuck did you know where we were?" Rome grumbled, his hand dropping away from my face to let Sincere pull me in for a hug.

"You share your location with us, remember? We just never had to use it before today because you're always in one of three places."

Romeo kissed his teeth and I didn't bother hiding my smile as Sincere pulled away from the hug to let his concerned gaze rove over me.

"Are you okay, love?"

"Yes," I breathed, my heart calming from his proximity.

Sincere had the most mellowing effect of anyone I'd ever been around. All I needed to do was be around him half a second and my chest didn't feel so heavy.

Lorenzo finally reached us, looking between me and Rome and then to Sincere.

"What's going on?" He pointed a finger at me.

"Your phone keeps going straight to voicemail." He turned to Rome. "And you haven't answered us since last night."

"I told you we were safe," Rome mumbled.

"You know that shit don't cut it with Sin. He looked up this location, saw y'all hadn't moved from the cliff in hours and assumed the worst."

Before Romeo could retort, Lorenzo's eyes locked on his chest and a smile stretched his lips. "Is that my hoodie?"

He fingered the fabric covering Romeo's shoulder and his smile broadened. "I knew you loved me. You should wear my clothes more often. They look good on you," he added with a sly smirk, looking Romeo up and down.

"Yo, Enzo, I swear to—"

"Who wants to go to breakfast?" Sincere interjected, lacing his fingers through mine.

Romeo diverted his attention from glaring at Lorenzo to look at us with the beginnings of a frown.

My eyes ping ponged between the three men I loved and giddiness filled my chest.

"Fine," Lorenzo conceded. "We'll go to breakfast and then back home to talk. We clearly have a lot of catching up to do."

I didn't miss the hint of hurt in his voice when he said that, but he quickly masked it by giving me a wink.

We were gonna be okay. I just needed to tell them how I felt and stick around long enough to hear their response.

"The Sleeping Owl is the only place open right

now," I shared, staring at the sky. From the sun's perch, I knew it couldn't have been later than seven a.m., and Bliss Peak was too sleepy of a town for anything substantial to open before ten.

Sincere nodded, wrapping me in another hug before he muttered, "Then The Sleeping Owl it is."

"I LEFT FOR TWO WEEKS AND EVERYTHING WENT UP IN flames," I joked, even though a pinch of tension tightened in my chest.

Goldyn smiled awkwardly and my husband barely registered my words.

If Sincere could find a way to be in Goldyn's skin right now, he would be. He hadn't stopped touching her since we found her with Romeo at the overlook this morning.

After breakfast, we came home and straight to my office. It was just the three of us, because Romeo said we needed the privacy, and I tried to think of the best way to break the ice.

Even though Goldyn had been with us nonstop for the past month and a half, it felt like we'd entered new territory and I didn't want to fuck this up.

Sincere's lips stamped loving kisses along the inside of her wrist, reminding me of that first day when we asked her to be ours. So much had changed since then. *Everything* had changed since then.

We'd both fallen in love with her and couldn't see our life moving forward without her in it.

"I think I should go first," Goldyn started, looking

from me to Sincere and back again. "This has been bothering me for weeks and I need to get it off my chest."

Sincere stopped kissing her and I sat up straighter, expecting the worst to fall from her lips.

"I don't think I can keep doing this with you two, feeling how I feel. I'm already too deep and I know what I agreed to, but I didn't expect it to get this real for me this fast. Apparently, I can't do casual. Not when the people are as great as you. And I'm tired of hurting my own feelings imagining the day I have to leave. So..." Her eyes flitted back and forth, the uncertainty in her tone amplified in the amber depths.

"Goldyn." Sincere and I spoke at the same time, but I nodded, giving him the floor because the emotion tangled in my throat was making it hard to form anything other than her name.

"Love, we don't want you to leave. That's what we were going to talk to you about before you left."

"You were?"

Sincere squeezed her hand, his eyes piercing and intense. "Yes. We were waiting for Lorenzo to get back from his business trip so we could tell you together. We've known for a while we didn't want you to leave. But we didn't expect his trip to last as long as it did or you would've known before it got to the point of you running away from us."

Goldyn's mouth dropped open. "Oh."

"Goldyn, I'm in love with you," he confessed, voice thick. "I can't imagine ever going back to the way things were before you showed up. And we don't want to. Right, Enzo?"

"Right. We can't do this without you. We need you."

"It was never supposed to be three months," Sincere confessed, rubbing his nose along the column of her neck before his lips followed the path.

I loved watching them like this. How easily he surrendered to the affection he wanted to give and how freely Goldyn accepted it. It was like they shared an invisible current, the love pouring freely into their connection and it made me happier they were both mine. They balanced me out while complementing each other. We'd unintentionally struck the perfect harmony.

"When we met you, I knew I wanted to see where this could go but I was too scared to tell you that upfront, so I masked it as a summer fling."

"Really?" Goldyn's eyes flashed to mine for confirmation and I gave her a nod.

"You mean too much to us to think we can't see it. Or that we're suddenly gonna stop wanting you after this summer. I'll *never* stop wanting you, Goldyn."

Pride pulsed through me as I watched him cling to her, not caring that his feelings were clear as day. He wasn't letting fear dictate his words and his eyes hadn't flicked to me for reassurance once while he poured his heart out. Who knew our little intruder would unlock Sincere's assertiveness?

"I'm in love with you, too. Both of you." She stared at me, biting her lip. "But I have a question."

"Anything, mamas."

"I'm in love with Romeo, too. I need to be with him

just as much as I need to be with you. Are you sure that won't cause any friction—"

"It doesn't change anything, Goldy. If anything, it makes this easier. You having a connection with all of us makes me believe this was supposed to happen. Regardless of how messy it started, this was always supposed to be how we ended up. Romeo deserves the love you give him and I'm just happy that he's letting it happen. You'll never have to choose between us."

"Okay."

"Now, back to you," Sincere said firmly, shifting the topic. "No more running, Goldyn. I couldn't sleep all night thinking you were leaving us and we couldn't reach you to find out why."

Goldyn cupped the side of his face and nodded. "I'll work on that. I shut down when I'm overwhelmed, and it's usually fine because I've always been alone. But I won't sneak out again. I'll tell you that I'm leaving."

His brow dipped at that compromise and I tamped down my laugh by adding my own conditions. "We're not tryna put a leash on you, mamas, but a text would save us a lot of stress. And your phone needs to be charged to do that." I finished with a pointed look.

She flashed a sheepish smile. "Sorry about that. The battery has been replaced three times since I got it and it's getting bad again. I'll take care of it."

"We could just buy you a new one," Sincere suggested.

Goldyn shook her head. "I love you for offering, but the only reason I haven't is because the last time I tried to upgrade, they told me I would lose my voicemails. Which doesn't make sense because when I upgraded from a six to the eight, the voicemails transferred without a problem." A crease formed between her brows as she thought it over and her voice took on a wistful quality. "The messages are from my grandma, I can't lose those. It's all I have left."

Understanding bloomed in my chest. This whole time, I thought she was holding on to that phone because of her...frugal nature, but it was deeper than that, and now that she'd said it, it made so much sense.

Sincere spoke before I could. "I think I know how to get those voicemails off your phone and onto your cloud so you can listen to them on your laptop or your new phone."

Her eyes lit with hope. "Really?"

He nodded. "Yep. I wish you'd said something a long time ago."

Goldyn crossed her legs, clearing her throat. "I have one more thing before I head to the shop for the day."

"What is it, love?"

Her throat worked in a swallow. "It's about Chance."

"I fucking knew it. Did he touch you?" I was on my feet, shoving my chair away from me as I strode around my desk.

"What do you mean you *knew* it?" Sincere balked at me and then swung his gaze back to Goldyn. "Goldy, what the hell is going on?"

"I'll fucking kill him," I promised.

"Enzo, please. Nobody is getting hurt." She dropped

her hand from Sincere's hold and reached out to grab my clenched fists.

I let her soft touch consume me, soothing me until my fingers relaxed against her palm.

The frown on her face told me she wasn't expecting my reaction and that confused me more than her cryptic opening. I would end anybody who hurt her, Sincere, or Rome without question.

"It's not like that. Nobody touched me."

"We're listening."

Uninterrupted, she revealed everything Chance told her yesterday. While Sincere's brows jumped on his forehead, apprehension tightened my jaw.

Goldyn finished and the weight of her sigh sat on my chest. I wanted to erase the despair shining in her eyes. "I was fine not knowing. That's how it was all my life and it was fine. It was safe."

My words came out before I could check them. "Tell me how to fix it."

She smiled up at me. "There's nothing you can do to make up for twenty-seven years of not knowing. That's the part I can't make peace with. I don't know what I'm supposed to do if I take a test and it turns out he's right. I'm not a child anymore, so a part of me feels like there's no point in knowing. What can a dad really offer me at this stage of my life? And yes, I *know*, relationships shift over time and adults are close with their parents. But we have no foundation. It feels like we're starting from scratch when we should be close to the middle of our story."

I tipped up her chin, and smiled when she turned trusting eyes on me.

"Whatever you want to do, we support it. I'll go with you to take a DNA test. I'll go with you to tell him you don't want to know if he's your father. I'll go with you to tell him that you do wanna get to know him, but on your terms. Whatever you decide, just know you won't have to do any part of it alone. We won't let you."

That Night

"I MISSED YOU," SINCERE RASPED AGAINST MY LIPS. HIS hand cradled the back of my head as he pumped into me and Lorenzo rocked into him.

"It was only one night," I whined, breath shuddering as he worked his hips, slowly pulling out of me and pushing himself back against Lorenzo's length.

His eyes rolled from the sensations hitting him from every side before he focused his heated stare back on me.

"One night was enough. You can't leave us." His other hand palmed my right breast, squeezing and tugging just enough for my nipples to strain against the stimulation.

"Oh…" I moaned when he pulled out of me before driving forward with a thrust that stole my words.

"Promise me, love." He rolled his body into mine, watching my face while the friction against my clit made black edge out some of my vision.

"I promise," I cried before his tongue tangled around mind, drawing out another moan. I was quickly on my way to becoming overstimulated, and I still couldn't bring myself to stop relishing in every delicious sensation.

I was on my side, chest to chest with Sincere. My right leg was thrown over his hip and Lorenzo held it in place, his grip tightening every time Sincere arched against his dick, leaving me wanting.

"I've been thinking about this all day." Lorenzo's throaty growl permeated the temporary silence as his hips bucked. "You taking care of our girl while I take care of you."

God, whenever he called me theirs, warmth spread throughout my body, blanketing every part of me I thought would never get to exist in this state of bliss.

Lorenzo sat up and scraped the shell of Sincere's ear with his teeth, his eyes trained on me.

Using the hand he had splayed over mine, he grabbed my fingers and threaded them with his.

"I love you, Goldyn." He fucked into Sincere, fucking into me. "I love the way you take us." He dropped a kiss on Sin's shoulder. "And I love the way you love us."

I couldn't snatch my gaze from his. I was falling into an abyss of his making, mesmerized by all the other unspoken words shining in his gaze.

"Love…you, too," I managed on a gasping breath.

"Ah, fuck," Sincere hissed between us. His hips bucked with abandon, pounding in and out of me as the notes of my declaration lingered in the air.

Knowing the harder he fucked me, the harder he fucked Lorenzo satisfied a need I didn't know I had before I met them. I didn't know I needed any of *this* before I met them, and now I couldn't imagine my life without it.

Skin smacking skin.

Panting breaths.

Needy moans.

Music to my ears.

I didn't think anything could top the first time we did this, but this insatiable pull in my core proved me wrong the second Sincere entered me.

This was different.

Better.

Deeper.

Nastier.

I could feel every. Fucking. Thing.

And I wanted to keep feeling it.

A sensual swipe of Sincere's tongue against the seam of my lips made me drop my mouth open. A silent invitation to kiss me deeper.

And he did, while sliding into my wetness with a hum that vibrated against my chest, synching our kiss with the rhythm of his hips.

"How does she feel, Sin?"

My eyes snapped open at Lorenzo's question and I watched Sincere's face while he tried to gather his words.

Pleasure and pain painted his handsome features, morphing into ecstasy. He slanted his lips over mine again, sucking my tongue into his mouth.

"She feels like home," he answered. "So fucking tight and wet for me. Every time."

Lorenzo's whimper wasn't the sound I expected to hear next, but it kissed my ears at the same time he untangled his fingers from mine and wrapped his hand around Sincere's hip, holding him in place while he rocked in and out.

"Oh, shit," he groaned, humping faster and harder. "I'm coming, baby. I'm...*fuck*."

That was the last word he got out before he froze, whimpering against Sincere's neck.

I was unraveling, completely captivated by the sight of Lorenzo's unexpected undoing.

His muscular body shook as he shot his release inside of Sincere, his face buried in the crook of his neck.

Still seated inside of me, Sincere hooked his arm around me and held me in place the same way Lorenzo held onto him moments before.

He worked his hips, grinding against Lorenzo as the last of his orgasm shook him with quiet spasms.

I couldn't take this. I was gonna come.

Could already feel it building low in my core.

Could already hear the blood rushing in my ears.

Could already see the stars forming behind my lids.

Sincere smirked when my walls clamped him tighter.

"You wanna come for me too, love?"

Fuck yes.

But I couldn't speak.

All I could do was bite down on my bottom lip and succumb to the torrent of pleasure consuming me.

"That's it, love. Let me feel how much you love it when we take care of you."

"Sincere, please."

"I'm right here, Goldy. And I'm not coming until you do. Let go for me."

I didn't bother pointing out that he and Lorenzo had already made me come three times before he ever slid inside of me.

He'd been there. And he knew it.

And I was still going to give him what he wanted. It was hard not to. I had a feeling Sincere could ask for the last breath in my lungs and I'd give it up, freely. Another part of me knew he would never ask because he was so used to sacrificing himself for others.

But I wanted to sacrifice for him. Wanted him to know that I wanted to take care of him the way he took care of everybody else.

Fuck, I loved this man.

Love and need and happiness rippled through me.

Sincere tucked my body against the front of his, grinding into me slowly.

I was so wet, the sound of his languid strokes echoed in the room, drawing me deeper and deeper.

"Fuck, Goldyn, I can feel you squeezing me." He freed a groan. "You feel so good."

"You feel good too," I choked out, just as my orgasm made a mess out of me.

I whined and Sincere captured the sound, licking into my mouth while Lorenzo ran kisses up and down his neck.

Wrung out, I didn't fight the pleasure surging through me or the aftershocks that quickly followed.

"I love you," I breathed, my hand on the side of his face while he watched me with a tender smile.

His dick swelled inside of me, and my sensitized walls spasmed around him. He dipped his head, kissing my chest, then my lips. "I know."

"Then come for me."

SEPTEMBER

APPREHENSION CLOUDED THE WHISKY ORBS I LOVED AS Goldyn rested her chin on my chest and peered up at me. It was my favorite way to be cornered by her. And there was nothing I could do about the smile tugging at my lips.

"I should just rip the bandage off, right?" Goldyn asked as we stood outside the only upscale restaurant in town, Noir. It was the same restaurant where Enzo, Sin, and I had celebrated Soulstice's anniversary before going home to find the woman in front of me asleep on our couch.

Only two months had passed, but nothing in my life was the same. This woman had filled a sacred space in my heart and made it her home.

The Monday after Lorenzo got back from his business trip, Goldyn decided she *did* want to take that paternity test after all. He'd had someone come to the house and collect her samples before sending him to Chance's office to do the same. By that Friday, the results were in our mailbox.

That was a week ago, and Goldyn still hadn't

opened the envelope to learn the truth.

Chance had agreed to let her set the pace, and dropped everything to come meet her today after two weeks of radio silence.

"I can do this," Goldyn cheered herself on, trying to slide out of my embrace. But I held her to me, nodding as our eyes clashed.

"Yea, you can. You're the bravest person I know."

"Not brave enough to open an envelope and find out if he's my dad," she followed up.

"That doesn't change the fact that you're brave. Look at how you kept going after all your biggest losses. A lot of people don't have it in them to move past it, but you do and you did. Every single time." I bowed my head and kissed her, unable to resist the pull of her soft lips. "You went to college, even though you thought it was later than you should have. You graduated. You stood up for yourself to your doctor and got the surgery you needed. You converted a whole fucking van by yourself and traveled the country for two years in it. You danced in clubs where you didn't know anybody. And now you're opening the bookstore of your dreams because you never give the fuck up. You think a damn test result cancels all that out?"

Goldyn bit her lip, and I knew tears were about to start welling. But before they did, she got out a whispered, "I guess you were listening to me talk all those times I made you have lunch with me."

"I'm never not listening to you, Goldyn. Even when it's not your mouth doing the talking."

In so little time, I'd conditioned myself to be in tune

with her. I knew what her sighs meant. I knew what her eyes were saying before she ever said the words. I knew her excitement as well as I knew her fear. The only person I knew better was myself. I didn't know how it happened, but I wasn't mad at the turn of events. Some things were just meant to be.

Smiling, she tried to hug me tighter but her arms were already holding me as snug as possible. "Thank you for being here with me."

"Stop thanking me. The only thing you ever ask of me is my presence, and I'm going to give you that every time, because you never leave me alone." Even in sleep, she found a way to tuck herself into my space.

Just this morning, I woke up with her in my bed, smelling like Sin and Enzo. We'd barely said good morning before I was feeding her my dick for breakfast, fucking her in slow, lazy strokes while she alternated between keening moans and sucking on my skin.

"I missed you last night, but I fell asleep before I heard you come back upstairs from the gym."

"You could have come to the gym and told me you wanted me in bed with you." My balls clapped against her lips and I retreated just to hear an echo of the sound as I pushed back inside of her.

"I didn't want to be clingy," she wailed, clamping a hand over her mouth. Her brows met in the center of her forehead and her hips worked to keep up with my increasing pace.

"Stop that," I ordered roughly, pulling her hand away from her face. "I wanna hear you, G. The same way I hear you scream for Enzo and Sin, I wanna hear you scream for me."

But Goldyn didn't scream. She gasped and her words came out raw and broken. "I love you. I love you. I love you."

"You love me fucking you when your pussy was just full of their cum?"

She nodded, face contorted in pleasure.

"You love knowing I would do anything for you?"

"Y-yes."

"You love knowing that I'm not going any fucking where?"

"Mmm, Rome," she sputtered when I swiveled my hips, hitting a spot inside of her that made her legs shake on command.

"You love knowing that you belong to us and we'll give you the fucking world?"

Finally, a scream loosed itself from her throat and she started convulsing around my erection.

"Fuck, Goldyn. You love coming for me, don't you?"

Thrust.

"You love knowing that we belong to you and letting us please this perfect pussy."

My own words mixed with the intensity of her release sent me spiraling into a climax that made me moan in her ear as my body enveloped hers, folding myself around her small frame until we were one.

Emptying everything inside of her, I kissed her hair and heaved a happy breath. "Fuck, I love you, woman."

"I love you too, Rome."

A few minutes later, I eased my softening length out of her and smiled at the drowsy curve of her lips.

"Will you come with me to meet with Chance today? I don't want to go alone."

"So you won't." I kissed her temple and rolled onto my side. *"What time do we leave?"*

"Twelve-thirty," she answered, covering her mouth as a yawn slipped out.

"Mmm." I nibbled on her ear. *"Enough time for me to make you come for me again before I run us a bath."*

"Okay," Goldyn exhaled, bringing me back to the present. "I'm opening it."

The sound of paper ripping pulled my attention down to her hands. The slight tremor in them didn't stop her from getting the envelope open and holding on to the folded results.

"What if he's not my dad?" Goldyn forced a laugh, but I could hear the hope clinging to her words. "What if we drove out here for nothing?"

"Open the letter and see, baby."

Goldyn swallowed hard and started fidgeting in place. "Right."

Hands a little shakier now, she unfolded the paper and read the results in silence before her eyes flashed to mine. I couldn't read anything except surprise in them, and I didn't know if it was good surprise or bad surprise.

"Well?"

"He's my father."

MY STOMACH CHURNED THE LONGER I STARED AT THE stuffed mushrooms on my plate. I was sure they tasted perfectly fine, yet the thought of putting anything in my mouth right now made bile rise to my throat.

If it wasn't for Romeo's steadying presence at my side, I probably would have thrown up breakfast on the table by now. His heavy hand against my thigh had a grounding effect, allowing me to sit here without jumping out my skin.

Despite my jumbled nerves, Chance sat opposite me, looking calm and collected, his smile confident and bright.

"Thank you for agreeing to meet with me. I haven't been able to get you off my mind for the past two weeks. And I want you to know that even if I'm not your biological father, there's no reason—"

"You're my father," I blurted,.

Chance's whole demeanor changed in the blink of an eye. That calm, cool, collected façade he'd been rocking earlier was replaced by a stunned expression and tears collecting in his light brown eyes.

Shit.

I didn't mean to make the man cry.

"When did you find out?" He asked, voice shaky as he stared at me.

"Just now, in the parking lot."

Chance choked out a laugh and the sound did something funny to my chest. He sounded…relieved?

He *wanted* me to be his daughter?

When I glanced over at Romeo, his head was cocked, watching our exchange with a contemplative expression.

"I'm your father?" Chance's voice was disbelieving, full of awe and more relief. "I thought…I didn't know… I just…wow."

He stopped trying to articulate himself and raised his elbows on top of the tablecloth, propping his face against his hands.

"You don't understand what this means to me."

I didn't understand what it meant to *me*, either.

But Chance's visceral reaction stirred something in me. It never occurred to me that someone could know I was their daughter—their flesh and blood—and be *happy* about it.

My mother really had set the bar in hell.

Because Chance wasn't running. He looked… overjoyed. And the tears in his eyes were starting to make my nose burn.

"I'm so sorry, Goldyn." The crack in his voice did nothing to help my shakiness.

Finding my voice, I asked, "Why are you apologizing?"

"Because I *failed* you."

His bottom lip trembled and sorrow fisted my heart.

"You didn't know about me."

He met my eyes—the eyes I'd only recently realized looked like his—and offered me a watery smile.

"But if I did..." Chance shook his head. "I'm so sorry."

"Please stop apologizing. The parent who knew about me decided not to be present. Don't put that guilt on your shoulders because she didn't tell you about me."

Romeo squeezed my thigh when I finished talking, and when I looked over at him, a hint of a smile was flirting with his lips. He turned to look at me and the pride in his eyes calmed me. Just a little bit.

Chance blew out a breath and pulled my attention back to him. "You shouldn't be comforting me. I—I just —I don't know what to say. I had a hunch, but I had no idea I'd be right. At the very least, I thought I knew your mom. I didn't know she had *you*—" His words broke off again and this time his shoulders were shaking as he hid his face with his hands.

When I tossed Rome a wide-eyed look, he inclined his head to the man opposite us and I got the silent message.

Sliding off my seat, I sat on the booth side of the table and wrapped my arms around Chance.

"It's okay."

He let me console him for a while, rocking gently until his tears ebbed and he turned to me with awe in his eyes.

"I've wanted a child all my life. That's all I wanted. To be a father. But it never happened and I accepted that. But *you…*" Every time he got to that word, his voice grew faint and another wave of emotion overtook him.

Seconds melted into minutes before he got his bearings again. The brightness had returned to his smile, but he couldn't stop shaking his head.

"I don't believe this." He touched his chin, shock still traveling over his face. "You're *mine.*"

That was all it took for the first wave of my own tears to hit me.

You're mine.

I didn't realize I'd been waiting my whole life to hear someone say that about me until it fell from his lips.

And he sounded so damn happy about it, it made me happy too.

Everything at the table blurred while I tried to play it off, but then Rome reached across the table to offer me a napkin and the dam broke.

Tears coasted over my cheeks unchecked until I could steady my hand enough to wipe them. Chance's hand found my shoulders, supplying wordless reassurance.

"So now we know," I muttered, lost on what else to say.

Chance seemed to read the uncertainty in my words and quickly followed up. "We'll take this at your pace. But I do want to get to know you, Goldyn. I want to know everything about you. I want to have dinners with you. I want to tell you about my childhood and your grandparents on my side. They would have adored you."

Some part of me wanted those things too, but there was still a lot up in the air.

"Um," I cleared my throat. "Did you tell Lilith?"

I still wasn't able to scrub our confrontation from my mind.

That woman did not like me.

And technically, I was her stepdaughter. I shivered at the thought.

"She knows it was a possibility. And she's really sorry about the way she blew up at you that day. I've never stepped out on that woman, I don't know what got into her, but…"

She could be sorry all she wanted, but the hate in her gaze that day wasn't anything I would just get over. This wasn't about her. It was about Chance. My *father*.

"I'd prefer that if we're going to build a relationship, it doesn't include her. At least for now. That means I won't be going to your house or anywhere she deems her territory."

Chance looked somber before nodding. "That's fair."

"This is new…to both of us. If I get dodgy just know that I'm processing, not trying to punish you with my absence. This is a lot to accept after twenty-seven years of not knowing."

Again, he nodded, his earnest eyes sweeping over my face. Was he trying to see which ones we had in common? Or was he drawing comparisons between me and my mother?

Speaking of which…

"The same way I'm not jumping to be in Lilith's presence, I'm not up for hearing about my mom or your relationship. At least not right now. This thing is just you and me. Let's keep it as simple as possible and see where it goes."

"Of course, Goldyn." Chance's smile widened before more tears welled in his eyes. "Can I hug you?"

Instead of answering, I opened my arms and welcomed his embrace.

"I'm proud of you," Romeo said as soon as we were back in his car.

He reversed while I stared out the windshield, still dumbstruck about the events that unfolded at lunch.

"Do you think I was too harsh about his wife?" Ugh, I couldn't even say her name again.

Romeo shrugged. "Your boundaries aren't harsh just because they might make someone else uncomfortable. You have every reason not to want to be around that woman, and now you won't have to be."

"We'll see," I muttered. There was always the chance she'd pull another pop up, but there was no use voicing my doubt. Dragging my eyes from the windshield to the passenger window, I peered through the dark tint at the blur of mountains and blue skies. Romeo handled every curve in the road with ease, reminding me of that first day he got stuck with taking me back to my van.

A smile tipped up my lips.

"What you over there smiling at, G?"

"How do you know I'm smiling? Shouldn't you be watching the road?"

He scoffed and the sound made me smile harder. "I know how to multitask. Now, what you smiling about?"

Relenting, I turned my body toward him as much as the seatbelt would allow. "I was just thinking about the first time I was in your car. Back when you hated me."

Romeo's jaw ticked. "I never hated you, G."

"Well, you didn't *like* me either. I had to wear you down."

He laughed dryly, not denying it.

Another quip sat at the tip of my tongue, but then my stomach groaned in protest. Thanks to my nerves at lunch, I hadn't eaten anything since the French toast Sincere made me for breakfast.

"Can we go get something to eat?"

Romeo didn't miss a beat. "Where?"

He slowed the car, waiting for my request.

"Lucky's."

All he gave was a simple nod, but it was enough to make peace settle in my heart. So much had changed since I climbed in their window. Every day I woke up showered in love I didn't think I'd ever receive. Life with Sincere, Lorenzo and Romeo was a lot of things, but most of all it was just…right.

Two Months Later

NOVEMBER

ROME NUDGED MY KNEE WITH HIS UNDER THE TABLE WHILE I was in the middle of dipping my first fry in cheddar cheese. When I looked up at him, he didn't say anything, but stared at me with imploring eyes.

"What?" I asked, confused. I knew there wasn't anything on my face because I hadn't started eating yet, but my fingers still flew to my chin, rubbing at nothing.

"You good?" he asked cryptically, his knee swiping mine again.

We were seated on the same side of the booth for four because we were waiting for Goldyn and Lorenzo to arrive. But Rome's warmth by my side was nice. His presence was *always* nice.

"I'm good." *Better than good*, but that was beside the point. "Why you asking?"

I ate my first handful of fries and cut him a look out the corner of my eye. Ever since Goldyn had introduced me to the food at Lucky's Tavern, I ate here at least once a week.

"Because I haven't in a while," Romeo answered, licking his lips. "Checkin' in and shit."

Cleaning my hands, I grabbed my ginger ale and nodded. "What about you? You good?"

The question felt redundant when I could *read* how he felt written all over his face. Romeo was the happiest I'd seen him in a while. Hell, I didn't know if I'd ever seen him this happy.

Goldyn had shown up and pored light into all the darkest parts of us until all we could do was radiate it. We were good before she came, but she made us better.

I expected a terse reply from Romeo, but he surprised me and said, "I've never felt like this before. About anything or anybody. It's scary, but most days I don't even give a fuck. I like being lost in her. I can't go back to what I was doing before she showed up. I thought I was happy, but I was just existing."

"You're in love," I supplied, picking up my burger. Chili spilled from the sides and my mouth watered at the sight.

"It's deeper than that. I don't even know if what I feel is healthy, but it gets deeper every day."

"As long as you don't wake up one morning and decide to run from it, we're good."

He scoffed until I cut my eyes at him again.

"I'm serious, Rome. Goldyn *loves* you. When we asked her to stay for good, she made sure we knew she was in love with you and wouldn't stop seeing you. Her heart and happiness are wrapped up in this too. And I know we promised to never let a woman come between us a long time ago, but you gotta understand

Goldyn isn't just 'a woman.' The same way I don't want her to hurt you, if you hurt her…"

"You never gotta worry about that," Rome assured me, his voice calm but unrelenting. I could hear the love lacing his words and my chest squeezed.

"Good. Now why aren't you eating?" I took a bite of my burger while I waited for his reply.

"Nervous," he mumbled, and if the place wasn't so quiet right now I wouldn't have heard it.

Thankfully, it was the lull between the lunch and dinner rushes, and no one was talking except us.

"What if she has to get surgery?" he asked lowly, and I dropped my burger, my appetite waning the more he made me think about it.

Lorenzo and Goldyn had been in Charlotte all morning for an appointment with her new OBGYN.

She'd had another bad episode earlier this month, and the heavy bleeding that came a few days after it scared the fuck out of Rome. To the point that he knocked on our bedroom door in the middle of the night and told us to be on standby in case we needed to go to the hospital.

But Goldyn had declined the hospital visit, saying she knew her body and the bleeding would get better in a couple days.

It did, but the thought of her being in bed for two days while her body waged war on her was still a mindfuck.

"She'll be fine. And if she has to have surgery, she'll be getting it from one of the best doctor's in the state."

He nodded, still looking unconvinced until I threw my arm around his broad shoulders.

"She's *fine*, Rome. Us worrying about it won't make it better, either. Just wait for her to get here and tell us how it went."

"Yea…right."

I wasn't used to Rome being the one in need of reassurance, but the worry emanating off of him was almost a tangible thing, wedging itself between us.

"Besides," I added, trying to lighten the mood. "Aren't you still working on a new tea for her hormones? Goldyn Hour or something?" I fully knew the name of the proprietary blend Romeo had formulated for our girl, but I hoped giving him a chance to talk about it would ease some of the tension bunching his shoulders.

And it worked. Little by little, he relaxed as he caught me up on the progress he'd made with it this week. "There's still work to be done before I let her try it. But I'm using Lottie as my guinea pig and she said it tastes good and her last period had mild cramps."

As if we'd summoned her, Goldyn appeared in the doorway to Lucky's a few seconds later. Her usual sunny smile was missing, but I was convinced that had more to do with how long she'd been up today. She and Lorenzo got on the road at seven o'clock this morning.

Her eyes glowed when they landed on us, and she made a beeline for our table.

"Hi, baby," she said with a radiant smile, leaning down to kiss me. Our lips brushed in a sweet kiss before she stared at me with unguarded emotion covering her face. Her hand caressed my jaw as she sighed and turned her attention to Rome. "Hey, lover."

"Hey, G. You okay?" he asked, the emotion in his voice thick and heavy with concern.

Goldyn paused to think for a second and sighed wearily. "For the most part yea. Got an MRI but won't have the results until next week, but the ultrasound was productive."

Before we could ask what that meant, Lorenzo walked in, tucking his shades into the open collar of his shirt.

I couldn't take my eyes off him as he approached and he smirked when he noticed my attention pinned on him.

Goldyn scooted into her place across from Rome and grabbed his hand over the table while Enzo bent to kiss me.

"We fucking missed you today," he said roughly, gripping my jaw to deepen the kiss. I would've been self-conscious about the chili and cheese clinging to my breath if he didn't lick into my mouth like I was his favorite flavor.

Enzo pulled away with a groan and gave Romeo a quiet nod in greeting, sitting down beside Goldyn.

Romeo and Goldyn were having their own hushed conversation, so I focused my attention on my husband. "How'd it go?" I asked.

"So many damn tests." He shook his head, scrubbing a hand down his darkly-stubbled face. "I was more anxious than her. I don't know if I can do that shit again. By the time we got to the pharmacy after the appointment, she was trying to calm me down."

I shot him a sympathetic smile, knowing exactly what he meant. All three of us were fucked up when it came to Goldyn. Romeo was the most extreme which was exactly why he'd been left at home today. But I wasn't far behind him. None of us liked the idea of her suffering and not being able to do anything about it.

Pushing my fries across the table, I motioned for Enzo to eat. If the rigid set of his shoulders was any indication, I knew he'd been just like Rome all day and wound too tight to feed himself.

Quietly, he started eating and I let my eyes roam over everybody at the table. All the people I adored in one place. The man I gave my last name. The woman who felt like home. And my best friend who was the mirror to my soul.

I flagged down the waitress and ordered more food for the table before I let my eyes rest on them again. Especially the woman who turned out to be the perfect missing piece for all of us.

Because of Goldyn, I was finally taking my baking seriously. When we met, I knew right away that I would do anything to help make her dreams come true. But I didn't know she'd end up doing the same for me. She was my partner in more ways than one, lifting me up and pushing me to do things I'd shied away from for too long.

We were in the middle of designing the bakery

connected to her store together, and every day I got to work on that, more of my former insecurities were laid to rest.

Loving the people at this table and letting them love me in return had given me everything.

JUNE...AGAIN

"I can't even get my lashes on!" I groaned, turning my back to the mirror. I was two seconds away from sliding down the side of the vanity when my eyes snagged on a pair already trained on me.

"Hi, Baby," I cooed, crouching down to scratch between my dog's ears.

A few months after she was born, Sincere went to collect her from Ms. Ruby's house and brought the Pit bull home to me.

He'd remembered my drunken confession about wanting a dog once I settled down, and I'd cried so hard holding her for the first time. Yes, I'd always wanted a damn dog. But it was more than that. Getting her meant I was gonna be here for a while. I had a home. A permanent place to exist with three men who loved me unconditionally. The puppy was just the icing on top.

She was almost a year old now and stared up at me with her little head cocked and her eyes focused so intently on me it tugged at my heart.

"I can just stay home with you and watch *Braxton Family Values*."

"You tryna flake on us, mamas?" Lorenzo popped up in the doorway, leaning against it as he stared at me with adoring eyes.

I had yet to get accustomed to the way he snuck up on me when I was lost in my head.

Lorenzo was always there. My constant in the midst of everything else in my life changing. He was so sure of himself and his place in this world that it was infectious, sneaking under my skin and branding me with a renewed confidence in whatever I was doing.

"Maybe," I mumbled, tossing the tube of lash glue on the counter behind me.

"You know I'm not letting you do that." He walked into the bathroom we shared with Sincere, his electrifying presence crowding the space in a way it usually didn't.

Baby shuffled two steps to the side, refusing to move out of my orbit. A smile quirked my lips. I loved my little velcro bestie.

"I'm so fucking nervous," I confessed, chewing my bottom lip.

My face was already in Lorenzo's hands before his silky smooth voice calmed me. "You have nothing to be nervous about. This is a year in the making."

When he bowed his head to kiss the top of my head, I sighed.

"Well, longer than a year," he amended. "But a year since you started working on it and I'm so fucking proud of you. So I need you to finish getting dressed and take your pretty ass downstairs so we can celebrate you tonight."

After months of construction delays and last-minute changes, Read the Room and Sinful Bites were officially opening their doors tonight.

Technically, Read the Room had been cleared for operation two weeks ago, but I didn't want to do this without Sincere. We were doing this together. Every nerve-racking, heart-clenching part.

So, tonight's soft opening was the culmination of everything we'd been brave enough to believe we could accomplish.

Nerves tangled in my gut and I freed myself from Lorenzo's hold to crouch down in front of Baby again.

She nuzzled my nose with hers and a rush of giddiness pulsed through my bloodstream.

"Come on, pretty," Enzo called from above. "Get up here and finish getting ready so we can head downstairs."

"I can't get my lashes on," I shared, rising to my full height. I kept the sullenness out of my voice, but Lorenzo tipped up my chin anyway and kissed my nose.

"I got you. Where's the stuff?"

Unlike mine, Lorenzo's hands were steady as he cleaned my lashes, used his breath to air dry them, and then reapplied the glue. He smirked at me while he waited for it to get tacky and then grabbed the clamp I'd thrown earlier and applied my left lash strip perfectly on the first try.

"What kind of witchcraft..." I muttered under my breath.

I tried to move around him to look in the mirror, but his grip on my jaw prevented that. So, I looked up at him, forever in awe of the way everything seemed to come easy to him.

When the right side was done, he kissed my lips briefly before moving so I could examine myself in the mirror.

"What else do you have to do?" He wanted to know.

"Um..." My heart hammered while I tried to come up with something, but I knew there was nothing else I needed to do. Lashes, gloss and blush were the extent of what I wanted to wear in this summer heat, so that was it. "Nothing. I'm ready."

With his hand wrapped around mine, Lorenzo lead me downstairs and we caught the tail-end of a whispered exchange between Rome and Sin. Romeo leaned forward to kiss Sincere's brow while he muttered something meant only for their ears and the show of affection had my heart hammering all over again.

Outside of me, Romeo wasn't the most physically affectionate man. He much preferred acts of service over physical touch. So, I'd seen him help Sincere build his herb garden week by week. I'd seen him buy Sincere an anthology they both loved in audio form. I'd seen him teach himself how to make Lorenzo's new favorite drink and create an herbal tea to help balance my hormones. I'd also seen the way he showed up for me while I navigated my relationship with Chance for the past year.

But there were brief moments, like the one I was witnessing, when he let his guard down and kissed Sincere. Or hugged Lorenzo extra tight even after they'd been bickering all day.

It was amazing to watch and made me appreciate the way he was with me even more.

They turned toward the staircase when they heard us approach.

Sincere's smile was instant and warm.

While Romeo's was gradual and understated.

Reaching the landing, I walked over and smiled up at them. "Hi."

"Hey, love. You look pretty." Sincere tucked a loose curl behind my ear.

I ran my eyes over his tailored slacks and champagne-colored silk shirt. "You look better," I told him.

"Impossible," he said, just before his lips covered mine in a chaste kiss.

Turning my attention to Rome, I beamed up at him and watched the way his features relaxed when my attention was pinned on him. It would never get old knowing how much he softened in my presence.

"You look amazing," I told him, resting my chin against his chest to stare up at him.

Had I really looked at his outfit? No, not really. But Romeo Wilde looked incredible in whatever he put on. And he smelled like sin, just adding to the effect.

Slowly, his lips stretched into a smile, revealing a diamond encrusted gold grill.

Got damn, this man knew exactly how to make me weak in the knees.

I was so lost in lust that it took me a minute to glimpse the iced-out initial resting on his right incisor.

It was a G.

What the hell?

"Romeo…"

"Hmm?" he asked nonchalantly.

"What is the G for?"

He didn't blink when he slid me a bored look. "What you think, Goldyn?"

"You got a grill customized for me?"

Last month, he'd surprised me with a scenic train ride across the state to King's Town to show me where he'd grown up. Before we left, he took me to his jeweler and had me fitted for a grill since I was always so enamored with his. I had no idea he'd put in an order of his own though.

"Why wouldn't I wanna rep you on your day?"

My face fell, but before tears could form, Baby sat herself on my feet and broke the moment.

Grinning down at her, I heaved a sigh and looked over at Sincere and Lorenzo near the banister.

"You ready for this?" he asked quietly.

Shrugging, I tried to play off the nerves and replied, "I'll do it if you do it."

THE END.

ACKNOWLEDGMENTS

I'm not gone hold you, I wanna thank MYSELF for finally sitting down to write this book. It's lived my head for months and months and months. I would start other projects, and it would be tucked away in the back of my mind, until one day I couldn't ignore it anymore. And I'm so glad I got it out.

I also wanna give a very warm shout out to my Patreon members. Sharing this with them in real time was a treat. They've been there for *Kharma, Just Right* and we're five chapters in with *This Time Forever*. Our little corner of the innanet is small but MIGHTY.

BOOKS MENTIONED IN THIS NOVEL

Glory by Aria Daze
The Air Between Us by Shameka Erby
Nobody to Love You Better by ML Bash
The Fifth Season by N.K. Jemisin

ALSO BY SHON

EROTICA

His Majesty: A Second-Chance Novella

Midnight: An Interracial Friends with Benefits to more
Novella

Yours: A Friends to Lovers Novella

Cravings: An Insta-love Novella

The Finale (Website exclusive): Even more King's Town
Content | Over 20+ deleted chapter PLUS read what
happened at the yacht party once Cravings ended

URBAN ROMANCE

Chubz & Kim: A Second-Chance, Age Gap Romance Novella
(King's Town)

SHORTS

KHARMA: An Arranged Marriage, Erotic Short

STANDALONES

Unconditional: A Second-Chance, Slow Burn Romance

Unstoppable: A Forced Proximity, Bodyguard Romance

Untouchable: A Small Town, Friends to Lovers Romance

E&J: A Brother's Best Friend Novella (website exclusive)

Heaven Sent: A Small Town, Marriage of Convenience
Romance

Roomie, Lover, Friend: A Small Town, Roommates to Lovers
Romance

This Time Forever: A Small Town, Second Chance Romance
(FALL 2024)

LEAVE A REVIEW

Thank you so much for reading this book!

Leaving a rating/review helps more than you know! Please consider leaving one for this book (and any other book you've read by me) on your favorite bookish sites. As an indie author, it helps other readers find me. Thank you so much in advance.

KEEP IN TOUCH

Check out my website for the latest updates.

Join my mailing list at my website for exclusive access to eBooks, special editions, and signed copies.